"Amanda Schrock had my heart from the minute she paid a call on the most uneligible bachelor in town. The multiple storylines were fresh, well-written, and simply adorable. *Green Pastures* is yet another example of why Patricia Johns is a true fan favorite."

New York Times bestselling author Shelley Shepard Gray

"Patricia Johns beautifully captures the struggles of three sisters trying to fit their dreams into the expectations of Amish life. You'll find yourself rooting for each of them as they navigate love, faith, work, and the push and pull of tradition."

Suzanne Woods Fisher, bestselling author
of *Anything but Plain*

"*Green Pastures* explores the ties that bind a community as three sisters navigate their way through romance, heartbreak, and marriage. Patricia Johns tackles tough topics, resulting in a poignant story of hope, faith, and love that shines a bright light on the Amish—and human—experience."

Leslie Gould, award-winning, bestselling author
of *A Brighter Dawn*

GREEN
PASTURES

GREEN PASTURES

The Amish of Shepherd's Hill 1

PATRICIA JOHNS

BETHANYHOUSE

a division of Baker Publishing Group
Minneapolis, Minnesota

© 2025 by Patricia Johns

Published by Bethany House Publishers
Minneapolis, Minnesota
BethanyHouse.com

Bethany House Publishers is a division of
Baker Publishing Group, Grand Rapids, Michigan

Printed in the United States of America

Library of Congress Cataloging-in-Publication Data
Names: Johns, Patricia (Romance writer), author.
Title: Green pastures / Patricia Johns.
Description: Minneapolis, Minnesota : Bethany House Publishers, a division of Baker Publishing Group, 2025. | Series: The Amish of Shepherd's Hill; 1
Identifiers: LCCN 2024041939 | ISBN 9780764244179 (paperback) | ISBN 9780764244544 (casebound) | ISBN 9781493448920 (ebook)
Subjects: LCSH: Amish—Fiction. | LCGFT: Romance fiction. | Christian fiction. | Novels.
Classification: LCC PR9199.4.J6364226 G74 2025 | DDC 813/.6—dc23/eng/20240906
LC record available at https://lccn.loc.gov/2024041939

Scripture quotations are from the King James Version of the Bible.

Cover design by James Hall
Photograph of model from Kirk DouPonce

The author is represented by the literary agency of Liza Dawson Associates, LLC.

Baker Publishing Group publications use paper produced from sustainable forestry practices and postconsumer waste whenever possible.

25 26 27 28 29 30 31   7 6 5 4 3 2 1

To my husband and son,
who are the center of my world.
You're my everything.

1

The metal gate slammed shut with a reverberating clang, and Tabitha Schrock pulled her dust-streaked cotton dress up to her knees, ready to jump up the side of the cattle-loading chute. A year ago, she'd done this job in blue jeans. Now she was back to a cape dress, pulled up to her knees to let her move more quickly, but with the same unerring instinct for injured cattle that she'd had all her life.

The black Angus limped ahead of her, swinging his head from side to side on muscular shoulders, his snorts getting louder as the bull's pain and anger grew.

"Tabitha, get out of there! I told you already. He's a killer, that one!"

She allowed her father, Abram, a quick glance, but that was all. He stood outside the chute, his straw hat clasped between his hands and his wispy white hair standing up all over his head. His white shirt was soiled with dirt, and one black suspender hung down his shoulder.

Tabitha needed her attention on that bull in front of her, though. He had a broken leg, and he could hardly touch the ground with his hoof. What he needed was a painkiller and a sedative, and then to have that leg set and splinted. But first, she needed him in the squeeze chute and the head gate, or she'd never be able to touch him.

The bull was a rented animal, and he was only supposed to be here for a few months to sire some calves. He'd done his job, but this injury would have to be healed before they returned him to his owners. All it took was a gopher hole to take down this mammoth.

The bull came to the end of the metal fence and turned back. He couldn't charge with one front leg curled up underneath him, but she could tell he wanted to. He lowered his head and hobbled forward. It was sad to see the proud animal reduced this way. He was still dangerous, but her heart went out to him all the same.

"Tabitha!" Her father's voice was full of warning. He meant well, but this wasn't her first cattle chute.

"Daet . . . let me do this . . ." She kept her voice low and calm, and she held a length of stick out in front of her. "Prod him this way, Amanda."

Her younger sister was twenty-seven this year. Her gaze fixed on the animal, and her thin lips pressed together in concentration. She had a stick with a few dried leaves on the end, and she poked it through the rails and swatted the bull's hind quarters with a thwack. The animal turned on her, and she squeaked and jumped back.

"Hey! Hey!" Tabitha called. "This way!"

"Tabitha, I'm coming in there!" Her father started hobbling in her direction.

"Daet! Let me do this!"

Her father was in no state to start playing chicken with a wounded bull. He had his own aches and pains slowing him down these days, and she was the actual expert here, as much as he was reluctant to admit that.

10

The bull started toward Tabitha, and she took one step back, her hand on the swinging gate. If he came at her, she'd have to jump. She eyed him, watching as he staggered when the hoof from his injured leg touched the ground.

The poor animal. The pain would be excruciating, and he wouldn't be thinking straight. Animals were like people that way—put them under enough pressure and you got the worst out of them, never the best.

The bull came at her, and Tabitha spread her arms wide and shouted. He veered left, straight into the chute, and she swung the gate shut with a clatter.

Amanda let out a whoop, and Tabitha shot her sister a grin. Her father planted his hat back on his head.

The job wasn't over yet, though, and she prodded the bull from behind to keep him moving into the squeeze gate. Finally, she dropped the last gate behind him and pulled on the handle that brought in the sides. His head came out the front, but he couldn't move farther, and the sides squeezing against him actually held him up to help support his weight and let her get to that leg.

"Hey, friend," she murmured. "I'm here to help."

The bull bellowed and struggled, but he wasn't able to move much. She had her medical bag waiting beside the chute. She pulled out a syringe and a bottle of Meloxicam. That was for the pain. She'd also give him a sedative to help him stay still while she inspected the leg and splinted the fracture. She could tell that the break was below the shank, which was the best possible location to work on for an animal this size.

Her father came up beside her, pulling up his suspender and eyeing the bull.

"Not bad," he muttered.

"That's all I get?" she asked, giving him a sidelong look before she pushed the needle into the animal's neck—the safest place for subcutaneous injections—away from large veins or nerves.

"I could have done it," he replied.

"Daet, you could have, but I'm a certified large-animal vet. You might as well use my skills, don't you think?"

He muttered something in Pennsylvania Dutch that wasn't exactly bad language, but it wasn't good either. She hid a smile. Daet was getting older, and the last time he attempted to get a cow in the chute, he'd injured both himself and the cow. He wasn't as quick or as strong as he used to be, and when he'd asked her to come home, she knew it was for more than his care for the state of her soul. He'd been struggling, and a man with three daughters didn't have sons to lean on. Tabitha's youngest sister, Rose, had gotten married, but her husband was working his own farm.

But first and foremost, Gott had been working. When she'd received her father's invitation, Tabitha had been ready to come home properly, and his letter had been the nudge she needed. In her ten years of *Englischer* freedom, she had missed the tight-knit community she'd been raised in. Even with her newfound relationship with Gott, it hadn't been replaceable. And having been back for two months already, she was glad she'd swallowed her pride and returned.

Tabitha pulled out another syringe and vial of medication. This was the sedative. She measured the amount and eyed the bull. He was already calming, the pain meds taking hold. Good. She'd get him comfortable yet. She rubbed a spot on his front shoulder, a nice thick muscle, and pushed the needle in. He moved a little—he felt that one—and she quickly injected the sedative. It didn't take long for him to stop moving around, his eyes drooping.

"There you are," she said. "I'll work fast."

Amanda crouched down next to Tabitha, and Tabitha glanced over at her. Her sister was tall and slim with strong hands and a keen eye. She crouched with her dress tucked between her knees, and she absently slapped at a mosquito that landed on her bare arm. Another one took its place, and Tabitha reached over and slapped it for her.

"Mosquito," Tabitha said.

"Thanks." Amanda leaned closer as Tabitha reached through the bars of the squeeze chute and felt down the bull's limb, her fingers expertly moving over muscle, tendon, and bone. "Does he feel that?"

"No, he's pretty doped up," she replied. "I'm feeling for the break to see how bad it is."

It wasn't too bad, as far as breaks went. Setting it wouldn't take much force at all.

"Daet, I have some fiberglass splints in that bag just over there," Tabitha said. "Could you grab them for me?"

"I have to tell Leroy Lapp that their bull is injured," her father said, handing her the splints. She put them on the grass beside her. Leroy was her brother-in-law's cousin. This wasn't just a business relationship. This was about family too.

"The bone will heal in a few weeks. He'll be right as rain when you return him, Daet. Don't worry."

"I have to tell him, all the same," he replied.

"*Yah*, but you're also getting top veterinary care at no charge, aren't ya?" she said.

"*Yah*, I suppose."

Tabitha knew that her father was a worrier. He always

had been. He worried about too little rain or too much. He worried about what people said and what they didn't. He worried about the beef market and the horse market and the health of his herd. When she'd been at home, he'd worried most about his daughters. When her *mamm* died when Tabitha was sixteen, her *daet* had worried about raising the girls without her. He'd gone easy on all three of them, and that was why he'd been convinced to let Tabitha get her GED in town when her *rumspringa* had started at seventeen. But in that GED class, Tabitha met the man she'd marry— Michael Logan.

Michael had been funny and attentive. He wasn't like the Amish men her age. He'd shown his affection openly and directly. She'd fallen for him head over heels, and after two years of dating—something her *daet* had loathed but could not stop—Michael asked Tabitha to marry him, and she'd said yes.

Her father had earnestly tried to talk her out of the wedding on several occasions. He'd even sat her down the night before the wedding and pleaded with her to just put it off for another year, but Tabitha was sure she knew best. Besides, she'd been in love, and Michael had been everything that the Amish world could not give her—excitement and adventure.

But while Michael had been an adventure, he had not been faithful. If only she'd listened to her father that night, because though divorcing Michael had given her respite from the heartbreak of his wandering affection, it also meant she'd never marry again in the Amish faith. Not while Michael lived, at least. Marriage was for life, and a very cautious choice to make. She'd made hers, and the consequences of her mistake were hers to bear.

Tabitha moved her fingers along the fracture in the bull's

leg, feeling again for where a piece of bone was angling away from its proper position. She used the heel of her hand and a strong push to get it back in place. When she felt the click, Tabitha nodded toward her sister.

"I need you to hold these splints in place while I wrap them, okay?"

Amanda leaned forward and did as Tabitha asked. The splints were the right length—there was no need to adjust that—and her fingers worked quickly to wrap the gauze, keeping it straight and unwrinkled as she gave that leg support. She had to be careful to make sure the wrap wasn't too tight, or it would hinder blood flow and cause other problems.

Fixing a broken leg was a job Tabitha had done dozens of times in fields, in barns, and once in the middle of a thicket of trees when they couldn't get the cow out into the open. This was a job she was good at, and one she was prepared for. But it wasn't the kind of job that a woman performed in Amish circles. The bishop had made an exception for her because of her marital status. She needed support, and she wouldn't have a husband to take care of her. Besides, the community needed a good vet who spoke their language and knew their culture.

She'd accepted a position under skilled veterinarian Dr. Brian Fuller when she'd decided to come home to Shepherd's Hill. Before that, she'd been living in Philadelphia, where she and Michael had moved after the wedding. It was where she'd gotten her veterinarian training, and the base she'd been working from since her graduation and her subsequent divorce. It was only an hour's car ride away from Shepherd's Hill, but it would take closer to ten hours in a buggy. The distance between Amish fields and *Englischer* city life was greater than miles, though. It could be calculated in that tense, uncertain silence between heartbeats late at night when she could feel Gott telling her that she wasn't where she should be. When she'd come home, that tension in her prayer life evaporated.

Tabitha was home, an Amish woman in good standing once more. Most lapsed Amish who left the faith didn't return, so Tabitha knew she was a reason for celebration. And even though this work of setting a broken bone was exactly the same as she'd done on *Englischer* farms in her last two years as a veterinarian, squatting here in her cape dress, her gray work apron smeared with dirt and mud, she felt like she'd shrugged off a blanket of constant low-level anxiety and she could finally breathe.

Her heart was in the lush green pastures, the simple Amish kitchens, the earnest belief in Gott's goodness, and the low sound of a cappella singing on Service Sundays. Her faith had begun out here in Amish country, and exploring the outside world hadn't brought any of the satisfaction that she'd hoped to find. Freedom had proved reckless, and home was a safe haven where rules protected them and the community pulled close together to take care of one another.

As Tabitha finished wrapping the leg, she looked up at the bull. His eyes were half closed, and he had given no resistance, which confirmed he wasn't feeling pain. Bulls, like a lot of people, didn't suffer discomfort quietly.

"I think I could be good at this," Amanda said, tucking the roll of gauze back into the medical bag. "Helping you with the veterinary cases, I mean."

Her sister brushed a stray wisp of hair out of her eyes. She had a streak of dirt across her cheek. Then whip fast, Amanda reached out and smacked Tabitha's arm with a stinging slap.

"Mosquito," she said.

Tabitha rose to her feet and shot her sister a smile, rubbing the spot where the mosquito had bitten. "You definitely are good at working with cattle, Amanda. I think we'll make a great team."

Two single Amish sisters—one incapable of marriage again and one who'd been passed over for some prettier girls in the community. Maybe they'd never marry, but their lives could be full, and they could support each other. Dr. Fuller had no problem with Tabitha arranging her own helpers for her calls, and she could even pay Amanda an hourly wage for her contribution. So together, the sisters could serve Tabitha's veterinary clients and settle back into the quiet, peaceful cycles of Amish life.

"Can you open that roll of fiberglass?" Tabitha asked. It was time to layer on the cast, immobilizing the leg so that it could heal.

Yah, Amish life came with fewer freedoms and more rigid restrictions, but perhaps, like a cast on a broken limb, it could give her the support Tabitha needed to heal too. Her *Englischer* years had provided her with an education that would build her future, but those years had also broken her heart.

2

After getting the bull back into a stall in the barn, Amanda and Tabitha stopped by the horse stable to check on Fritz. Amanda used to be nervous around the big gelding. He'd been nippy, and while it was only because he was sick, a horse's teeth could leave a nasty bite. Her sister had been doing wonders with their draft horse, who had gut issues. Daet had been intent on getting rid of him until Tabitha arrived and took over with him, though it was likely that Fritz would never be used for farmwork again.

But Tabitha had both healed and calmed Fritz, and he was like a completely different horse now. Amanda had watched her sister carefully choose the horse's diet and even personally check the pasture for harmful weeds before sending him out to graze. Tabitha was a good veterinarian. There was no getting around it.

Amanda brushed a mosquito off the back of her arm as she and her sister trudged together toward the house. The June air was muggy and overly warm, and beads of sweat stood out on Amanda's forehead. She glanced over at Tabitha—hair pulled back under a surprisingly white *kapp*, not a speck of dirt on it after all they'd done that morning. Her sister was pretty, Amanda thought to herself. It was a shame she couldn't marry a nice Amish farmer now.

But Tabitha had ruined more than her own ability to marry in their community. No nice Amish boy had wanted to take the chance on the younger sister of a runaway. Tabitha had married Michael just as Amanda had entered her own *rumspringa*. There had been scandal attached to their family after that. And it seemed like Tabitha and Michael had the worst timing for coming home for a visit, because just as a boy would show Amanda some interest or the community seemed inclined to gossip about something else, Tabitha and Michael would arrive in their blue jeans and cowboy boots, and waggle their *Englischer* selves under everyone's noses again.

Amanda walked half a step ahead of her older sister, and she hit the stairs first that led up to the side door at the house. She stepped out of her rubber boots and picked up the thick bar of homemade soap at the mudroom sink. She lathered up and rinsed, then dried her hands while Tabitha did the same behind her. Then Amanda led the way into the bright kitchen.

The windows were cranked open, a grass-scented breeze wafting through, mingling with the scent of cooling cinnamon rolls. Amanda had left with the dishes done, and they were piled high in the drying rack on the counter, but her glance took in several more chores that needed doing. The woodstove needed a thorough cleaning one of these days, but she'd been putting it off. And the cupboards needed a good scrubbing, as well as the floors. Downstairs in the basement, laundry was piling up too. These were all Amanda's responsibilities.

Daet sat at the kitchen table eating a cinnamon roll with his fingers, peeling off a layer, rolling it up, and pushing it into his mouth. He winked at Amanda as she took off her outdoor work apron and replaced it with a white kitchen apron.

"Daet, that isn't good for you," Amanda said. "You know what the doctor said."

Tabitha wordlessly swiped the plate away from him and ignored the sour look he cast her. Tabitha didn't care if Daet was pleased with her or not when it came to his special diet to lower his cholesterol. But then, she also said that she understood the science behind it, and while science never trumped Gott, science definitely trumped Daet's feelings.

"You need protein, Daet," Tabitha said. "We've got some leftover roast beef. You can have that."

"I wanted Amanda's good baking." Daet licked his fingers and shot Amanda a smile.

Daet loved Amanda's baking. He used to say that she'd have suitors banging down their door for her strudel back when she was a teenager. He didn't say that anymore. No one had come knocking after Tabitha left, regardless of the quality of Amanda's baking.

Outside, the sound of hooves on the gravel drive drew all of their attention, and Amanda went to the window and squinted through the screen. She recognized her younger sister Rose's buggy. Rose was a lovely, petite woman. She had bright eyes and pink cheeks, and she'd been every boy's first choice back when they'd been girls waiting to be asked to be driven home from an evening of hymn singing—regardless of Tabitha's shame. And she'd been married by the age of twenty-three.

Rose reined in her horse and hopped down. Even the act of jumping down from the buggy looked cute when Rose did it.

"Rose is here," Amanda said.

"That's good timing," Tabitha said. "We're back from the fields, at least."

Amanda turned away from the window again. She'd spent her entire adolescence being mildly jealous of Rose, but it seemed like a waste of energy now. What good would it do Amanda to resent her own sister's happiness? Besides, they had Tabitha back again, and while the road Amanda had hoped to travel toward marriage and motherhood now seemed closed to her, a new opportunity had opened up. Amanda could help Tabitha with her veterinary duties. It was exciting, and Amanda liked the idea of being able to travel all around the countryside, helping to cure ailing animals.

"Hello." Rose's voice echoed cheerfully as she came inside.

"Hi, Rose," Tabitha said, and she went over to give their sister a hug. "What brings you by?"

"Can't I miss my sisters?" Rose asked with a smile. "Aaron is at work, and I've got the housework done."

There was always more to do. A mental image of their own laundry tickled Amanda's mind. It wasn't like an Amish woman was ever lacking for work to do around a house. But then Rose didn't have any *kinner* of her own yet, so Amanda imagined sitting in that house all by herself might get lonely, even if she had plenty to do.

Daet pushed himself to his feet. "Will you stay a bit?"

"*Yah*, a little while." Rose smiled again.

"I'll go take care of your horse, then," Daet said. "I'll leave the kitchen to you girls. I have a cattle trailer due shortly. I'm heading out to the auction."

"You're buying something?" Tabitha asked, her interest piqued like it always seemed to be when it came to men's work. If anyone talked cattle or horses, Tabitha was in the middle of it, but their *daet* had a way of keeping his own business to himself. The cattle trailer was news to Amanda, too, but she didn't give it another thought.

"I'll be back" was all he said as he headed out the door. When the screen clattered shut, Amanda shot Rose an inquiring look. Rose always had a reason to stop by, even if it wasn't a reason she'd voice in front of their father. "Well?"

"All right," Rose said. "I come with news."

That was more like it. Rose tended to pick up the local scuttlebutt faster than Amanda or Tabitha ever managed to. She pulled out a heavy kitchen chair and took a seat. Amanda did the same.

"What about the auction, though?" Tabitha asked, and she took a couple of steps toward the door.

"Never mind the auction," Amanda said. "What have you heard? Is it about Tabitha?"

Tabitha turned back and met Amanda's teasing grin with an annoyed look. "You might as well tell us what you heard."

"You remember Menno Weaver, of course?" Rose said.

"*Yah*," Amanda replied. Who didn't? The Weavers were a family with scandal all their own. The Weaver men had struggled with alcoholism, and everyone knew. But Menno had been attending Alcoholics Anonymous meetings in town, and Amanda had even seen him coming out of one of those meetings on a Tuesday afternoon. They were held in the Presbyterian church basement. There was no other reason for an Amish man to be coming out of a Presbyterian church.

"He's looking for a wife," Rose said, then leaned back with a satisfied look on her face.

Amanda's pulse sped up. Menno Weaver . . . He never came to any social gatherings or mingled with the community, but every Service Sunday Menno sat in his spot right between Rose's husband, Aaron Lapp, and another young married man. When the last hymn was sung, he'd leave again without a word.

"He wants a wife?" Tabitha finally sank into a chair opposite Amanda.

"He's at that age," Rose replied.

"Is he still drinking?" Tabitha asked.

"Not anymore," Amanda broke in. "He's going to AA meetings now."

Tabitha nodded slowly. "What do people think of him? His father and his uncles used to drink and gamble. I know of three separate times they were shunned before I left."

Amanda didn't answer. She knew it was true, but Menno wasn't the same as his father and uncles. None of the older generation had gone to AA meetings like Menno did. It was important for a man to face his weaknesses.

"He can't help being born a Weaver," Amanda said. Any more than any of them could choose the family they were born into. But the Weavers *were* a family with problems.

"I always thought he was a bit strange," Rose said. "Has he said anything to you in the last five years? Because he hasn't spoken to me. Aaron said Menno never says more than hello to him, and even then only when Aaron presses him into it."

"Who told you he's looking for a wife?" Amanda asked. "It could just be gossip."

"Katie Hochstetler was going to Elder Yoder's home for a quilting circle with her *mamm*," Rose said, "and she saw Menno leaving. She overheard Elder Yoder tell his wife that Menno is looking to get married. I suppose he wanted the elder to help him find someone."

It certainly sounded that way, Amanda had to admit.

"Is there anyone the elders would suggest for him?" Tabitha asked. "I recognize I'm not exactly marriageable, either, but I can't think of anyone who'd suggest their own daughter for a Weaver these days."

"I saw him in town," Amanda said, and suddenly her voice sounded too loud. She cleared her throat.

"And?" Rose's eyebrows went up.

"And . . . he was coming out of the Presbyterian church," Amanda said. "He was talking with some *Englischers*. He seemed comfortable enough around them. Very friendly and open."

Her sisters both went silent, their gazes locked on her. Amanda felt her face start to heat. They were drawing conclusions, she could feel it.

"But he won't talk with the men in our community," Rose said after a beat. "He won't say two words to Aaron."

But then, Aaron was reserved and earnest—a combination that Amanda found rather off-putting. Maybe it was the same for Menno.

"I'm just saying, it isn't like he's weird," Amanda said. "Because I've seen him with others, and he seemed very pleasant and cordial. He has it in him."

Tabitha and Rose exchanged a look.

"Would you stop doing that?" Amanda demanded.

"Are you . . . considering him?" Rose asked cautiously.

"No, I'm just saying that we can't judge him unfairly. His family has a lot of problems. We know that. But that doesn't mean he's all bad. We've got to be fair about it, at least."

The side door opened with a creak, and their father came back inside, boots thumping on the wood floor. They heard him washing up at the sink. Then he dropped his hat on the hook by the door to the mudroom.

"Why the ominous silence?" Daet asked with an indulgent smile. "What were you all clucking about like a bunch of hens, huh?"

Yah, Daet's old joke about his little chicks. He'd adjusted his joking to allow for them growing up, at least.

"Menno Weaver," Rose said.

"What's he like, Daet?" Amanda asked hurriedly, cutting her sister off before she could explain further.

"He's running a hog farm," he replied with a shrug.

"We know that much," Amanda replied. "What else? What is he like?"

He shrugged again. "He's like a pig farmer."

Daet ambled back through the kitchen and stopped at the counter. He pulled out some bread, and then headed for the fridge.

"He keeps to himself," he went on. "I've seen him in town a couple of times. And he looks . . . thin. Like he could use a good meal."

That thought tugged at Amanda's sympathy. When someone got too thin, people knew they weren't happy. A happy man ate.

"Should we do something?" Amanda asked.

"Like bring him a meal?" Tabitha asked. "He'd think you were there for his wife hunting plans. I wouldn't risk that. Someone older and more matronly should bring it to him."

"Like you?" Amanda teased.

Tabitha laughed. "I actually would be safer. So, *yah*, someone more like me—completely unavailable."

Daet had the roast beef out of the refrigerator, and he was assembling a sandwich with butter, sauerkraut, meat, and cheese. He added another dripping forkful of sauerkraut on top, and then pressed down the top piece of bread.

"Listen to your sister," he said. "Sometimes men are like bulls. It takes a squeeze chute and a large dose of sedative to set them straight. And as a woman, you shouldn't have to be either of those things."

Daet was meaning to joke and lighten the mood, but Amanda wasn't joking. A man looking for a wife after he'd been passed over was not amusing to her. She'd been passed over, too, and while she was determined to get used to it, she could empathize with a man who hadn't made his peace with it yet.

"Set him straight from what, though?" Amanda asked. "I'm just curious. How did Menno go wrong?"

"He's just . . . odd," her father replied, heading back toward the table. "He's antisocial. He doesn't seem to trust anyone. He won't come out to any gatherings here in the community, and I overheard the bishop say that, Gott forgive him, he thought Menno was absolutely hopeless. No one really knows what happens up there at that hog farm. His brothers come and go sometimes, I've been told, and they're up to no good."

"*Hopeless* is a strong word," Amanda replied.

"Perhaps a moment of weakness on the bishop's part," her father agreed, and he took a jaw-cracking bite, chewing a few times before he continued talking. "But the fact remains, while Menno has remained Amish—he certainly hasn't jumped the fence—he's only as involved as he absolutely must be without being disciplined. And what are we without our neighbors?" He took another bite of sandwich.

A risk. *Yah*, Amanda heard it well enough. Menno Weaver had sealed himself away on a pig farm on the outskirts of the district, and the beauty of the Amish life lay in their close Christian community. They cared for each other. They supported each other. They mourned together and celebrated together, and did their best to make everyone feel valued and appreciated. Menno didn't take part in that.

Rose turned toward her. "Are you sure you aren't considering that man for yourself?"

Was she? Amanda had wondered if she'd ever marry. Every family had a maiden aunt or two—women who hadn't married but who'd stayed a part of things. They enjoyed their nieces and nephews, pitched in with younger *kinner* when someone gave birth, and were generally helpful. In fact, Amanda's favorite Aent Dina had never married. But she was cheerful and fun, and always had time to sit down with Amanda and talk about life and feelings. These were women who stayed single and just never had the family of their own—no husband, no babies—but there was always someone who needed extra help, like their *daet*, who would have no one to take care of him in his old age if one of them didn't do it. It had occurred to Amanda that with Tabitha home again, that burden wouldn't be hers alone. They could take care of Daet together.

"I wasn't thinking about me marrying him," Amanda said. "I think my days of finding a husband are behind me."

"That can't be true," Tabitha cut in, but Rose had the sense to look at her feet. "Daet, tell her it isn't true."

"It is true," Amanda insisted.

"Well . . . it was a problem with numbers, really," Daet said slowly. "When she was born, so were a lot of other girls, and there weren't as many boys. Then we had some families move away who had mostly boys, and . . . well, it was a numbers thing, like I said."

Numbers? Amanda watched her father take another bite of his sandwich. Was that the story he told Tabitha?

"It's not numbers, Daet," Amanda said. "When Tabitha

left, things were complicated, and I just wasn't pretty enough to make up the difference."

Her father harrumphed and dabbed at the corner of his mouth with a napkin.

"What?" Tabitha frowned. "I visited. I came around."

"That was part of the problem," Amanda said, turning back to her sister. "Every time a boy looked my way, you and Michael would show up, and it would remind everyone that my older sister had jumped the fence."

Besides, Amanda knew that she was to blame too. She'd loved her older sister, and she'd stood up for her time and time again, telling people gossiping about her that she wasn't a heathen or no longer a believer. She'd just decided to live differently, and she had a right to it. She wasn't shunned. So Amanda couldn't really blame Tabitha for all of the fallout. But she wasn't going to pretend she was more marriageable than she was either.

"Marriage isn't everything," Rose said. "Marrying the wrong man is worse than not marrying at all."

"That's not entirely fair either," Amanda replied. "You're married. You have a home and a kitchen of your own, a garden of your own . . . You're one of the married women in the community—and you know it's different."

"I think she's talking about my situation," Tabitha said. "And she's right. Marrying the wrong man is more painful than not being married at all."

And that was a proper warning. Tabitha had left the Amish life to marry an *Englischer*. Everyone had warned her against him, and when she married him, the women in Shepherd's Hill had whispered that she might not have done it if her mother were still alive to give her some much-needed advice, mother to daughter.

Then Michael had lost interest in her, Tabitha had told them later, and she didn't understand why he was away from home so much. Until her friend told her that she'd seen Michael out at a restaurant holding another woman's hand. And when Tabitha confronted him, he admitted it all and said he wouldn't give the other woman up.

It was shocking. Horrifying. What could a woman do if her husband simply ran around on her? What choices were left? Amanda couldn't blame Tabitha for refusing to live with it, and when she divorced him, Michael married the other woman. Insult ladled on top of injury.

That was what came of marrying the wrong man. Or, if you listened to the people in this community, that was what came of jumping the fence and marrying an *Englischer*. And Amanda had to agree—if Mamm hadn't died, everything might have been different.

3

Tabitha picked up her father's plate from the table. The screen door bounced as he headed back out to meet the cattle trailer that had just pulled up. It beeped as it backed up, Daet waving the trailer in. He would be selling some beef steers at auction, and it still rankled Tabitha a little bit when her father refused to give her that kind of basic information. He didn't have to be that secretive. They were a family, after all. They were all working together.

Daet looked older these days, though. It still took Tabitha by surprise when she noticed the stoop in his shoulders and the complete whiteness of his hair. No more iron gray. Her father was tired, but he did seem happier when all three of his daughters were around. And perhaps he ate better when Tabitha could share some of the cooking duties too.

There was something about being a family again that was comforting for Tabitha.

Amanda pulled out a paper bag of baking flour and a package of dry yeast. A small glass bowl thunked onto the counter next, followed by a big metal bowl. Amanda's lips were pressed together in a firm line. She filled the glass bowl with some warm water and poured the yeast into it. Then she stood there with hands flat on the counter, seeming to stare straight through it.

"What do you think of the Menno situation?" Tabitha asked.

Amanda straightened and reached for the flour. "It's interesting. That's all."

Rose stood to the side, her attention focused out the window, watching the truck pulling the cattle trailer drive down the dirt road toward the cattle barn. Tabitha picked up an apple, rubbed it over her clean apron, then took a bite.

"Do you want to help me hitch back up?" Rose asked. "I promised Aaron I wouldn't be too long, and if I don't go now, I might get blocked in by the truck."

Rose's gaze flicked toward Amanda, but Amanda didn't look up.

"Oh, of course." Tabitha took another bite of the apple and followed her sister out the side door. She'd give the rest of the apple to the horse. He'd like the treat. From inside the house, she could hear a whisk start up inside the metal bowl.

"Do you think Amanda might still have a chance at finding a husband?" Rose asked as the screen door banged shut behind them. A breeze cooled Tabitha's neck, and she flapped the front of her dress to let in a bit more cool air.

"I have no idea," Tabitha replied. "Did I really hurt her reputation that badly?"

Rose sobered. "*Yah*."

Not the answer Tabitha had expected, and she felt a wave of defensiveness. "Really? You're married. You'd think I would have done just as much damage to your life as hers, if that was the case."

"There was a bit more time for things to die down before I was old enough to start courting. Besides, Amanda is . . ." Rose licked her lips, then lowered her voice. "She's not known for her great beauty, is she? Then you count something like our older sister jumping the fence, and there were risks men wouldn't take."

Rose wouldn't quite meet Tabitha's gaze, and her face colored.

"So just my visits—"

"You were flaunting the fact you jumped the fence by wearing blue jeans. You didn't have to. You could have worn a dress, even if it wasn't a cape dress. Then there was the time that Michael sat outside with our cousins and tried to convince them to jump the fence. He was telling them how much happier you were now that you were free of the Amish restrictions."

"He didn't!"

"*Yah*, he did. We thought you knew."

"No . . . I didn't." Tabitha sighed.

"And he was rather . . . flirty with Amish women."

"He didn't understand our boundaries—" Tabitha started to say, and then she felt heat hit her face. "I always defended him. I didn't want to see what he was doing, because if I really faced it, I'd have to do something about it, and I didn't know what to do. I do remember him being flirtatious with our cousins. We used to argue about it on the way home again, and I'd be so frustrated with him. He always said he was just being friendly and it was a cultural difference, that was all. He made me feel like the stupid one. I guess I hoped you all hadn't noticed."

Rose pressed her lips together. "We noticed."

"I'm so sorry."

32

"You don't have to apologize for your husband's bad behavior," Rose replied.

"So I was a bigger problem than I realized. We were. My visits, at least . . ."

"It was complicated," Rose confirmed.

Rose was being kind. It was more than complicated. Tabitha could see how her visits home would have shaken people up. No one would want Michael as a part of their extended family, causing trouble where there hadn't been trouble before. And Tabitha was the one bringing him home on a regular basis because she missed her family, and they should be able to visit.

"Maybe now I can help her," Tabitha said.

"How?" Rose raised a hand to shade her eyes from the sun.

"Maybe I can help her find a husband. I visit enough farms. I might find someone who'd be a good match."

"Like who?" Rose asked.

"I'm not sure yet. But I might spot someone who'd be good for her."

"She's made her peace with not marrying," Rose said.

"And that's just sad. I'm the one who has to make my peace with it, not her. Maybe she's afraid of more rejection, but I'm not giving up on her."

Rose just shook her head. "I'm not sure that's a good idea."

They fetched Rose's horse from the corral and brought him over to the buggy to hitch up. Rose held out her hand to the horse. He nuzzled toward her, and she stroked his nose.

"Why is finding a match for Amanda such a bad idea?" Tabitha asked. "Amanda is hardworking, a great cook, and, like you say, I held her back. I'm in a unique situation here. I'm not going to have a husband or a home of my own. I'm back with Daet, and I can take over helping him out and let Amanda have her chance at a family of her own."

"Amanda has gotten . . . prickly," Rose said.

"Prickly? I don't see that in her."

"Trust me. She's gotten used to doing things her own way."

"She can adjust," Tabitha replied. "Any of us can adjust to changes, especially if it means getting the very thing you've longed for. Don't you remember when we were little girls, and we used to pretend we were getting married?"

"And we'd make the dog stand in for the groom, and we'd take turns being the bride," Rose said with a chuckle. "And Mamm told us we'd be better off practicing our homemaking skills than marrying the dog every afternoon."

Tabitha remembered those hot summer days when she and her little sisters used to put on their best white aprons, promising Mamm they wouldn't get a speck of dirt on them, and go stand in a row by the chicken coop and take solemn vows of fidelity and faith to their black lab named Thunder. They'd set up wedding dinners with biscuits and jam at the kitchen table, and they'd give each other marriage advice that they thought was very wise indeed. Mostly it consisted of feeding their husbands well—it was the only thing they knew made a husband happy.

Tabitha laughed. "And when Aent Marie got married, and we sat at the table with her husband's cousins. Do you remember that boy who'd been quite keen on Amanda?"

"It didn't last."

"No, but she was only fourteen or something like that," Tabitha replied. "All I'm saying is that men have found her attractive before, and she wanted marriage as much as you and I did. I messed up my chance at a united Amish marriage, but she's been a good daughter and a good sister. She deserves the same happiness you have."

Rose met Tabitha's gaze, and something uncertain swam in the depths of her brown eyes, but then she nodded.

PATRICIA JOHNS

"She does. And you're a loving sister to try to help her," Rose said.

"I really believe Gott wanted me to come home," Tabitha said. "And I don't think that is just for me. I mean, I missed you all, and I missed the life I was raised to, but I think that Gott has more for me to do that obviously doesn't involve a husband and *kinner* of my own. Maybe I'm supposed to help Amanda."

"Maybe so," Rose said thoughtfully. "Gott's ways are above ours. Maybe there is a plan at work."

"There is always a divine plan at work," Tabitha replied with a small smile. That was one thing she'd become most sure of during her time away. Her life was not over, even though her marriage was. There was a set of verses that had sunk deep into her heart as she'd struggled with her own mistakes: "If I take the wings of the morning, and dwell in the uttermost parts of the sea; Even there shall thy hand lead me, and thy right hand shall hold me."

Philadelphia wasn't so far that Gott couldn't reach her. Divorce wasn't so shameful that Gott couldn't give her a new future.

"I'd better get back home. It's wash day, you know," Rose said. "Just be careful when it comes to Amanda. I think your heart is in the right place, but she's more sensitive than you think."

Fine. She'd heard the warning, but she wasn't giving up on her sister either.

"I'll see you, then," Tabitha said. "Tell Aaron I say hello."

Rose nodded and pulled herself up into the buggy.

Tabitha was home in Shepherd's Hill again, but there was nothing simple about making a place for herself in the community she'd left. Everyone had changed. Her father

35

was older, and her little sisters had both grown up, and Tabitha was no longer the eager, optimistic young woman who thought that life would treat her gently just because her family had. If she'd learned anything, it was that life was not gentle, a man couldn't be her savior, and the only one she could truly rely on was Gott above. Gott was the One with the plan.

4

For the next few days, the Schrock sisters were busy. Amanda and Rose went along on several farm visits with Tabitha, and the rest of Amanda's time was spent catching up on household chores and doing the weekly deep clean to prepare for a restful, worshipful Sunday.

That Saturday, Amanda bent over a bowl of bread dough. The smell of warm, foamy yeast had always soothed Amanda's heart in a way nothing else could. And yet this morning it wasn't enough to smooth over her jostled emotions. She poured the yeast mixture over the flour in the big metal bowl and watched as it soaked in. Eggs were next, then milk. Then oil. She used a strong wooden spoon and some muscle to stir.

The clock ticked comfortingly from the kitchen wall. Next to the clock was a calendar, and next to the calendar was a large piece of embroidery that had been made by their *mamm*. Amanda's memory of her mother was foggy, and she couldn't quite recall her face anymore. But she remembered her hands—the long, slim fingers, and the way she'd wear a thimble when she worked on a piece of stitching. Amanda remembered her mother working on that very piece of embroidery—the full twenty-third Psalm, surrounded by leaves, vines, and flowers. Her mother's initials were stitched neatly at the bottom: *VS. Vannetta Schrock.* Her mother's touches were still around the house—quilts she'd stitched, scarves she'd knitted, baskets she'd woven. Amanda treasured those handwritten recipe cards, too, little pieces of Mamm left behind that reminded her how much Mamm had loved them all.

Amanda leaned into stirring the dough, scraping flour from the side of the bowl into the soft, sticky mass in the center. Scrape, fold, scrape, fold. She changed hands and repeated the process.

The side door opened, and she glanced up as Tabitha came inside.

"I stopped by Rose and Aaron's place on the way back from the Bernhart farm," Tabitha said. "And Rose will come with us to do those calf vaccinations at the Peachy farm Monday morning."

"I thought she'd be busy with her own home," Amanda replied. "Monday is wash day. Rose never misses wash day."

"It's wash day here too," Tabitha said. "We'll make it work. Isn't it nice to do something as the three Schrock sisters again?"

But it was odd. Rose had been coming along for almost all of the veterinarian visits she could. She even went when Amanda was staying home to bake and scrub floors. If Amanda had her own husband and home, she wouldn't be running off with Tabitha to vaccinate cattle, that was for sure. Even though she enjoyed it. Even though she felt like she was good at it.

"What's going on?" Amanda asked.

"I don't think anything is going on. She wants to help."

"It just seems strange to me," Amanda said, leaning into the mixing again. "Why wouldn't she be working on her own home and garden? What about Aaron? If she has extra time, she could be sewing him an extra shirt or going out to keep him company. I mean, a man always needs someone to open and shut the gates—"

"Amanda, she's fine," Tabitha interrupted. "She wants to help. What's wrong with that?"

Technically, nothing.

"You two used to hide things from me when we were *kinner*," Amanda replied.

"Oh, those were just silly things. We were teasing you."

Amanda met her sister's gaze, and Tabitha blushed.

"I'm sorry," Tabitha added. "I suppose we were being cruel back then. I'm not doing that now." She paused. "I was telling Rose that I wanted to find you a husband."

Amanda blinked. "Me?"

"Why not you?" she asked. "You're plenty old enough to marry, and I'm here now to help with Daet."

It was true. Tabitha being home again did free Amanda up, but that thought was both exciting and terrifying. Taking care of Daet had given her a job to do. With Tabitha back home and repairing the family name, if a man still didn't want her, it would sting more. It would feel like a more personal insult.

"It might not be taking care of Daet that is holding me back," Amanda said.

"Then what?" Tabitha asked. "I want to help. I know I made things worse for you when I married Michael, and I want to help set things right."

"I'm twenty-seven." That was a fact, and it needed to be faced. Women in their community tended to get married young. When Rose got married at twenty-three, she was considered a little on the old side.

"And you're also not dead yet," Tabitha retorted, meeting her gaze. "*Englischer* women get married at all ages. In fact, they're getting married much later these days because they're getting educations, starting careers, and pursuing things that interest them. When I was married at nineteen, I was considered shockingly young to have taken those vows."

"I'm not *Englische*," Amanda replied. As interesting as it was that the *Englischers* did things so differently, it didn't affect their community.

"But you are an attractive woman who can bake up a storm," Tabitha said. "What man doesn't want a wife whose food tastes as good as yours? And while you're perfectly pretty, a face only lasts so long, but quality strudel? That's for life! So let me help."

Amanda couldn't help but laugh at her sister's description, but it did make her feel a bit more hopeful.

"The problem is, there aren't a lot of men to choose from out here," Amanda said. "Unless you can whip up some men from other communities and transplant them in Shepherd's Hill . . ."

"Actually, that's not a bad idea. We could reach out to a matchmaker," Tabitha said, brightening. "You've just got to let me sell you a bit, point out everything you have to offer."

"I don't like the idea of being sold," Amanda said, making a face. "But maybe I should put myself out there more."

"You should," Tabitha said.

"It's hard, though," Amanda said. "If I do that, and they still don't want me—"

"Don't think like that," Tabitha replied. "You're wonderful, and the right man will see it."

Tabitha's return had brought some excitement back to this old house, but it also brought whole new dynamics between the sisters, and maybe that was a good thing. Amanda had settled a little too comfortably into her rut, and maybe it was time that things changed for her.

She pressed her lips together and continued stirring. There was one man she knew of who was looking for a wife . . . and Menno was kind. She remembered back in their childhood when some of the boys at school had been teasing Amanda, Menno had stood up for her. They'd turned their teasing onto him then, but he hadn't seemed to mind. She'd never forgotten that he'd taken the brunt of a day's teasing for her.

And then there had been a youth group event at a deacon's farm when they were in their young teens, and a cat had given birth to kittens. One was a runt, and it didn't look like it would survive. Menno had asked permission to take it home and bottle feed it. He'd had a gentle heart back then, and if that kindness was the foundation of his character, she couldn't imagine that he'd be so bad now.

"I meant to ask you earlier," Tabitha said. "What's going on with Daet and Nathaniel Peachy?"

Her sister's question pulled her out of her thoughts. Amanda poured a drizzle of oil around the edge of the bowl to loosen the sticky dough, and she used her fingers to pull the dough off the spoon.

"Nothing more than usual. They still don't like each other," Amanda replied.

"But why?"

Amanda looked up at her sister and considered for a moment. "I honestly don't know. You're older than me. Do you remember what went wrong between them?"

Tabitha shook her head. "No, Daet was never one to talk about those things, was he?"

"Daet doesn't talk about anything," Amanda replied.

"We need to change that," Tabitha said.

Amanda laughed. "That's not likely to happen."

Their father was a stubborn, stoic, good-hearted man. He meant well, and he loved his family fiercely, but there were some parts of his nature that simply would not change, and Daet didn't talk about his personal issues. Ever.

"I remember when they used to be seated next to each other on Service Sunday," Tabitha said. "That was before Nathan Glick moved to our community, and he ended up between them. But Daet and Nathaniel Peachy used to sit shoulder to shoulder, and Daet wouldn't look at him once. Just sat there and stared straight ahead. I didn't remember it ever being different, so I didn't question it."

The Amish always sat in order of age in the Sunday service, so a man could sit between the same two men for his entire life in one community. It all had to do with when his birthday fell. So when a man deeply disliked the fellow he was sitting next to, that was more than awkward. It was wrong. He had the duty to make amends. Daet and Nathaniel Peachy never had.

"I remember that," Amanda said. "But Daet has told us for years that he doesn't trust Nathaniel Peachy as far as he can throw him. So whatever happened to turn Daet away from him must have happened a very long time ago."

"Do you think Daet would hold that kind of grudge?"

"Whatever happened between them must have really made Daet mad," Amanda said. She sprinkled more flour into the dough and used her fists to knead it in.

"Anger covers pain," Tabitha said. "Whatever happened

hurt him. Hasn't the bishop or the elders tried to make them talk this out? That's their job, isn't it?"

Amanda shot her sister a wry look. "This coming from the woman who has been gone for ten years?"

Some color touched Tabitha's cheeks. "I still remember how things are supposed to work. They're supposed to help people sort out their differences. They're supposed to insist upon it."

"Things don't always work that way," Amanda replied. "If two people have a grievance but they don't pull anyone else into it, why would the bishop get involved?"

"Because it's not the Christian way." Tabitha's flush deepened.

Her sister was right, of course.

"I'm being naïve, aren't I?"

"A little." Amanda shrugged. "We do our best, but everyone has flaws, including our own *daet*."

It was ironic that Amanda, the younger sister, understood their way of life better than Tabitha did at this point, but that decade had made a big difference. Amanda spent her adult years here. Tabitha had spent hers out with the *Englischers* and had come back with a broken heart and ridiculously high ideals, as if the Amish life could heal everything that had been broken inside of her.

But Amanda knew better. Their life was beautiful, but it didn't fix everything. And their ideals didn't always pan out either. They certainly hadn't for her.

"I still think that two Amish men who can't stand each other goes against everything we believe in," her sister said. "It's not right."

Amanda eyed Tabitha thoughtfully.

"What?" Tabitha asked.

"Do you regret coming back?"

"Why would I regret it? I knew what I was doing when I came home."

"You left Shepherd's Hill for a bigger life," Amanda said.

"I did. I thought I was terribly smart. The teachers said I was gifted, and they were amazed at how fast I could finish my GED with top grades. They told me that if I applied myself, I could do anything I wanted. I . . . believed them."

"You are smart, Tabitha."

"For whatever that matters. *Yah*, I was able to get the education I needed to be a veterinarian, but it doesn't set me above anyone else. If anything, I was ridiculously naïve, and that was more damaging by far. I truly believe that our way of life is what Gott wants for us. I followed my heart to my own detriment. I'm home because it's where I belong."

"It's not perfect here, though," Amanda said. "People are still lonely. People still have grievances."

"I know that. Where is this coming from?"

"I don't know. I'm sorry." Amanda shook her head. She didn't want to become a suspicious, bitter woman. That was why she needed to make some changes of her own. Her current path wouldn't end well for her. But this chance to work with Tabitha was an interesting opportunity.

Tabitha sighed. "It isn't right that Daet and Nathaniel have fostered this animosity all these years. I stand by that."

And Amanda had to agree. But with close neighbors and people who had to rely upon each other for everything from help with their chores when they were ill to raising a new barn after a fire, maintaining those relationships sometimes meant keeping mouths shut. Right now, Daet and Nathaniel Peachy could sit on the same bench during Sunday service, and they could manage to work on opposite ends of the property when helping an elderly couple with their chores. And that was worth something.

Amanda shrugged. "If you meddle where you shouldn't, you might find yourself being sat down by the bishop."

That wasn't unheard of either. If the bishop came knocking, it was normally to let someone know they needed to adjust their behavior somehow. Amanda had never had the bishop sit her down before, but she'd had a friend who'd been sat down because of her too-short hemlines.

"So what issue would make you stand up and say something?" Tabitha asked.

"My own future," Amanda replied. "I'm not so different from you, you know. I don't have any desire to jump the fence, but that doesn't mean I don't have hopes for my own future. And they don't involve just keeping house here for the rest of my days either."

"What do you want to do?" Tabitha asked.

"I want to help you with your veterinarian work," she said. "I like the freedom of it. We can see three farms in a day and make a big difference. I can do more—learn more. And if I'm not going to be married, then at least I can find other places to be useful."

"That's what I'm doing too," Tabitha said, and the sisters exchanged a smile. "I'm glad we'll do it together. I missed you."

Amanda patted the ball of dough and tossed a tea towel over the bowl.

"But don't cling too much to the idea of not getting married," Tabitha said. "Not if deep down you'd really like a husband. Because I think you can find a good man."

It was almost a cruel hope to dangle in front of Amanda, but her sister looked utterly sincere. And Amanda couldn't help but think of Menno, who was equally unmarriageable around here, but who she also remembered having a good heart.

Was it foolish of her to wonder if she should renew their acquaintance?

She looked down at the bowl of dough. Today she was making dinner rolls, but one treat she was particularly good at making was cinnamon rolls. They were her specialty, and if she was to renew her acquaintance with Menno, she could bring them as a gift. They'd be her very best foot forward.

If she dared . . .

5

That week was Service Sunday, and Tabitha had been looking forward to it and dreading it in equal measure. Service Sunday and Visiting Sunday alternated weeks, and everyone looked forward to Service Sunday because they got to see everybody all together. It was a whole day of worship, singing, and visiting, and it was another opportunity for Tabitha to settle back into the regular rhythms of Amish life.

That was the part that put her stomach into knots. She was back, but she was just still adjusting, and her old friends were welcoming and kind, but they held back too. Tabitha looked forward to the day when all of this was behind her and she was just another Amish woman seeing her friends.

Gott, may that day come soon.

Menno Weaver attended every Service Sunday, and Tabitha took notice of him this time. He sat in his usual spot during the service, and he nodded to a few of the men. His gaze moved over the young women a few times, and Tabitha wondered if there was a particular woman he had his eye on. If there was, he didn't talk to any of them to give Tabitha a hint. He murmured a hello to a group of women in their twenties, and they looked at him in mild surprise, their conversation suspended until he carried on past, his face ablaze, and Tabitha's heart went out to him.

He was trying, and she could sympathize with that. She was trying too.

But when Tabitha attempted to say hello to Menno, he didn't hear her and beelined for his buggy while everyone else starting milling around the food table. So maybe Menno had it worse than Tabitha did these days. At least Tabitha had people making conversation with her.

Amanda didn't want to stay as long as she usually did, and Tabitha was happy enough to head back home midafternoon. As soon as they stepped into the house, Tabitha pulled on her apron to get cooking.

"I'm going to do some baking," Amanda said. "Do you want to start tonight's supper?"

"Sure," Tabitha said. She went downstairs to the refrigerator and pulled out some chilled beef to make stew. This was one meal that turned out beautifully on an *Englischer* electric stove or a woodstove. Tabitha couldn't ruin this one.

That evening, their father clomped back into the house after chores and pulled off his rubber boots. The kitchen was filled with the fragrance of the beef stew, corn bread, and sizzling sausages and potatoes. Tabitha could just see into the mudroom where her father leaned over the sink to scrub his hands with that thick bar of yellow homemade soap.

Tabitha set their places at the table—three heavy stoneware bowls and matching plates. This used to be a full set of twelve place settings. Tabitha remembered them from her girlhood. Mamm had loved these dishes, and she'd said over and over how they'd outlast all of them, they were so sturdy. But there were only a few left now. Tabitha couldn't help but think that things never quite turned out the way people expected.

"I'm hungry," Daet announced as he came out of the mudroom and pulled out his chair at the table. "It smells wonderful, girls."

"*Danke*," Tabitha said. "Amanda did the baking."

Amanda shot her a smile. There were cinnamon rolls in the oven, cream-cheese frosting waiting on the counter, and a tray of oatmeal date bars. The bars would be good for Daet to eat, but the cinnamon rolls would only be an unnecessary temptation for Daet. That was something to discuss with her sister later.

When they all sat down, they bowed their heads for silent prayer. When Daet cleared his throat, Tabitha raised her head and waited as Amanda served their father first.

"So what is your plan for tomorrow?" Daet asked, then added to Amanda, "*Danke*."

"I'm doing the vaccinations at the Peachy farm in the morning," Tabitha said, holding her bowl out to Amanda to fill. "*Danke*, Amanda."

"As in Nathaniel Peachy?" her father asked.

"*Yah*, the very one," Tabitha said. "Amanda and Rose are going to come and help me."

"Shouldn't Dr. Brian be the one doing those vaccinations?" he asked.

"This is my job, Daet," she said gently. This had become an old argument. Her father accepted that she was both educated and qualified, but he hadn't fully made his peace with her working full-time as veterinarian. Most of the men in these parts struggled with it.

"What does Dr. Brian even do?" her father demanded. He

accepted a wedge of corn bread still warm from the oven and slathered a thick layer of butter on it before he dipped it into the stew. "It sounds to me like he sends you off doing the real work, and he's just sitting in an office somewhere. Men should be putting their backs into some proper hard work. That's the way the good Lord intended it."

"He's not sitting around," Tabitha replied. "He's running the clinic. There are plenty of people bringing their animals to see him there too."

"Dogs and cats and the like?" he asked.

"*Yah*, probably. Maybe even a gerbil or a parakeet," Tabitha attempted to joke.

"You should be doing that, not him," Daet said. "One of these days you're going to get hurt. That's not women's work."

"Daet, this is about Nathaniel Peachy's farm, isn't it?" Tabitha asked.

Her father didn't answer, but he pressed his lips together disapprovingly.

"I know you don't like him—"

"You can't trust him," he said.

"Why do you always say that?"

"Because I know him," her father stated.

"What happened between you two?" Tabitha pressed. "He's a part of this community. His cattle need veterinarian care, just like everyone else's."

"Nathaniel Peachy cannot stand me, and you are my daughter. And maybe I don't like you going out there and putting yourself into the position of being talked about. I don't want him criticizing you behind my back."

"I'm sure he wouldn't be the first," Tabitha said. "I jumped the fence, remember? I was the source of more than one gossip session over the years."

Amanda nodded soberly. "They did talk. A lot."

Tabitha glanced over at her sister. She sat with her back straight, her spoon hovering over the bowl.

"I'm back now," Tabitha said. "They'll stop talking eventually."

She'd come home—what else could she do? She couldn't erase the past, and even if she could, she wasn't sure she wanted to. She took a bite of stew, savoring the delicious mix of potato, beef, and fresh rosemary.

"Since Rose will be there to help you, I think I'll stay home tomorrow," Amanda said.

Tabitha swallowed. "I thought you wanted—"

"I've got some things to do," Amanda said, and her expression softened. No harm was intended. "I know I said I wanted to go with you, but since Rose is going, you won't miss me, will you?"

It *was* wash day. Someone had to do it.

"I should be okay with Rose's help," Tabitha said. "You're a better assistant than Rose is, though."

Amanda smiled at the compliment. "I do believe that." She glanced toward the open door that led to the summer kitchen on the porch. "Just a minute. I think the cinnamon rolls smell like they're done."

Amanda put her spoon down and swiped the oven mitts off the counter as she headed back toward the door.

"Gossip can ruin lives," Daet said, his voice low. "Remember that. We're connected, this family. We affect each other."

And Tabitha had already affected her sister's life—the message was clear. But suddenly she had to wonder what her leaving the community had done to her father. Somehow she'd expected Daet to remain just as she remembered him—strong, immoveable, stubborn, kind—but that was hardly fair, was it?

51

"I'll do a good job, Daet," Tabitha said, her voice low. "I'll be professional. There will be nothing at all to complain about. I promise you."

Her father met her gaze. It would have to be enough, because it was all that Tabitha could offer.

6

The next morning, Tabitha checked her satchel and leather medical bag to make sure she had everything for the day's duties. She mentally ticked off a list as her eyes moved over the supplies—*vaccine vials, syringes, extra syringes, stethoscope, stomach tube, scalpel* . . . She wouldn't need the emergency supplies, but she should always be prepared.

Behind her, Amanda wiped down the last counter, and Rose stood by the door looking antsy.

"You're done with the cleanup," Tabitha said. "You might as well come with us to the Peachy farm."

"No, no," Amanda said. "I have some sewing I have to catch up on. I'll work on that. Plus, there's the laundry."

"I can help you with that later," Tabitha said. "It'll go faster with two of us."

"You might be late, and it has to be done."

Monday was wash day—there was no arguing that—and as if to prove her intent, Amanda hung up the dishrag and headed for the basement stairs.

"I'll just go start separating the colors out," Amanda said

brightly, disappearing down the staircase. "You two have a good time."

Tabitha eyed the worn, wooden stairs for a moment, then sighed. She didn't have time to figure out her sister this morning anyway. She gathered up her satchel of vaccination supplies and picked up her medical bag in her other hand, then headed out the side door. There was work to be done, and a new reputation to prove. Her family was right that people talked, and a person's mistakes traveled faster and farther than any of their virtues.

Tabitha and Rose sent Rose's horse into the corral and hitched up Tabitha's buggy. Her horse was used to the veterinarian work and less likely to spook if they took the buggy out into a field. Besides, Tabitha preferred to hold the reins. This was her career, her future, and her new clients, whether they fully accepted her or not. Sometimes a woman needed to take the reins of her own life and get moving in the right direction.

"Amanda wanted to do laundry?" Rose asked as they rattled out of the drive and onto the gravel road.

"*Yah*. That's what she said."

Rose was silent.

"Did I do something to upset her?" Tabitha asked.

Rose shook her head. "I doubt it. Amanda has her own idiosyncrasies. She's been living alone with Daet for too long, if you ask me, and she can be very particular about her schedules and ways of doing things."

"That's not her fault," Tabitha countered.

"No, of course not," Rose agreed. "But Daet is peculiar, and Amanda has been dealing with his moods and expectations on her own ever since I married Aaron, and she's turning into a peculiar one herself."

"You mentioned that before," Tabitha said. "Haven't you tried to set her up with anyone?"

"I've suggested her for two of Aaron's friends, but she questions them too directly. She has absolutely no ability to be demure and flirt." Rose sighed. "And she won't take advice from me. Besides, most of the single men I know are five years younger than her. Maybe some older widower in another community would be a good match for her."

Some older man who'd already been married before . . . maybe even a man their father's age. It seemed like even Rose had given up hope for Amanda, and that didn't sit well for Tabitha. Amanda needed people on her side who believed in her.

First they headed into town to the clinic, where they picked up the vaccines, then they headed back out to the Peachy farm that was nestled in next to a train track on the west side of the property. She could see the straight stretch of tracks from their vantage point at the top of the hill before they started down toward the farm. The tracks were fenced off to keep the cattle clear of danger, and Tabitha remembered only one time that the cattle had broken down the fence. A young heifer had been killed on the tracks. That was back in her school days when Nathaniel's son, Jonas, had been in her class, and he'd missed a few days of school helping his *daet* fix the fence. The location of their farm in relation to the railroad tracks was not ideal, but people could get used to anything, as could a herd of cattle.

The rest of the farm was a compact little arrangement of barns, a big white house, and a patchwork of fields. Cattle grazed along the verdant spread, and Tabitha could make out a sizable flock of chickens milling around a chicken house. The Peachys sold eggs too.

"Jonas Peachy is single," Tabitha said as they neared the drive.

"*Yah*, he is." Rose shifted on the hard bench seat.

"And he's only a bit older than Amanda," Tabitha said. "He's good looking too. I can't believe I didn't think of it before."

"Jonas and Amanda?" Rose shook her head. "I don't see it happening."

"It might need a nudge," Tabitha agreed. "But Amanda needs our help, Rose. She's not good at this, you know."

"*Yah* . . ." Rose shrugged. "But you'll see what I mean. Go ahead and try. Amanda is a tough one to match, and not only because there are so few eligible men for her. She's . . . difficult."

And maybe she was, but she was also a good woman with a big heart.

"I'll never have grandchildren of my own," Tabitha said, forcing a smile. "So I'd better get you two having babies. I need to be someone's favorite *aent*."

Rose paled. She'd been married two years now with no sign of a baby. Tabitha shouldn't have said that.

"I'm not pushing—" Tabitha winced. "Rose, I'm not trying to pressure you into having a baby. I know that these things happen when they happen. I'm sorry."

"It's fine," Rose said, but her voice was as tight as a clothesline.

The best of intentions seemed like a pasture littered with cow pats, and Tabitha exhaled a sigh of relief as she pulled up next to the large, freshly painted Peachy farmhouse. Cattle were less complicated by far.

7

What was Tabitha Schrock doing here? Jonas leaned closer to the kitchen window. Her hair was neatly pulled away from her face, and he found himself drawn to those dark, soulful eyes. She was a woman who'd come home, but before her return, she was a woman who'd been painfully humbled.

Jonas hadn't gotten his nerve up to talk to her yet. She'd been home for two months already, and he'd seen her from across the service at Sunday church gatherings. She seemed so calm and collected, so much more confident than he'd expected her to be when he heard the gossip that she was back. He'd listened to her confession before the congregation too. Even confessing her mistakes, she'd held herself with the poise of a bishop's wife. Her painful past shone through her eyes, but it hadn't bent her neck.

Tabitha's sister Rose rode in the buggy beside her. He was friends with Rose's husband, Aaron. Jonas would have assumed the women were here to visit his *mamm*, except then Tabitha jumped down and pulled out a brown leather medical bag.

Dr. Brian wasn't coming today, was he?

"Is that the vet?" his mother asked. Mary Peachy's cheeks were red from the heat of sterilizing jars for canning green beans. She dabbed at her forehead with a handkerchief.

"It's Tabitha Schrock," he replied.

Jonas had been used to Tabitha being the source of head shaking and gossip, but she'd done what very few others had. She'd returned, contrite and ready to admit defeat. He doubted she'd stay, though, in all honesty.

"Is she doing the vaccinations?" Mamm frowned.

"Looks like."

Mamm shook her head and sighed. "That's what happens when a girl jumps the fence."

What exactly his mother was referring to, he could only surmise, but he was glad his *mamm* was the one in the house when Tabitha arrived and not his *daet*. Daet would have had some strong opinions, Jonas was sure, and not only because she was a woman. She was Abram Schrock's daughter, and anyone associated with Abram Schrock was tainted to Daet. Mamm headed back to the counter where she had lined up glass jars. In a clapboard addition to the house, the summer stove had a big black pot steaming away, filled with jars of sealed green beans, no doubt.

"I'd better head out, then," Jonas said.

His mother gave him a distracted smile as she started filling the jars with cut beans, and Jonas went out the side door. The windows were all cranked open to let some air flow through the kitchen, and the screen door clattered shut behind him.

Tabitha gave him a nod as he came down the wooden steps. "Jonas Peachy."

"Tabitha Shrock." He smiled faintly. "Are you our vet today?"

"For sure and for certain."

"Where is Dr. Brian? My *daet* will ask." His father would more than ask. He'd rant about it and wonder if she'd report back to her father about the state of his farm. His mother would murmur and calm him. Jonas could already play out the scene in his head.

"He's otherwise busy," Tabitha replied. "You've got me today, or you can reschedule with him. It might take a few weeks to bring him out, though. Whatever your *daet* prefers."

Jonas was dealing with the vaccinations today. Daet was at a horse auction that had been going on for the last few days. A lot of the local men had been heading over to see what was for sale, and they needed a new horse come harvest time.

Rose shot him a small smile. "Good morning, Jonas."

"Morning, Rose," he replied. "How is Aaron?"

"Working hard. I'll tell him you said hi."

"*Yah*, please do." Rose was the perfect little Amish wife—dutiful, sweet, pretty. Aaron had mentioned in confidence that the marriage wasn't easy, though.

"Shall we get moving, then?" Tabitha asked, eyebrows raised. No dutiful meekness there. There was a flicker of the girl he'd known in grade school, the rebel waiting for an escape. Her face had matured, though, and her gaze was unwavering.

"*Yah*," Jonas said. "Do you need me to carry anything?"

"I'm fine," Tabitha replied, shouldering her bag. "Lead the way."

Tabitha Schrock was the new veterinarian. That was going to take some time to adjust to. They'd heard she was stepping in, and some of the men had mentioned that she'd been at their farms, but somehow seeing her here in her professional capacity made it all seem a little more real.

He led the way toward the cow barn. There were thirty cows to be vaccinated today, and yesterday had been spent rounding them up and bringing them into the small pasture so they'd be easier to access.

"How long have you worked as a veterinarian?" he asked.

Tabitha fell in next to him, Rose coming up behind them. Both women were neat as pins, and he wondered how long that would last with the work today.

"I've been a full vet for two years." She cast him a side glance, but he saw the glint in her eye. She was proud of herself. If she'd lived Amish for longer, she'd hide that. That was the *Englischer* influence coming out, and he wasn't sure how to respond to it.

"Was the schooling hard?" he asked.

She shrugged. "I suppose so. *Yah*. I had to buckle down and really focus."

She'd always been smart, though. Everyone knew that Tabitha Schrock took to books like a fish took to water. There had been talk that she could be the new schoolteacher if the current one got married. And then when she'd been getting her GED, Jonas had assumed that she planned on teaching. He'd been very wrong about that.

"How is your *daet*?" he asked. It was mostly a way to change the subject.

"Fine." Her smile faded. "Jonas, I wanted to ask you about that."

Behind them, Rose cleared her throat loudly.

"Rose would rather I didn't bring it up," Tabitha said.

"Bring up what?" he asked. His first thought was that his father had overstepped with hers somehow. The two older men were constantly grating on each other, but if she thought he had any influence over his *daet*—

"I understand that our fathers still don't get along," she said.

Jonas almost laughed, although it wasn't a laughing matter. "We don't talk about that."

"No one does," Tabitha said. "But it's a problem, and I think we should help them to get over it."

Jonas slowed his pace as they reached the barn, the pasture of waiting cattle just beyond. The first several animals were already in the stalls, though. He looked over at Rose, and she dropped her gaze, not to be pulled into this apparently.

"We?" he said. "As in you and me?" He wasn't about to get in the middle of this either. It had been years of tightly restrained animosity.

"Who else will do it?" Tabitha asked. "It's been decades, and from what I can tell, our *daets* are both good, hardworking, family-centered men. Your mother is a kind and considerate woman. All of us *kinner* are decent people. There is no good guy and bad guy here. Not that I can see."

"Rose, are you wanting to do this too?" he asked, glancing back at the younger woman. Rose's lips were pressed tightly shut.

"No," she said. "This is Tabitha's plan."

Jonas pulled open the barn door, and they headed into the dim interior. The cattle barn was an older building, while the horse barn had been fixed up recently. But this barn, while old and worn, was kept clean and well organized. Daet was a stickler for every tool being cleaned, maintained, and put back in its place along one wall. White paint outlines showed where each item belonged. The loft above held hay bales and cattle feed, the bales getting low at this time of year. In the stalls that lined both sides of the barn, cattle shuffled while they waited for their injections.

"I'm glad you give my *daet* some credit," Jonas said.

"Of course." Tabitha handed her sister one of the bags from her shoulder. "Where should I set up?"

There was a row of waist-high cupboards topped with a wooden counter, rubbed smooth with beeswax and mineral oil, on one end of the barn that would give her a convenient work surface, and he gestured in that direction.

"I don't think either of them want to leave this life with an enemy," she said. "And I want us to help mend that rift."

"How?" he asked.

She put her leather bag down on the counter, and then placed the black insulated bag next to it. She unzipped the insulated bag, revealing a selection of vials. She pulled out the first bottle and tore open three sealed syringes. Rose came up next to her, and Tabitha filled two syringes, covered their sharp tips, and handed them to Rose. The women had done this together before, it would seem.

"How?" he repeated.

"I'm not sure." Tabitha raised her gaze to meet his. There was nothing demure about her, and Jonas couldn't help but feel disconcerted. How was he supposed to relate to this woman who barely retained any Amish mannerisms? "But if an opportunity presents itself to help our fathers make peace, I hope I can count on you to back me up? And vice versa, of course. If you see a way, I'll support you."

She was serious. She wanted their fathers to stop this bitterness between them, and he couldn't help but be impressed by her determination.

"I'm not sure it's that easy," he said.

"With Gott, all things are possible," she replied. "We can pray on it."

Try to argue with a woman when she quoted Scripture.

"If there's a chance for them to make peace, I will encourage it," he said.

A quick smile made her eyes sparkle. "What are we if we don't have community? Our close relationships are what set us apart and make us different. Even the *Englischers* talk about our sense of community. Did you know that?"

She was newly baptized. He'd been baptized into the church a decade ago, but she'd only just returned and was still on fire for the faith. Maybe he should appreciate that.

"The first stall?" Tabitha was back to business again, and she gestured toward a heifer patiently chewing her cud.

"*Yah*, wherever you want to start." He picked up a clipboard with the cattle's ear tag numbers to document their vaccinations.

"Is that why you came back?" he asked. "For some real neighbors?"

"*Yah*." Tabitha picked up the third syringe. "It's exactly why. And because I believe our way of life is right."

Tabitha looked a little frailer in the light of that revelation. She'd come back for their Amish ideals. But neighbors, family members, and friends were all she could have. He knew she was divorced, and with no husband, she'd be looking for friends and family to fill every empty hole in her heart. What happened when she was faced with Amish reality again? What happened when those friends and family weren't enough? Because they hadn't been before.

If Jonas had to guess, he'd say that Tabitha Schrock would be back over the fence again in six months.

8

༄

Amanda looked down at the four perfectly arranged cinnamon rolls in the Tupperware dish. They were buttery brown, and cinnamon and brown sugar oozed from the spiral of dough. Was it better to squeeze in one more roll, or to leave them looking attractively arranged? What would a man like more?

She used a butter knife to edge them aside, and she squeezed in the fifth. It wasn't as pretty, but at least he'd have more baking to stretch a few days. One more roll to enjoy while thinking of the woman who'd baked it. She drizzled some white icing on top of each bun—pretty little lines to contrast with the dark sugar and cinnamon. She paused, eyed them, then dumped the icing, slathering each bun in a splash of icing that sank into the cracks and spirals.

Less attractive but tastier. Appearances were not as important as the gooey, tasty depths of a cinnamon roll. That was much like people too. The depths mattered. Even the Bible talked about how a woman without discretion was "a jewel of gold in a swine's snout," and that true beauty came from character, but the men Amanda knew hadn't stopped to look deeper for her.

Amanda felt a flood of heat hit her cheeks. This was the point she was at now, luring a man with her baking. She'd waited for an interested man to come calling on her, which was the right and proper way for things to work. She should have been able to smile nicely at social functions, add her pie to the lunch table on Service Sunday, and have some nice young man ask to drive her home from singing. But smile as she did, and no matter how many pies she put out, no matter if a young man might stop and talk to her a little bit or offer to help carry her basket of dishes back to her buggy, no one asked her for that all-important drive home from singing. There had been one young man who'd come to help her *daet* with mowing the lawn, and that had looked promising for a couple of weeks, but then Tabitha and Michael had come home for a visit, and he'd never come back. So here she was, packing up Tupperware containers of her best baking to drive up to a hog farm on the edge of their church district.

Uninvited.

That was the part that pricked her pride. He hadn't asked her to come. He hadn't shown her any interest whatsoever. Menno Weaver tended to keep to himself, and he'd never so much as struck up a conversation with her since they left school. He might be no different from any of the other young men whose gazes had slid right past her.

She pushed the lid down on the container and put it on top of another container of blueberry muffins.

Menno Weaver had always been a little standoffish with everyone, though. But then, his family had been the problem family in their district. His *daet* drank heavily, as did his uncles. His *mamm* left the family once the boys were teenagers, which left his *daet* to raise him and his brothers alone. People talked—oh, the thought of a woman walking out on her own *kinner*—but every woman had her limit, and Linda Weaver had reached hers. She'd gone back to her parents for a few months, and they'd reported to the bishop that she'd had a nervous breakdown. She was a shell of herself, shaking and trembling and jumpy. Then she left them, too, and no one heard from her again. She was out there somewhere, but what she was up to, no one knew.

Ironically, Linda Weaver wasn't shunned. She should have been. She'd done the unthinkable. But she'd also had to live with the unthinkable in that house full of drunken men, and she'd broken. There was always hope she'd come back now that her husband was dead, but she hadn't. She might not even know she was free of him.

And young Menno had been raised in that home, but he'd broken some of the patterns already. He'd stopped drinking. He went to AA meetings in town. Service Sundays, he sat in church with his head bowed. It wasn't his fault he was born into such dysfunction, any more than it was Amanda's choice to have a fence-jumping sister. And she believed in second chances.

Gott, am I doing the right thing?

But Gott was silent today, and looking at her containers of baking, she realized that if she was going to go out without her family knowing about it, now was the time. Because tomorrow, her sister might need her help, or Daet might be at home more, or someone might come visit. Anything might get in her way. The baking would get stale, and then she'd have to bake again and try to find another crevice of time to slip away.

If she was going to do this, she'd best get to it.

Amanda gathered up her containers and headed for the side door. There was no time like the present. If she overthought this, she'd never do it.

What harm could one visit do?

But before she could even put on her shoes, she heard her father's boots on the step. The door swung open, and Daet thumped inside. Outside, the clothesline was laden down with the laundry that Amanda had washed that morning, working feverishly to finish as quickly as she could. Dresses, shirts, pants, sheets, towels—all fluttering in the warm June breeze.

"It's a hot day," he said, pulling off his hat and mopping his forehead with a handkerchief. His face was red from exertion, and he tossed his hat on a peg by the door. "Where are you off to?"

"Me?" Amanda shrugged feebly. "Um, I was going to go visiting now that the laundry is done."

"Has working with your sister lost its shine?" Her father headed past her into the kitchen.

"No, it's not that," she replied. "I do like working with Tabitha. But it's her job, isn't it? I need to do some things on my own too."

"That's true. How are things going with Tabitha? Is she settling in all right?"

"*Yah*, she's fine. She lands on her feet."

She exchanged a smile with her father. They'd talked about this before. No matter how difficult life got, Tabitha was resilient. She was like a cat tumbling out of the hay loft— she'd twist and flip, and every time, she seemed to land on her feet and walk away. Or this time around, she'd walked home . . . and they were grateful for that.

"I think you deserve to have something new, Amanda." Daet stepped on the heel of his boot to pull a foot out, then bent down to pull up his sock.

"Something new?"

"Some new cloth for a dress?" he suggested. "A new apron?"

He stepped out of the second boot and arranged them on the mat. He tugged up his second sock, and then turned to the mudroom sink.

"Why the generosity?" she asked with a short laugh.

"I know it's been hard," he said. "We're so glad Tabitha's well and truly home again, but things aren't easy for you. Rose is getting closer to Tabitha, and I can see that you're getting frustrated."

He lathered up with the homemade soap, his attention on his dirty, calloused hands. Amanda watched him scrub, the bubbles gray with dirt, and her containers of food getting heavier by the second.

"I suppose Tabitha does like to have her way around the house," Amanda said. "I'm used to doing things my way, and having her home again means that there is more than one woman in the kitchen."

"It occurred to me you might feel a little bit like the prodigal son's older brother," her father said, turning off the water and drying his hands. "You stayed home. You did your duty, and you made good choices. Your sister left, made mistakes, and is back home again to the great celebration of everyone around. Including your *daet*." He looked at her meaningfully. "I have all but killed the fatted calf."

Amanda smiled wanly. "It's all right. I'm happy she's home too."

"But I want you to know that I appreciate all your hard work around here," he said. "You have been a good and dutiful daughter. I don't know what I would have done without you in this home, and your sister's return does not change all you've contributed around here. I am not blinded to it. I am grateful."

"Oh, Daet." Tears misted her eyes. What would he think of her traipsing out to the Weaver farm after all he'd said? She adjusted her burden to rest on one hip for support.

"So if you want to get yourself something, put it on my tab at the store. A treat for my daughter."

"*Danke*, Daet," she said. "Can we afford it?"

"We?" He arched an eyebrow at her. "My dear girl, I always tell you that when you have your own home, you can worry over the money. This is my home, and I'm the provider. I can afford it, yes."

She rolled her eyes. "Of course, I know. I shouldn't ask about the money. It's just that I don't need a new dress yet. I'd enjoy making one, but I don't need it. That's all I meant."

Her father patted her shoulder affectionately. Ever since Rose got married, it had been Amanda and her *daet* facing the world together. Daet had given her a few lessons in personal finance. If there was no husband to take care of it, she'd better know how to take care of the money herself. And she'd been grateful for the lessons. But with Tabitha's return, one thing had been proven: miracles still happened. And if that was the case, maybe Amanda could get hers too.

"I sold a horse," he said. "So there will be some extra as soon as I get the payment. But it's coming. There's no worry there."

"Which horse?" Amanda asked. There were two horses they used for buggies in the stable, and then down in the barn there were three others used for farmwork. And, of course, there was Fritz. Which horse had been sold?

"Never mind the details, Amanda," he replied. "Go to town and nose around the sewing shop. You deserve to forget about your worries for a little while. Go on, now."

When Daet got into a good mood, he tended to treat

Amanda like a teenage girl. She was far from her teen years, but she appreciated the sentiment all the same. Since he was sending her out, it was best not to stay and pester him with more questions. If she was wanting out of the house, she was getting her wish.

"Leave that sweet baking alone, Daet!" she called over her shoulder before the screen door clattered shut behind her. "The date oatmeal bars are for you!"

He likely wouldn't listen to her, and she didn't have the time to stay home and argue either. Tabitha was the one who insisted that cholesterol mattered so very much. Amanda didn't see how a treat now and then could be so terrible for a man's health, although she did agree that their father should follow doctor's orders.

But Daet was sending her off to do something nice for herself. She wouldn't be choosing new cloth for a dress just yet, but she would do something for herself, and her stomach flipped with nervousness. What was she supposed to say when she arrived at Menno's hog farm with two Tupperware containers full of baking? She headed over to the buggy and pushed the containers into the back. Miracles still happened, but Tabitha's experience had shown that miracles happened once someone stepped out and tried something new. A cat didn't land on her feet without first falling out of the loft.

Amanda headed for the corral to fetch the horse to hitch up the buggy, and she scanned the horses. Fritz wasn't there, but her mind spun forward to her own concerns.

She knew the road that led to the Weaver farm, although she hadn't actually been to see the Weavers before. But finding the right place wasn't the worry that had her heartbeat skipping all over the place.

When she did arrive, how did a woman introduce herself as a prospective marriage partner to a man she hadn't spoken to since their school days? Was Amanda going to have to say it in so many words, or would two Tupperware containers full of baking speak for themselves?

9

The barn was warm and stuffy, dust dancing in the sunlight that pooled in through some windows near the door. Tabitha looked over Rose's shoulder at the clipboard, watching as her sister carefully copied down the ear tag number, then the vaccine vial number next to it. She'd taken over for Jonas since Rose was more accustomed to the long vial numbers. This job was easier with Rose's help, and Tabitha was glad she'd come along.

This stuffy cattle aroma was a comforting scent for Tabitha. She'd always been more comfortable around animals than around people. She remembered skipping hymn sings and youth gatherings so that she could be there for the birth of calves or nurse an ailing animal back to health. Her parents had urged her to go out with friends, and she'd thought they just didn't understand her. Lately she'd been wondering if her parents hadn't been wiser than she thought. Maybe she would have been a little wiser to Michael's hollow charms before she married him if she'd spent more time with people than livestock.

But he'd been so attentive to her. He looked into her eyes

and listened to her talk about just about anything. He told her that she was adorable and that she filled his heart, and that he couldn't think about anything but her. He insisted that she was brilliant, and that she owed the world more than she could give in her Amish life. He said that few women were as intelligent as she was, and that she'd always regret it if she didn't use the gifts she'd been given. According to him, she was more beautiful, more intelligent, and more intoxicating than any woman around her. Heady words for an Amish girl who'd been raised to be humble.

And then the teachers had pulled her aside and told her so seriously that she was uncommonly bright. They'd help her get scholarships. They'd write letters on her behalf. But please, please pursue more education.

The *Englischers* saw no problem with one person rising above others . . . if she was worthy of it. The Amish kept everyone on the same level, no matter how gifted a girl might be. That chance to rise higher had been the hook for Tabitha.

But the extended education that was so outside of Amish norms and ideals had given her this dream come true. She was a veterinarian and could work with the animals in her community. And she never could have done this job or used her gifts this way if she hadn't gotten the education outside of her Amish community . . . outside of what her community would have permitted. So there was a little bit of nagging guilt that followed her. The job that filled her heart and made her feel like she was living up to her potential had only been acquired with rebellion. Had leaving been part of Gott's will in her life, or had this career been Gott's merciful redemption of her mistakes? She only knew that she was so grateful for this job that it left her filled to overflowing with gratitude, however Gott had given it.

And yet it had come with a cost too. An image of handsome Michael rose in her mind. *Yah*, it had been a painful cost.

Tabitha inserted the syringe into the cow's thick skin and pushed down the plunger. The big girl shuffled her hooves, so she felt it, but that was all. The vaccination was an important one for Infectious Bovine Rhinotracheitis and Bovine Viral Diarrhea viruses. Both illnesses could bring down a herd quickly, so keeping up with vaccinations was a priority for farmers. She removed the syringe and rubbed the spot.

"There you are," she murmured. "You'll be okay."

Cattle had feelings, too, and she liked to leave each animal reassured and calm again. This was the twentieth cow, and she swapped out the needle every ten injections so that the point stayed sharp and there was less risk of a broken tip.

"Rose, I need the sharps box." Rose passed over the yellow plastic box that held used syringes and other sharp medical implements, and Tabitha pushed the syringe into the box, then took the last syringe and peeled open the sealed packaging. It was broken.

"Rose, you know my little black bag in the front of the buggy?" Tabitha asked.

"I'll go get it," Rose said.

"*Danke*," she replied.

Rose headed out of the barn, and the door hung open for a moment, then swung shut. Tabitha looked over at Jonas, who stood with his arms crossed over his chest, leaning against a stall rail.

"What is it like being back?" Jonas asked.

"It's coming home," she said. "What else can I say?"

These were the green fields she'd missed so much when she was away—like the prodigal son, longing for everything he'd taken for granted at his father's home. That was Tabitha. Even farm chores had gained a rosy glow in hindsight.

"But it's been a long time," he countered. "Everyone has grown up, changed."

That reminder stung. A lot had changed. Life had moved on without her. Somehow, when she had thought about her return to Shepherd's Hill, she hadn't taken that into account. She wasn't picking up where she left off.

She cast him an amused smile. "When we were teens, Susan Lapp talked a mile a minute about youth group gossip. She still talks just as fast, but now it's about her *kinner*."

Jonas smirked at that. Aaron's sister was known for her chatter. If she got nervous, she only chattered more.

"What about me?" Jonas asked. "Am I any different?"

"I don't know." She met his gaze. "You're locked up tighter than a jam jar."

Jonas smirked again. "I've grown up."

"I'll give you that. So how come you aren't married yet? Everyone else in our class got married. Your sisters are all married now."

Jonas pushed himself off the rail and headed for the window. He glanced out.

"You sound like my mother," he said after a beat of silence.

"Too personal?" Tabitha asked. "Sorry, I guess everyone heard the worst of my time away when I confessed in front of the church. You know all of my mistakes."

"And you want to know mine?" he asked.

"Nope." She shook her head. "Just curious why you didn't get married. You're a good-looking guy. You're running a farm with your *daet*. You come from a good family. . . . You seem like good husband material for someone nice."

"I was courting Miriam Yoder," he said.

"You and Miriam?" She hadn't heard about that. "What happened?"

"We had a private agreement. I was going to save up more money so we could get married," he said. "And then this guy from Indiana came to the community—Jake Miller. He had a new courting buggy, money in the bank, and was looking for a wife."

"He stole her?" Tabitha said.

"She married him, at least," Jonas replied. "Don't know if you can say a woman was stolen or not. She had a choice in the matter. She made hers."

"How long ago was that?" she asked.

"Three years, I guess."

"And you didn't find another girl?"

"Again, you're sounding a whole lot like my *mamm*."

"Maybe your *mamm* talks sense," she teased.

"I want more than just a girl I could reasonably get along with," he explained. "Sometimes people get married, and it's not a great match. It's difficult and challenging—more than it should be. I see that in friends, and it makes me more careful."

The door opened again, and Rose came back into the barn. Color bloomed on Jonas's cheeks, and he retreated to the rail again and leaned against it. Rose didn't seem to have overheard anything, but it did make Tabitha wonder if he'd been referring to Rose and Aaron. Rose shut the door behind her and waggled the little black bag that held extra supplies.

Tabitha shot her sister a smile.

"*Danke*," she said. "Let's get the last of these cattle vaccinated."

She glanced over at Jonas, but he didn't meet her gaze. It

seemed like he was cautious now. He'd had his heart broken, and he wasn't about to launch himself into a marriage without being sure. Tabitha couldn't find fault with that, except that he was nearly thirty, and the women his age would be married off. If he wanted to marry later, it would be more difficult. She wondered if he'd ever considered Amanda.

Tabitha readied a new syringe and moved over to the next stall, where a young steer was waiting.

"Hi there, young fellow," she said. "This won't be bad. Don't worry."

"Your sister is concerned that I'm not married yet," Jonas said to Rose.

Rose laughed. "We're all concerned that you're not married yet, Jonas."

"Are you really?" he quipped back.

"By the time you're ready to get married, you'll be the strange old bachelor," Rose joked. "You'll be like Menno Weaver."

"Do you know him?" Tabitha broke in, looking back at Jonas.

"Menno? *Yah*. You knew him too."

"He was younger than us," Tabitha said. "So I knew who he was, but I didn't know him personally."

"I talked to him now and again."

"And?" Rose raised her eyebrows.

"And what?" he asked.

"You know he's looking for a wife, don't you?" Tabitha asked.

"I heard something about that," he replied. "Why, are you looking for someone for Amanda?"

"We are not wanting a match between Amanda and Menno," Rose said.

Tabitha moved on to the next stall—a young heifer. This animal was more antsy, and Tabitha put a hand on its shoulder and stood quietly, waiting for the heifer to settle.

"Menno had a tough time growing up," Jonas said. "He was the one who called the cops on his father."

Tabitha looked over her shoulder. "He did?"

The Amish did not call in law enforcement unless absolutely necessary. They dealt with their own problems.

"He couldn't take it anymore," Jonas said. "His *daet* was a mean drunk. There was never any food in the house either. He called the police from the phone hut, and his *aent*—his *daet*'s sister—had to move in for the next couple of years to be the adult in the home. His *daet* wasn't allowed back unless he stopped drinking and followed some orders from social services."

"I thought he drank himself to death," Tabitha said.

"He did," Jonas replied. "Just not at home."

"Oh . . ." She turned back to the heifer and inserted the syringe. "How did people react to him calling in for *Englischer* help?"

"They had mixed opinions. It was complicated."

Yah, she could only imagine.

"He had a tough time of it for sure," Rose said, "but that doesn't make him the man for Amanda."

"Amanda's a good woman," Tabitha said, although her words weren't meant to encourage a match between Amanda and Menno. "She's a tremendous cook too. And she's smart. She's good with money, she's a good seamstress, and she knows what's right and wrong, and she's determined to live the right way."

"You're sounding like my *mamm* again," Jonas said dryly.

"Is your *mamm* suggesting you court Amanda?" Tabitha asked in mock surprise. Amanda was a worthy woman, and she was just as single as Jonas was.

"Are you suggesting I court your sister?" Jonas countered.

Amanda had been passed over, and it wasn't fair. Here was Jonas—strong, good looking, smart, a little jaded—and Tabitha couldn't help but think that if the two of them thought rationally, they might see a match there.

Rose shuffled her shoes against the floor. "We aren't trying to meddle in your life, Jonas."

Rose cast him an apologetic smile. *What was that for?* Tabitha wondered. Well, Jonas was a few years older than her. Maybe she didn't feel quite at ease with him. Jonas didn't intimidate her, though.

"Maybe I am," Tabitha cut in. "Suggesting you court Amanda, that is. Not meddling in your life. My sister is a wonderful woman, if you take the time to get to know her."

"I don't need a matchmaker," Jonas replied.

"Amanda seems to," Rose murmured.

"It's just a thought," Tabitha said, moving on to the next stall. She knew enough to leave a seed alone once it was planted.

And who knew? Maybe Jonas just needed a little nudge. He'd had his heart broken, and maybe he'd seen the hard side of marriage. So had Tabitha, for that matter. But if she were permitted to marry, she'd take the leap again. Marriage could be difficult. It could be downright crushing when it wasn't the right marriage. But she'd also seen people who were kind and considerate to each other out there. She'd seen grace and forgiveness, old folks who held hands, young folks who got each other coffee, and couples who were wrangling kids together, working as a team. She'd witnessed true, deep, committed love. It existed in the *Englischer* world and the Amish one too. Tabitha didn't have a chance at experiencing that loving, sacred commitment anymore, but she still believed in marriage.

And Jonas could do far worse than Amanda.

10

When the vaccinations were finished, the three of them walked back through the farmyard toward the buggy. They'd left it hitched up, and the horse's ears pricked up and his coat shivered in anticipation. He was eager to be moving again. Tabitha put her bags into the back, and then she and Rose got up into the buggy.

"*Danke* for the help," Jonas said.

"My pleasure," Tabitha said, giving him a nod. "Watch that last heifer—the one that was so skittish."

"I will." Jonas tipped his hat at them, and she eased off on the reins, letting the horse take the lead and get moving up the drive once more.

"How come you're trying to set up Amanda and Jonas?" Rose asked.

"Why not?" Tabitha asked. "Amanda is lonely, and she wants a home of her own. Jonas needs a wife—"

"Jonas hasn't expressed any interest in her whatsoever," Rose interrupted.

"Maybe he needs a nudge."

"Maybe he just isn't interested."

Tabitha shot her sister a wary look. "You don't think they'd be a good match? What's wrong with him?"

"Nothing. He's a nice man. He's got lots of potential."

"So it's Amanda, then?"

"I just think that if two people are going to be attracted to each other, that will happen on its own. If you push this and Amanda gets rejected, it's going to really hurt her."

"That's true." Tabitha sighed. "If she'd been the only daughter and had brothers instead of you and me to overshadow her, do you think things would have turned out differently for her?"

"Actually, I don't," Rose replied. "I really tried to show her how to be soft and sweet to attract a husband, and she just wouldn't cooperate. She could have put a little more effort into smiling and agreeing instead of arguing with boys she disagreed with. You didn't see her while you were gone. She was purposefully contrary."

"About what?"

Rose fell silent.

"In defense of me?" Tabitha guessed.

"It doesn't matter what," Rose replied.

"It matters to me," Tabitha said. "So she was defending me when people talked about me leaving? Is that it?"

"*Yah.*"

Amanda had been disagreeing with boys her age and making herself bothersome because she hadn't wanted people talking badly about Tabitha. . . . It brought a lump to her throat.

"I take it you didn't defend me, then," Tabitha said.

Rose's face paled. "Oh, Tabitha, I—"

"It's okay," Tabitha flicked the reins to speed the horse

up to a trot. "I understand. I've got a thicker skin than that. Your way got you married, didn't it?"

Rose had learned how to be agreeable and sweet. She'd learned how to sidestep the gossip too. It had worked for her, and Tabitha wasn't going to begrudge her success in moving her life forward.

"But let's just be honest here," Tabitha said. "Amanda is loyal. She'll stand by us through anything because we're family. And she deserves a little more loyalty from us."

"She's a good sister," Rose agreed. "There's a husband for her out there, and I'm glad you're home. I wasn't any good at setting her up. You might have an easier time of it. You're the oldest. She might listen to your advice when she wouldn't listen to mine."

They fell into silence, the horse's hooves clopping out a relaxing rhythm. They moved into the shade of some over-hanging branches, and a twig scraped along the canvas top of the buggy. A dog barked from a farmhouse and ran up to the fence, loping along cheerily to match their pace until he hit the barbed wire of the field and stopped.

At the big stop sign ahead, a buggy turned onto the road and came toward them. It was moving more slowly, though, the driver reining in a horse that looked eager enough to break into a trot. When it came closer, Tabitha recognized Nathaniel Peachy, Jonas's father. Her heart-beat sped up in some unbidden anxiety, and she took a couple of deep breaths to slow it back down again. He was her client. Like her or not, she was the veterinarian working on his herd. She'd best get the balance with him right from the start.

As her buggy got closer to his, she reined in and gave him a wave.

"Good afternoon, Nathaniel," she called. "I'm just leaving your farm."

"Are you?" Nathaniel reined in, too, and she saw the reason for his slow progress. There was a horse tied behind the buggy.

"The vaccinations went well," she said. "I left a card with your son to contact me if you have any problems. There is a phone service set up, and I check the voice mail there a few times a day."

"So you're the main veterinarian, are you?" Nathaniel eyed her with pursed lips. His beard was gray but rather sparse, and his face was tanned from the sun.

"*Yah*, I am. Dr. Brian is slowing down these days. He's getting tired and wants to spend more time with his family," she said. "So folks around here will be seeing more of me."

He stroked his thin beard. "So if I call Dr. Brian to come look at a horse for me, he'd send you?"

"For the next couple of weeks, *yah*," she said. "And after that, it depends on his schedule. I'm qualified, though. I'm a full veterinarian."

Nathaniel sighed. "I'd rather have a man I know than a girl I don't."

As if he didn't know her . . . but what people did know of her wasn't glowing either.

"I have something to prove around here, and I know that," Tabitha said. "But you'll see that I'm educated, I know herds, and I'm good at what I do. I'm also dedicated. You come fetch me, day or night, and I'll come to help you out. I'm local, and I'm willing to work my fingers to the bone to prove you can trust me."

The horse started to step forward, and she reined him back again. He was getting antsy, eager to open up and get moving.

84

"I bought a horse," Nathaniel said. "I got him for a steal at the auction. He's back there, and he looks like a sound, fine animal to me. Maybe you can look him over."

That sounded like an opportunity to prove herself.

"*Yah.* Of course," Tabitha said. "I'll turn around, and I'll follow you back."

"I'm not calling you Doctor," Nathaniel added, then he flicked the reins, and his horse started forward again. Nathaniel Peachy would never call her Doctor, and that was no offense. The Amish didn't use titles. They used first names—everyone equally valued. Everyone belonging. Everyone needed. That included Tabitha, even if her community didn't quite understand how she fit in yet.

Tabitha watched as the newly purchased animal clopped on past, and her breath caught in her chest. The horse turned liquid eyes on her as it plodded on past. *Fritz.*

Rose reached over and clasped her wrist in an iron grip.

"That's our horse," Rose whispered.

"I thought he was selling cattle!" Tabitha hissed.

"Maybe he sold both?" Rose just shook her head. "You know Daet. He keeps his business private."

Even from them. Tabitha's stomach sank.

"Fritz has had gut issues, Rose. And Nathaniel and Daet are already feuding. This can't be good."

"Is Fritz still sick?"

"He hasn't had any flare-ups in the last few weeks, but I can't guarantee that he won't have more."

"What will you do?" Rose whispered.

"We'll go on back, and I'll check him out," Tabitha said. "And hopefully he's okay."

"Will you tell Nathaniel about Fritz's history?" Rose asked.

That was the question, wasn't it? Would she tell Nathaniel who had sold a sick horse at auction? Or would she keep her mouth shut? The problem with the latter was that the truth always came out. The auction kept records. Someone would have to tell Nathaniel, and in Tabitha's humble opinion, it should be her father.

"Not yet," she said.

Tabitha flicked the reins to go forward again. She needed to find a place to turn around and head back to the Peachy farm.

But she also had a chance to help her father and his Amish brother make peace, and while the situation was a prickly one, she could not let that opportunity pass her by.

11

A tin mailbox with *Weaver* written in white block letters on the side of it sat precariously on top of a wooden post next to the drive. The box wobbled to one side, and the post was both dented and leaning as if it had been driven into by some *Englischer* vehicle. These things happened when *Englischer* teens came joyriding in their parents' pickup trucks out on the back Amish roads.

That wasn't the only sign of the Weaver hog farm, though. The smell alone had announced its presence a mile off, and from the road, she could see a large outdoor pig pen with sows lazily lounging on some hay, a herd of half-grown piglets running around. There were a couple of nearly grown barrow pigs, and one large, intimidating-looking boar standing like a king on a mountain. He must be the sire of the young ones. There was a water trough that appeared to be running over with a hose stuck inside, and a large sow sprawled in the mud next to it.

The pigs looked well cared for to Amanda, but she wasn't the expert on these things. She reined in the horse and looked down the drive. She could make out a small house with peeling white paint, a stable that looked in better repair than the house, and a rusted old pickup truck with no tires, resting on blocks.

Menno Weaver had an *Englischer* vehicle? That gave her pause. If she hadn't driven all this way, she might have turned back, but then she saw Menno walk past the pig pen and pause to toss something into a trough. He saw her at the same time and put a hand up to add some extra shade to the brim of his straw hat.

"I've come this far," she murmured to herself. She flicked the reins and tugged on the right hand one to turn the horse down the drive. She licked her lips nervously. There'd be no time to gather her thoughts now, and they were slopping around inside of her like a wringer washer full of laundry.

She should have thought up a clever introduction, something that might let her off the hook if he wasn't interested. The horse clopped forward, and she reined him in next to the house just as Menno appeared around the side of it.

He wore a pair of dirty rubber boots, and his blue shirt was rolled up to his elbows, his forearms tanned golden brown. He wasn't a large man—maybe a couple of inches taller than Amanda was, if that. He eyed her uncertainly.

"Good morning," Menno said.

"Good morning." She swallowed hard.

"Can I help you?" he asked.

"I'm Amanda Schrock." It was a ridiculous thing to announce, but it was the only thing she could think of.

"*Yah*, I know who you are, Amanda Schrock. We went to school together." A smile touched the corners of his lips.

Amanda hopped down from the buggy and tied the horse to the hitching post. Menno's gaze stayed locked on her, and she dropped hers, looking down at her running shoes, her face starting to heat. What on earth had she done? This was a fool's errand to be sure!

"I—" She forced herself to look up again. "I did some baking, and I thought you might like some."

"You baked?" He looked surprised. "What did you make?"

"Cinnamon rolls and . . . muffins." It sounded over the top now. She wished she'd just stopped at the cinnamon rolls. Then she could leave the other container in the back of the buggy and not ever have to mention it.

"For me?" he asked.

"*Yah.*" Her face was blazing hot now.

"That's very nice. *Danke.*" He looked furtively toward the house. "It's not guest ready in there, but if you wanted to come in, I could put on coffee."

Amanda looked toward the house again. It was small—a two-story house with a sagging porch that looked like it needed both repair and a lick of paint. There was an overturned crate next to the clothesline, obviously meant to give someone a step up when hanging their clothes, and a few towels and two pairs of pants hung in the sunlight.

"I'd like some coffee," she said. "I'll just get the baking from the back of my buggy."

Menno stood back and watched as she pulled out the containers, piled them up one on top of the other, and headed toward the house with her armload. He eyed the containers curiously, but he didn't offer to carry them for her. Was that a sign of how he felt? Or just an awkward man?

He went ahead and opened the side door, disappearing inside and leaving the door propped open. Amanda had to feel her way up the steps since she couldn't see her feet past her Tupperware containers. When she came inside, Menno was clearing some papers off the kitchen table. She put the containers on the space he'd cleared and looked around.

The kitchen wasn't dirty, but it was cluttered. Clean dishes were piled on some dish towels laid out across the counter. There was an odd collection of jars and containers on the last couple feet of counter, with two used baby bottles sitting next to them.

Then she heard a soft oink.

On the ground in a crate filled with hay, she spotted a piglet.

"Oh, what's this?" she said, squatting down next to the animal.

"That's a runt of a litter," Menno said. "The sow just about crushed him, and he couldn't compete for milk, so I took him inside."

"Are those regular baby bottles?" she asked.

"*Yah*. They work for pigs." Menno gathered up the dirty bottles and headed for the sink. "He's about due for a new bottle, if you wanted to help feed him."

He was a cute piglet, perfectly pink with a twitching little snout. He oinked at her, tiny hooves tapping at the side of the crate. Amanda bent down and scooped him up. His rump fit into one of her palms, and the piglet blinked at her.

"What did you name him?" she asked.

"I didn't."

"Why not?"

"He's part of the herd. Once he's big enough, he goes back out with the rest of the piglets. No need to get attached."

"Are you telling me you aren't attached?" she asked.

Menno returned with a filled bottle of milk and gave her a grudging smile. "Maybe. But I shouldn't be."

He handed her the bottle, and she popped the nipple into the piglet's mouth. She had to wiggle it around to get the piglet to start to suck.

"I think he's sick," Menno said. "He's not doing well."

She could see that. In addition to his size, he seemed a bit lethargic. She pulled the piglet in close against her apron to hold him more comfortably like a baby. Menno crossed the kitchen and opened the top Tupperware container.

"These look good. I like blueberry muffins," he said.

"I'm glad," she replied.

"I haven't had them homemade in a long time," he said. "I get them at the bakery sometimes."

"Homemade is best," she said, casting him a smile.

Menno took out a muffin and took a bite. While he chewed, he opened the next container.

"Oh . . ." he said, his mouth still full, and she felt a little thrill of pride.

"Cinnamon rolls are my specialty," she said.

"They look delicious," he said. "This is very nice of you to come by." He glanced over and met her gaze. "What made you come?"

Amanda's heart thudded in her ears. "I, um . . ." Her head still seemed to be full of wet, slopping laundry, and she couldn't put a coherent thought together—at least not a clever one. "I heard you were looking for a wife."

Menno coughed, swallowed, and then coughed a few more times. Had she just said that out loud? She felt her face heat again, and if she could have sunk straight through the floorboards, she would have.

"Did Elder Yoder send you?" he asked, his face red from the coughing fit.

"No, I just heard."

"Oh . . ." Menno licked his lips. "Does your family know you came?"

"No." The piglet spat out the nipple, and she put the bottle onto the table next to an unlit kerosene lantern. "I didn't tell them."

"I see."

Menno started arranging the percolator, and he bent down to rustle up the coals in the belly of the stove, then added another piece of wood. His cheeks were still red.

"I didn't want anyone to meddle," Amanda explained. "That's why I didn't tell them. I'm twenty-seven and single. I got passed over. It happens. My younger sister, Rose, is married. My older sister, Tabitha, jumped the fence and got divorced. So it's been hard for me to meet someone who will look past my family."

"I know that feeling," he said.

"I thought you might."

Menno came back to the table, and he picked off a piece of cinnamon roll and put it into his mouth.

"I'll get us plates if you take the pig," she said.

Menno looked up and smiled timidly. "Okay."

She passed the piglet into his arms and went to the sink to wash up. "The thing is, I've passed the age that anyone thinks I'm marriageable. I don't know if age matters so much to you—"

"I'm twenty-eight," he said. "It's not like I'm younger than you are."

That was a good thing. "I cook well. I bake even better. I can take care of a home too. I've got a head on my shoulders, and I won't pretend I'm dumb to make you feel manlier."

"Okay."

She dried her hands and opened a cupboard. She gave up

after the third and fished some clean plates and forks out of the sea on the tea towel–covered counter. When she returned to the table, Menno put the piglet back in the crate. She put her attention into serving the cinnamon rolls onto two plates. He accepted his and took a bite.

"This is good," he said past a mouthful.

"*Danke.*"

Menno swallowed. "You said you thought your family might meddle if they knew you were here. Would they try to stop you?"

She'd tried to sidestep that, but maybe it wasn't fair. It was best to be up front.

"They might. They wouldn't understand," she said. "They're afraid you're a drunk."

"What makes you think I'm not?" he asked, and his dark gaze caught hers again. He had an interesting face, she decided. It wasn't traditionally handsome, but it had character, and she liked it. She tried to imagine him with a married beard, and she looked away quickly.

"I saw you in town," she said. "You were coming out of an AA meeting. And you were . . . warm. Happy. Comfortable. I assumed from that you aren't drinking anymore."

"I'm not," he said. He fished in his pocket and pulled out a little blue circle. "That's my token for seven years sober." He pocketed it again.

"That's really good," she said.

"*Danke.* I'm proud of it."

"We aren't supposed to be prideful," she said.

"I'm not prideful," he countered. "I feel good about the choice I made to quit drinking, and I'm pleased that I've stuck to it. Gott gave me strength, and I'm proud of where I am now. I won't apologize for that."

"It sounds almost *Englische*," she said.

He just shrugged.

"I'm not criticizing," she said. "I suppose the AA program is *Englische*, so . . ."

"*Yah*, it is," he agreed. "And it saved my life. They tell you to trust in a higher power to get the strength you need to quit drinking."

"I didn't know that."

"These AA meetings are put on by the Presbyterian church. So that higher power is Gott," he said. "But Presbyterians see things a bit different than we see things."

"How?" She squinted at him.

"Well, I got to know some Christian *Englischer* men there, and they see Gott as their friend."

That sounded almost disrespectful to her ear. That wasn't an idea they were raised with here. Gott was their maker and their king. He was so far above them that they fell in worship.

Amanda blinked. "Gott is our creator, our father . . . not our pal."

"They don't see him as a pal," he replied. "It isn't like that. But their relationship with Gott is very personal. They see Gott as a closest confidant. They see him as the first one they speak to each morning and the last one they speak to before falling asleep. It's more familiar than we tend to see Gott, and as a result, they gain a strength from Gott that I admire. Gott truly held them up in the worst of their temptations to drink."

Amanda picked at a snag in her thumbnail. Here in Shepherd's Hill, they worshipped Gott as a community, together. They knew Gott's love because they saw it in each other. "Is it . . . heresy?"

"No, just different. And I found that I liked it. I spend

a lot of time alone, and Gott is who I talk to most often. I rely on him to give me the strength to stay away from drink, and it's a very personal battle." His face colored again. "I'm saying too much."

"No, you aren't," she assured. "I imagine it would be a personal battle. I'm glad Gott gives you strength."

Gott as a friend . . . Something inside of her perked up at that thought. She had her own personal battles these days too.

Amanda watched as he ate another two large bites of the cinnamon roll, and she could see him savoring the treat. She'd done well on this batch—plus the extra frosting never hurt.

"So you're looking for a husband?" he asked when he had swallowed.

"*Yah*," she said. "I suppose I am. If I wait around, it won't happen. I know I'm not as pretty as the other women, so—"

"Says who?" he asked.

"What?" Amanda blinked.

"Who says you aren't pretty?" he asked.

"Most everyone."

"The same people who think I'm a drunk?"

"I guess so," she agreed, and he shot her a wry little look that made her laugh.

"Can I get another one?" he asked, pointing his fork at the container of cinnamon rolls.

She served him another roll and watched as he unwound a strip of cinnamon-crusted dough and popped it into his mouth.

"The thing is," he said, chewing, "I can't be a girl's secret. Her family has to be on board with this. I know how it can be when a family doesn't like a man. I went to Elder Yoder and asked if he could help me. I wanted to make sure it was all appropriate and approved."

"Oh . . ." Amanda looked over at the piglet in the crate.

He had curled up and was dozing. He hadn't had enough milk, though. "Then I'll tell them that I came."

"Would they approve, though?" he asked.

"I don't know," she admitted. "But I'm old enough now that if I wait for their approval, I'll never get a home of my own. That's the honest truth of it. They want to be helpful, but they just aren't helping."

Menno nodded. "I know a thing or two about that too."

"Does your family know you're looking for a wife?" she asked.

"Who, my brothers?" He shook his head. "No. I didn't pass it by them. But they don't care what I do. But the bishop and the elders know."

"That's very proper."

"I meant it to be."

Amanda took another bite of her cinnamon roll, but she hardly tasted it. She watched as he finished the second roll on his plate, then wiped his lips.

"I shouldn't stay too long," Amanda said. "People talk, you know."

He nodded. Perhaps he understood that more than most.

"Could I ask you to do something for me?" she asked.

"Maybe. Depends on what you ask," he replied.

"Name the pig," she said.

A smile tugged at one corner of Menno's lips, and he shrugged. "I did already. His name is Zeke."

"You did?"

"*Yah*. He's cute. He needed a name."

"Will you put him out with the herd again?" she said.

"I have to. A full-grown hog is a large animal. He can't be a pet. And I can't spoil him too much. He has to learn how to get along with other pigs."

"*Yah*, I understand that," she replied. "He'll be happier that way too."

"If he survives." Menno looked over his shoulder at the little pig in the crate. "He's doing his best."

"I could get my sister to come look at him," Amanda said.

"I don't know if I can afford a veterinarian visit for him."

Right. There were monetary concerns when it came to calling in the vet. Piglets died sometimes—that was part of life on a farm. But this little piglet had a name now, and he was a good excuse to see Menno again too.

"It would be for free," she said. "We wouldn't charge you."

"*Yah?*" He looked uncertain. "I should pay."

Amanda wasn't about to start quibbling about payment right now. She wanted to bring her sister here, and she wanted to help little Zeke. And she wanted to see if tomorrow, Menno might be just a little warmer toward her after he'd had time to think this over.

"Well, sleep on it, then," she said. "But I can bring her by, if you want."

"*Danke*," he said. "Maybe she can help."

"She's very good," Amanda said. "If anyone could, it would be Tabitha."

And if anyone could accept Amanda's fence-jumping sister, she had a feeling it would be Menno. He knew what judgment and public censure felt like. And besides, Menno liked Amanda's baking.

That was a good start—sadly, the best start she'd had so far in all of her experience with men. *Yah*, maybe tomorrow she'd get a hint as to what he felt about all of this. But he was looking for a wife, and she was looking for a husband. Some matches had started on less.

12

Tabitha crouched down next to the summer stove on the porch and poked a stick of wood into the coals. The summer stove was smaller than the main stove in the kitchen, and it was located outdoors so that it wouldn't heat up the house during the warmer months. She blew into the firebox, making the coals glow hot orange, and the edge of the piece of wood started to brown. She tossed in some shavings and some more wood, then blew again. There was a flicker of flame, and the wood caught fire.

Cooking on a wood-burning stove did not come back like riding a bicycle. With Amanda out, that left the starting of supper up to Tabitha. She was used to using microwaves now and cooking on electric stoves. She was used to setting temperatures with buttons, not by stoking up a fire, and this evening coming home to no food started and knowing it would take her at least an hour, if not more, to put together a semblance of a meal left her feeling grumpy. For the last while when cooking, Amanda had made sure the stove was stoked up for her. Today, she was on her own.

There wasn't any meat thawed in the refrigerator. She

could heat up some soup, but Daet would complain that soup alone wasn't meal enough after a long day of work, and he wouldn't be wrong either. Maybe she could find something for sandwiches and take some sausage out of the propane-powered freezer. It would be a start.

"The horse was just fine!" Daet called from the kitchen indoors. The door was open between them, and Tabitha shot her father a frustrated look. He stood by the table with a tall glass of cold meadow tea in his hand. "You make it sound like I sold a sick horse. I did not."

Tabitha pushed another stick of wood on top of the rest and leaned closer to blow into the depths of the stove. They'd been arguing about this ever since they'd both gotten home.

Gott, give me patience! she silently prayed.

Her father looked offended, but he wasn't the one who had checked over a horse she knew wasn't well and had to give it a clean bill of health because he was currently showing no symptoms. Fritz had not been a healthy horse, and she'd looked for symptoms. Her conscience wouldn't let her be anything but thorough, especially with Fritz. But for the time being, the horse seemed fine.

"Daet, you know that Fritz has digestive issues." Tabitha closed the stove door and stood up. "I was treating him for gut problems."

"You treated him. He's better," he insisted.

Some days Tabitha felt like she could throw something, she got so frustrated. This was the part of coming home that she hadn't anticipated. A ten-year absence changed a lot, and right now Daet absolutely refused to listen to scientific fact. Daet saw things the way he saw them, and he wouldn't budge an inch. Had his attitude always been this bad, or was it a new development?

But Tabitha had changed too. Her education showed her the reasons why things worked the way they did. For example, a horse with a gut problem could do very well with the right diet. That was why Fritz was doing so well now. It wasn't a matter of a sick horse or a well horse. Health was not always so cut and dried. But when she tried to explain these things to her father, he said she was being disrespectful and talking down to him. That wasn't her intention, but the truth of the matter was, she knew more than her father did in this area.

"I treated the horse's symptoms," she said, trying to keep her voice moderated. *Englischer* women could raise their voices. Amish women could not. "He's vulnerable to more intestinal flare-ups."

"I prayed for that horse's healing, and he's better."

"He's been treated. That doesn't mean he's cured." Tabitha pushed herself back to her feet and went into the house. "It comes down to maintaining a very specific diet, like people do if they have medical issues. Just because you're doing well doesn't mean you don't have a tendency toward high cholesterol. It just means you've been balancing your diet properly. If you ignore your diet, your cholesterol climbs. It's the same for Fritz. He has gut issues that I've been managing with a specific diet. He is not cured."

"Do you believe in answer to prayer?" Her father crossed his arms over his broad chest. "Did you lose all your faith while you were gone? Because I do believe in prayer. When we wake in the morning, it is because Gott has granted us another day, not just some scientific reason that you learned in one of those college classes. They'd have you believe that we make ourselves or that we heal ourselves or we decide how many days we have on this green earth. We are not Gott. I'd rather trust myself to the hands of Gott than to the opinions of your scientists. And I believe that horse is healed."

Daet hadn't asked Tabitha's opinion on the horse's health. Was she one of the scientists he so distrusted? If it had been Dr. Brian who had treated Fritz, would Daet have consulted with him?

"This is not a matter of faith. This is a matter of an animal's health. I'm not discounting prayer, Daet, but that horse was not in good enough health to sell, and now Nathaniel Peachy has spent good money on him."

Her father shook his head and turned away. Conversation over. He'd done this when she was a child. When Daet spoke, it was decided. But she was no longer a girl, and this was more than him going against her medical advice.

"He already thinks the worse of you, Daet."

"I didn't sell him to Nathaniel Peachy specifically!" Her father turned back. "I sold him at auction. Whoever bought him, bought him. I had no control over that. I didn't take the horse to Nathaniel and offer to sell to him. It's different."

"And what happens if the horse gets sick again?" she demanded.

"He won't."

"What if he does?" She threw her hands up. "You didn't ask me if I thought that horse was ready to sell! I don't know the future for Fritz, but there is a significant likelihood that he will develop symptoms again."

"And I'm not asking you now," Daet snapped. "I'm not asking you how to run my farm or how to sell my horses!"

The sound of the door opening jerked Tabitha's attention away from her father, and Daet and Tabitha both turned to see Amanda standing with one hand on the doorknob, eyes wide. Her dress had a streak of dirt down the apron and what looked like a wet stain on the skirt. She had one empty Tupperware container in her hand, and her gaze snapped from Tabitha to Daet and back again.

"You're back," Tabitha said.

"*Yah*, I'm back. What's going on here?" Amanda asked.

"Nothing," Daet replied.

Amanda shut the door behind her.

"What happened to you?" Tabitha asked. "You're dirty."

"Nothing." Amanda looked down at her skirt though and gave it a little shake.

"So none of us are up to anything, are we?" Tabitha said and sighed. "I'm arguing with Daet about a horse he sold that I think shouldn't have been sold. That's all that's happening here. Where did you go?"

Amanda put the Tupperware container on the counter with exaggerated care. She stayed there with both hands resting on the lid, her expression wary.

"Amanda?" their father said cautiously. "Is something the matter?"

Amanda turned slowly. "Nothing is wrong, Daet. Everything is fine. I was at the Weaver farm today. I brought some baking to Menno."

"You . . . brought him baking?" Tabitha's hand fluttered up to her throat.

"Amanda, it'll look like you're trying to interest him in courting you," Daet said with a short laugh. "I appreciate your compassion on a man in his situation, but we have appearances to consider."

Amanda didn't answer, but she did look over at Tabitha, her gaze locking onto hers in silent pleading. What did her sister want from her? And then suddenly, she knew, and her stomach sank.

"Are you really interested in a life with Menno Weaver?" Tabitha asked.

"I think he could be a good man," Amanda said.

Could be. What did Tabitha even know about him now? A woman's future was in her husband's hands, and that could be a very dangerous prospect. All Tabitha wanted was to protect her sister from the pain she'd gone through.

"Amanda, his family is known for being drunks," Daet sputtered. "Do you know what it's like to be married to an alcoholic? He'll spend all the money on booze and be drinking instead of working. For all you know, he'll be a mean drunk, to boot. If you're married to him, you're stuck with him. There is no changing your mind. Why would you even toy with this?"

Amanda exhaled a slow breath. "He's not drinking, Daet. I know that for a fact. He's been going to AA meetings, and he's going straight now."

"An alcoholic is like a pickle, Amanda," Daet replied. "Once he's a pickle, he can't go back to being a cucumber. Alcohol will always be his weakness."

"Maybe so, but he can stop drinking," she said. "Gott can give him strength."

The irony here was that Daet had just been arguing in favor of faith, and now Amanda was doing the same. Tabitha shot their father a pointed look and raised her eyebrows.

"Dear girl, I have been praying for the husband you will marry since you were born," their father said, his voice softening. "I believe in Gott's willingness to help us too. But I'm looking to my daughter to trust in Gott, not anyone else. Gott will provide for you. He always does. He answers our prayers, especially the earnest prayers of parents. Just trust him. You don't need to investigate Menno Weaver for a husband."

Amanda's chin trembled, and she nodded. "Daet, I understand your worry. I do. But I'm ready to find a husband, and Menno Weaver is looking for a wife. I owed it to myself to go talk to him."

"And you satisfied your curiosity?" Daet asked.

Tabitha watched her sister's face. Oh, let her have satisfied her curiosity!

"Almost," Amanda said quietly.

Daet rubbed a hand over his beard. "Tabitha? Will you talk some sense into her?"

"What about Jonas?" Tabitha blurted out.

Amanda blinked. "Jonas Peachy?"

"He's just as single as Menno Weaver," Tabitha said. "Why not him?"

"Is he interested in me?"

"Is Menno?" Tabitha asked.

Tears suddenly welled in Amanda's eyes, and she stomped across the kitchen, turning her back at the sink.

"I didn't mean it like that," Tabitha said. "But Jonas is single. He's a good man. He's had his heart broken, but he'd make a good husband. His family wants to see him married, and you're a quality woman."

"The Peachy family has their own problems," Daet said. "Jonas may be a nice young man, or he may be more like his father than you might hope."

"Jonas doesn't see me that way anyway, Daet," Amanda said, washing her hands, then turning off the water. "And Menno . . . might." Amanda turned toward Tabitha and grabbed a towel to dry her hands. "He's got a piglet that was the runt of the litter, and he's bottle feeding it. The little thing isn't doing so well. I said you could look at him without charge—a favor."

"What?" Tabitha shook her head. Either she had her father discounting her veterinarian opinion, or her services were being offered up for free.

"A piglet." Amanda's shoulders dropped. "It's just a tiny runt piglet, and it's so small. If you saw the little guy sucking on a baby bottle, your heart would just about break."

"Is he feeding?" Tabitha asked.

"*Yah*, but he's lethargic and seems sickly to me. He didn't drink enough milk, even from the bottle."

Tabitha nodded slowly. A sickly runt piglet. It might need more supplements than it was getting. It could need more warmth, or it might be overheating. . . . The lungs might not be mature enough or the stomach. She couldn't tell without doing a proper exam.

"I wanted you to—" Amanda swallowed. "I wanted you to meet Menno and tell me what you think of him."

Tabitha went to the cupboard and pulled down a jar of canned chicken, some powdered soup stock, and a can of mushroom soup. She'd make a hearty soup, at least.

"Daet?" Tabitha said. "What if I went up to the Weaver farm with Amanda? No more sneaking."

"And do what?" Daet asked curtly.

"We'll look at the pig," Tabitha said. "For free, apparently." She cast her sister an annoyed look. "And I'll tell my sister honestly what I think of Menno Weaver."

Daet sucked in a slow breath, then met her gaze meaningfully. "Tell her straight what you think of him."

"Of course, Daet," Tabitha said. "We'll go first thing in the morning."

If there was one thing that Tabitha had learned in her years as an *Englischer*, it was how to say exactly what she thought. *Englischers* didn't demure. They didn't wait for others to see what they needed first. They didn't hold back and wonder if they were bothering others around them. They said what they wanted, and they expected results. That had been one of the biggest culture shocks Tabitha had had to get used to out there in regular American society, and one of the hardest habits to try to let go of upon her return.

And Amanda needed a reality check. If Tabitha went with her to the hog farm and met Menno properly, this would be a good way to give it to her.

"Are you making soup?" her father asked, his gaze sharpening on the pot she'd started to fill.

"*Yah*, Daet. I'm making soup and sandwiches. We've got some sausage to go on the side too."

Food on the table, a clean and orderly home, a well-managed garden—those were luxuries afforded to Amish homes that had a woman to provide them. And in the *Englische* world, the men would be pitching in to get that meal on the table. Back at home in Shepherd's Hill, making the meal might fall under Tabitha's domain as a woman, but their home was far from traditional.

"You make soup," Amanda said, grabbing an apron. "I'll put together a casserole with that sausage. We'll make a meal of it."

Tabitha shot her sister a grateful smile. Daet muttered something that sounded petulantly hungry, and he headed out of the kitchen. Of the two of them, Amanda was the better cook. Jonas could do far worse than Amanda when he settled down.

13

Amanda sat up late that night in the sitting room, hunched next to the golden pool of kerosene light so that she could see her careful stitches on some ripped seams in her father's broadfall pants. She angled the fabric toward the light and pushed the needle through. Overhead, she could hear the creaking floorboards as her father and sister got ready for bed in their respective bedrooms.

She was finally alone, and she could think through her day. So far, she was thinking about Menno, going over the things he'd said and remembering the tone he'd used when speaking to her. He'd softened his voice for her—that hadn't been her imagination. He'd been gentler. Just a little, but it was something. And he'd liked her baking very much.

They hadn't exactly established anything, but they'd both acknowledged that they were looking for marriage, and that was the bravest she'd been in her entire life. She still couldn't believe she'd spoken so plainly. Her pulse sped up just remembering it.

And while Menno hadn't answered her directly, he had told her what he was looking for, and that included a supportive family.

She glanced up at the creaking ceiling. A woman came with a family, and up until this point, her family's reputation had held her back. Now she needed her family's unwavering support. Her father was against the idea, but surely Tabitha would be willing to look at it a little more rationally. Tabitha, of all her family members, would support a woman taking a chance, wouldn't she? Or maybe she wouldn't. Her risk had been a painful one, and she'd come home ready to live her life the Amish way. But even now that Tabitha was back home again, she was different. She wasn't going to be a wife and mother. She was working a man's job and shaking things up.

Would anyone support Amanda's rather rash hopes of marrying Menno?

Amanda didn't know Menno very well, but she liked his eyes. They were kind and thoughtful, and a man with eyes like that must have a good heart underneath it all. What would it be like to be a married woman with a home of her own and a husband to take care of?

In her mind's eye, she could see herself thoroughly cleaning out that kitchen and organizing everything to her liking. She could see the piles of clean dish towels and bath towels. The brand-new bedding and linens, the sunlight coming in through the windows . . . and a husband with kind eyes.

That gave her a shiver, and she settled back in to stitching. She wanted to be mending her husband's broadfall pants, not her father's. She wanted to be canning food for her own pantry and letting Tabitha can the food here. She wanted to be knitting tiny sweaters for a baby on the way. . . . She wanted the blessings that came with a home of her own.

And Menno, while a risk, did have kind eyes.

14

The smell of pigs was already in the air as the buggy came over the hill that led to the Weaver hog farm, and Amanda wondered if she'd ever get used to that and not notice it anymore. She wasn't fond of that smell, but if it meant home was near, maybe she could get used to it. Sort of like the Peachy farm that nestled in next to the train tracks. She'd heard Jonas say he didn't even notice the train going by, and neither did the cattle.

Tabitha had the reins. Whenever Amanda rode with her sister, her sister had the reins, it seemed. But at least Amanda was getting Tabitha out to the Weaver farm. That was a start.

"Just try to be open-minded," Amanda said.

"I'm always open-minded," Tabitha replied. "And it isn't like you know him very well, Amanda."

"Neither do you."

Tabitha shot her a veiled look and loosened the reins, letting the horse trot faster as they came down the hill.

They turned down the Weaver drive, and Amanda glanced at Tabitha as her older sister scanned the area, waiting for her judgment on the place.

"It looks like it needs some paint, but otherwise it's pretty sturdy," Tabitha said.

"*Yah*, I thought so too."

"Whose truck is that?" Tabitha asked.

The rusted pickup truck on blocks drew both of their eyes.

"I don't know," Amanda replied. "But no one is driving it, obviously. I'm assuming it belongs to one of his brothers. He doesn't seem to get along with them."

"They're troublemakers in town," Tabitha said.

Amanda didn't answer the uncomfortable thought. Menno was connected to some unsavory family members, and while he was no longer drinking, he had family members who were. She'd never grown up around alcohol. Daet didn't touch a drop of the stuff. But some of the boys in her teenage years had had some wild parties out at the old ice house beside the lake, and she'd seen belligerence, vomiting in bushes, fumbling, groping, offensive joking. . . . She'd avoided those parties. They made her skin crawl.

Was that what Menno's family was like?

Tabitha parked the buggy next to the house, and they both hopped down to tie up the horse and get Tabitha's bags. The stable door opened, and Menno came outside with his straw hat pushed back on his head and a shovel in hand. Amanda couldn't read his expression when he spotted them, but he did lean the shovel against the side of the stable and come in their direction.

"Good morning," Menno said. He gave Tabitha a nod, and when his gaze landed on Amanda, a smile touched his lips. "You're back."

Was that a happy statement or just a wry observation? She wished he'd show more on his face, and she dropped her gaze.

"My sister is here to see Zeke," Amanda said.

"*Danke* for coming," Menno said, and his gaze included Tabitha that time. "The piglet is inside the house. I cleaned out his crate this morning and hosed him off a bit."

"And fed him?" Amanda asked feebly.

"*Yah.* That's why he needed hosing."

Menno led the way into the kitchen. This time the table was completely cleaned off and had been scrubbed. The kitchen was swept, dishes were done, and there had been an obvious cleaning effort since she'd been here yesterday.

Zeke was in his crate, and there was fresh hay inside and newspaper flyers on the floor beneath the crate. Menno crossed his arms as Tabitha bent down next to the crate and picked up the squirming piglet in her arms.

"He's the runt," Menno said.

"Amanda mentioned that," Tabitha said. "Has he been growing?"

"*Yah*, he used to fit in the palm of my hand," Menno replied. "And now he's—well, he's that big. So he's eating and growing. But he seems . . . I don't know . . . tired."

"*Lethargic*, we say," Tabitha said. "Amanda, would you hold him while I give him an exam?"

Amanda stepped forward and accepted the little pink pig into her arms. She watched as her sister tested the pig's range of motion in his joints, opened his eyes to see the whites, checked his sucking reflex on one of her fingers, and then inspected some of his droppings inside the crate.

Menno stood there, arms crossed, watching her mutely, and Amanda let her gaze wander around the kitchen. The second Tupperware container that had been filled with muffins was empty now, too, and it sat on his counter, washed out. Had he eaten them himself last night? It was an oddly bittersweet thought to think of Menno hunched over those muffins, alone at his kitchen table.

"He looks fairly healthy," Tabitha said. "I can run a couple of tests to make sure he doesn't have any parasites. I can also give him a shot of vitamins to give his immune system a little boost. You've done well with him, Menno."

"*Yah*? He's okay?" Menno asked.

Tabitha handed the piglet back to him, and Menno looked down at the animal fondly. He really seemed attached to him.

"I saw the pigs outside," Tabitha said. "Is that all of them?"

"I have the sows with small piglets in the farrowing barn," Menno replied. "It gives them some quiet and lets the little ones eat undisturbed while they get bigger."

"Good, good," Tabitha murmured. "It's a lot of work on your own."

"I don't have much else to do," Menno said. "I might as well work."

"So you live here alone?" Tabitha asked.

"*Yah*."

"Your brothers don't live here with you?" She cast her gaze around the kitchen.

"No, I live alone." Menno's tone emphasized the repetition.

"Do you see much of them?" Tabitha turned a direct gaze onto Menno.

This was why Tabitha was here—as Amanda's sister. She was supposed to be asking the questions that Amanda felt too shy to ask.

"They're my brothers. I see them from time to time," Menno said. "But if you're asking if I drink with them, the answer is no."

112

"I'm actually asking if they spend much time here at your home," Tabitha said. "I know I haven't been back long, but even I've heard the rumors about how wild they are."

Menno met her gaze, but his jaw tensed. "They don't find me much fun."

"That's a good thing," Amanda cut in, and she cast Tabitha a warning look. There were less aggressive ways to get answers. "Don't you get lonely?"

Menno shrugged. "I work a lot and do see people. I bring the pigs to market, and I go into town for supplies and to—" He licked his lips. "I go to weekly AA meetings. So I see people. I'm not completely alone."

Tabitha pulled out a small syringe and a bottle. "This is the vitamin mix. Amanda, can you hold him for me?"

The piglet started when Tabitha gave him the injection in his rump, and he struggled to get free again. When Amanda set him down in the crate, he squealed and cried for a few seconds, then settled into his hay.

"You didn't like that, did you, Zeke?" Amanda asked. "You'll be okay."

Amanda squatted down next to the crate and scratched the top of his head. She was glad that the runt would be all right, and he'd grow up to be a big fat hog. But, as cute as he was, he wouldn't stay a baby for long.

"Tabitha, did you want to see the rest of the farm?" Menno asked. "I don't mean to keep you if you have other appointments, but I'm happy to show you around if you're interested."

Was Menno trying to show Tabitha that he wasn't a man to be worried about? Was this . . . for Amanda's sake?

Tabitha put her supplies back into her bag. "*Yah*, I'd like to see it."

Menno looked over at Amanda, and for just a moment, his gaze met hers, and she saw something sparkle there.

This *was* for her.

"I can show you the sows in the barn," Menno said. "Maybe you'll have some advice about keeping them as healthy as possible."

Tabitha brightened, and Amanda smothered a smile. That was the sort of thing that would make Tabitha happy—a farmer dedicated to the health of his animals. For a man who didn't spend much time with his Amish community, he did seem to have a sense about how to impress the right people. There was more to Menno. She was almost positive.

15

⚜

Menno Weaver's farm was in good shape. *He must work constantly to keep it so clean and organized*, Tabitha thought.

The six sows in the barn were clean, dry, and happily suckling large litters of piglets. The farrowing pens were a good size, about eight feet square. One corner in each pen had a little safety zone for the piglets and a heat lamp to attract them to the safe area, where the big sow couldn't accidentally crush them. The heat lamps were run by the battery energy collected by solar panels on the roof of the barn—perfectly permissible in their community. And without the heat lamps, the piglets would have no reason to gather in that safety zone, and Menno would inevitably lose piglets. The other walls of the pen had bumper boards so that if the sow lay down next to a wall, there was a protective rail that would provide a little wiggle room for the piglets to get away. There were clean wood shavings on the floors of each pen, and the sows were snorting comfortingly to their broods. The setup was a sound one and up to date with the latest safety measures.

This was a growing herd, and if Menno kept taking such

good care of his animals, he'd develop a strong reputation for animal husbandry in these parts.

If he could keep it up. That was the worry, wasn't it? That despite his good intentions, he'd fall into his family's habits. Even the best starts didn't matter a whole lot if the man couldn't maintain it.

Tabitha leaned against a railing. Amanda and Menno were looking at a different pen, and she could make out some of their words across the soft oinks of the sows and piglets. Menno was explaining about the bumper rails.

Amanda looked a little bashful, her feet pressed close together and her shoulders hitched high. She was nervous, and Tabitha's heart went out to her. Tabitha had dated a couple of *Englischer* men since her divorce, and she understood the uncertainty. But when Tabitha had gone out with those men, she'd realized that their different upbringings were a bigger hurdle than she'd thought when she was a girl dating Michael. They couldn't completely understand her view of the world or her view of faith, community, and family. She was foreign to them, and she'd known then that she'd have to come home if she ever wanted to be fully understood again . . . by anyone.

The last date that Tabitha had been on was with a divorced single dad. He'd been quite bitter about the breakdown of his marriage, and he'd complained a lot about his ex-wife. It was all her fault, in his eyes. The ex-wife had expected too much. She'd been uncooperative. She'd been withholding. Tabitha had left that dinner feeling uncomfortably aware that he wasn't ready to move on, and that maybe she wasn't either.

Because while she hadn't talked about Michael besides relaying the pertinent information that he'd been cheating on her and she'd had to leave him, she'd had her own bitter feelings stored up inside of herself—her own recriminations that she hadn't voiced.

There had been two of them in that marriage, and while she could blame Michael for having married a naïve Amish girl, for having been unfaithful, for having been less of a man than she'd expected him to be, she'd been in that marriage too. And she'd made mistakes. She had expected him to behave like an Amish husband—to be protective, to take pride in providing, and to work as hard as he could to keep them comfortable. She'd expected him to be fiercely loyal and to come to her for his emotional needs. But maybe she'd needed to meet him where he was at, too, instead of just being surprised when he didn't act the way she thought all husbands acted. She hadn't communicated her expectations very well either. Instead, she'd just gotten her feelings hurt over and over again.

How did Michael describe her behind her back? For all she knew, he might describe her as a little withholding too.

Tabitha didn't want to think about that. Her gaze moved back toward Amanda and Menno. They were heading in her direction again.

". . . it's at the Blank farm," Amanda was saying. "We're going to have a strawberry shortcake party. We'll all make our own little personal cakes with fresh strawberries and whipped cream on top."

"Oh, *yah?*" Menno's attention was fixed on his boots.

"What do you do for fun?" Amanda asked.

"I don't know." Menno shrugged, and his cheeks grew red.

"You must do something," she said.

"I . . . work a lot," he replied. "And I have some friends from AA. We go out for a burger sometimes."

"*Englischers?*" Amanda asked.

"*Yah.*"

She nodded. "Well, if you're free Saturday night, come to Jared Blank's farm. It will be fun. People will be glad to see you."

Menno rubbed at his chin uncertainly and gave Amanda a half smile. Did he believe anyone would be glad to see him? The three of them headed for the barn door, and as Tabitha emerged into the sunlight after her sister and Menno, she sucked in a deep breath of fresh air. The pigs in the grassy pen nosed around and sunned themselves next to a muddy watering hole.

"Do you have any advice for me?" Menno asked, turning toward her.

"You have a good setup," Tabitha replied. "You've got all the safety protocols in place, and your animals look to be in excellent health."

"And Zeke?" he asked.

"Just keep bottle feeding until he's bigger. You can put him in with the other pigs once he's big enough to hold his own, and you can bring his bottle to him, then. He's going to need to be socialized with the other piglets if he's going to get along in the herd and not end up being bullied."

But Menno knew that. This wouldn't be his first bottle-fed pig.

"Honestly, Menno, that might be my advice for you, too, if you want to hear it," Tabitha said. "You've got to get back into community again. You can't just sit alone on the farm. It's not good for you."

Menno pressed his lips together and dropped his gaze. She looked over at Amanda, and the color had drained from her cheeks.

118

"You should come on Saturday," Amanda said with some forced brightness. "It'll be fun."

They headed across the farmyard toward their waiting buggy, and Menno stood back while they got up onto the seat.

"Will you send me the bill, then?" Menno asked.

Tabitha looked over at Amanda, who was looking pointedly down at her hands.

"It's on the house," Tabitha said.

"What?"

"That's an *Englischer* expression. It means there's no charge," Tabitha said.

"I'd rather pay. You treated my pig."

Tabitha shrugged. "Okay, I can send a bill."

"*Danke*. Oh, just one minute. Can you wait?"

Menno loped off toward the house, disappeared inside, and then emerged again with the empty Tupperware container. He handed it up to Amanda with a smile and a nod.

"The baking was very nice," he said. "*Danke*."

He stepped back, and Tabitha flicked the reins. She pulled the buggy around, the horse plodding back up toward the road. Amanda sat rigid and silent, and when Tabitha looked over at her, her sister's face was granite.

"Did I do something wrong?" Tabitha asked.

"You agreed to bill him too soon," Amanda said. "You should have insisted that it was free of charge."

"I think it was about his personal honor," Tabitha said. "He doesn't want to be in our debt."

"Okay . . . so that means this visit was just a veterinarian visit for him?" Amanda asked.

Tabitha sighed. "I have no idea. You were the one talking to him. Is there a spark between you?"

"I don't know. How am I supposed to know that? I've never been out with a man before."

Her younger sister's face was blotched with color, and she turned her attention out the window as they turned onto the road and back in the direction of their own home. Tabitha wasn't sure what she'd expected from their visit to the Weaver farm. Perhaps she'd expected less competence from Menno—more of a floundering bachelor than he appeared to be.

"Amanda, you aren't out with a man now either," Tabitha said, carefully. "You brought him a gift of food and have talked with him. You've asked him to come out to a community event, and he's all but declined. I know you want a husband of your own, but I don't think this is the way to get one."

"Why not?" Amanda demanded. "Should I wait at home? Should I look demure and sweet at Sunday service for another year or two? Do you think that will bring me an interested suitor when it hasn't worked for the last ten years?"

"He's a big risk, Amanda," Tabitha said.

"He was polite. He showed you his farm. He was clean and organized—"

"He's a Weaver, and—"

"*Yah*, he's a Weaver, but I remember him from our school days, and he was a good boy then," Amanda said. "He's kind and decent now. He's got nice eyes."

Tabitha sucked in a calming breath. Her sister didn't want to hear the truth. What she wanted was some encouragement toward a man who seemed only nominally interested. He might just be shy, or Menno Weaver could end up being Amanda's cross to bear for the rest of her life.

"Can I tell you something that no one in our Amish community will tell you?" Tabitha said quietly.

"Fine."

"Every single man on Gott's green earth is attractive in some way. Every last one."

"Tabitha!"

"Ah, that sounds like I'm lusting after all of them, does it?" Tabitha laughed. "I'm not, I assure you. There is something attractive in every man that can spark something in a woman. Even Menno. He can give you a little smile or meet your gaze, and your heart skips a beat. Because for that moment, his eyes are only for you. But you still have to be incredibly careful."

"He's not Michael."

"Don't throw my ex in my face," Tabitha retorted, "and hear me out. Right after Michael and I split up, I went out with some friends from work one night, and I left earlier than they did. I wasn't having fun anyway. I just wanted to go home. I was walking to a bus stop to get back to my apartment, and it was not a safe part of town. There were a group of motorcycle toughs standing in the street, and they started saying crude things to me. I was terrified."

"What did you do?"

"I prayed! And one of them told the others to back off. He was tall with long hair and a big pot belly. He had this grisly, unkempt beard, and he was wearing black leather. But he met my gaze, and he said he wouldn't let them touch me. And in that moment, I saw more than a threatening appearance. I saw . . . a man."

"Tabitha . . ." Amanda sounded disapproving, but Tabitha wasn't going to be put off. Her sister might have stayed Amish, but she lacked romantic experience.

"Every man has at least one attractive quality about him," Tabitha said. "Even that guy in the street. Now, would he have been a wise choice in a romantic partner? Of course not. Should I have ignored all of my better instincts and attempted to get to know him better? No. The point is, just because a man has some attractive qualities you didn't notice before doesn't mean he stops being a massive risk. Do you understand?"

"Menno isn't some motorcycle gang member," Amanda said.

"I know. But you get my point, don't you?"

Amanda was silent, and Tabitha kept her attention fixed on the road. Her father would want her to point out Menno's shortcomings. He'd want her to tell Amanda the dangers.

"I see what you see," Tabitha said after a moment of silence.

"You do?" Amanda turned toward her. "Really?"

"*Yah.*" Tabitha sighed. "I still think he's got a family to be wary of, and a history to be wary of, too, but . . . I can see the attractive qualities. He's got a quiet confidence, he's a good farmer who takes proper care of his animals, and, you're right, he does have nice eyes."

"He does, doesn't he?"

"*Yah*, I see that much." Tabitha shot her sister a smile. This was the first time they'd discussed a man that Amanda was interested in as grown women, and it felt almost like a milestone between them. Back when Tabitha was dating Michael, Amanda had been a girl of fifteen, and she'd had a few crushes on boys. But this was the first time she might be able to do anything about it. Before her *rumspringa*, it was forbidden.

"Will you tell Daet?" Amanda asked.

"That he's got nice eyes?" Tabitha laughed. "I hardly think he'll be interested in that."

"Tabitha, I'm twenty-seven and single," Amanda said, sobering. "You got married. You had your chance. If I don't change something, I will live at home with Daet until he dies of old age. I'll never get a husband or a home of my own. Ever. And I don't want that life."

That was the very life that Tabitha had in front of her now. She'd never have another husband. She'd be the veterinarian and live with Daet until he died of old age too. And she'd be a cautionary tale to girls thinking of jumping the fence for a handsome *Englischer*.

"I don't mean that as an insult to you," Amanda went on. "You've already been married. You've had that experience, even though it wasn't a happy one for you. I just want my chance."

"It might be better to never get married at all than to go through the heartbreak I went through," Tabitha said, her voice tight.

"But isn't that my choice to make?"

Tabitha cast her sister a sad look. Amanda had no idea how gutted a woman could be after the man she'd entrusted her heart to crushed it under his boot. She had no idea how far Tabitha had had to crawl to get her head above ground again. She hadn't seen Tabitha's sense of self eroding as she sat at home alone, knowing her husband was with another woman and knowing he wouldn't even deny it. But it didn't have to be unfaithfulness that crushed a woman. There were other ways to do it just as efficiently. Amanda didn't know. . . .

Tabitha swallowed past the lump in her throat. "Just be careful."

16

Amanda settled back in the buggy seat as her sister drove toward home. Amanda was used to driving herself around. Their *daet* was normally busy on the farm, and Amanda certainly didn't have any interested bachelors pleading for the pleasure of driving her anywhere, so sitting on the passenger side of the buggy, watching the lush pasture slip by, felt strangely uncomfortable. She preferred to hold the reins herself. That might be part of her problem.

"There's a big pothole up there," Amanda said.

"*Yah*, I know," Tabitha replied. "I'm used to the area again, you know."

Amanda normally took another way home to avoid the pothole. The farmer who lived here always filled it in again, but every rainstorm hollowed it back out. Now that Tabitha was the veterinarian, Amanda had yet another person holding the reins in her life. Tabitha was her sister, and when they were out on a veterinarian visit, she was her boss too.

She shoved back the simmering discontentment. Tabitha didn't think that Menno was interested in her, but she thought her sister was wrong. She'd sensed something there between them. Would he come to the strawberry shortcake social? She knew the party sounded silly, but it would be delicious and fun. And if Menno wanted to find a way to see her again, he would be at that social. If he cared enough. That was the part that put a knot in her stomach. So far she'd driven out to his hog farm twice. She'd brought him baking, and she'd brought her sister to look at his piglet. And he'd sent her home with her Tupperware.

This could be the end of it—interactions concluded. He hadn't even kept the Tupperware in order to have an excuse to stop by. That would have been a way for him to come see her. But maybe he wasn't very good at these things and didn't know that the Tupperware could be used to see her. Was that all it was?

And if he didn't come to the gathering . . . would that be his way of telling her that he wasn't interested in more? If Amanda had any dignity at all, at that point, she should let it go. A woman didn't go throwing herself at a man—it wasn't proper. At least, not any more than she already had.

"Do you think he'll come to the strawberry shortcake social?" Amanda asked.

"Hm?" Tabitha seemed to be lost in her own thoughts.

"Menno—do you think he'll come to the social?"

"He hasn't come to any kind of gathering since he was young," Tabitha said. "I don't know. All you could do is offer."

Amanda smoothed her hands down her dress. "All right. If he doesn't come, should I find a way to run into him again?"

"Do you want to be like Aent Linda?" Tabitha cast her a meaningful look.

Linda had been in love with a man who hadn't returned

her feelings. She'd chased him from event to event, flinging herself into his path repeatedly over the years until he moved away to a new community and promptly married another woman. She'd made quite a spectacle of herself.

"No, I suppose not," Amanda said. "If he doesn't come, then I think we can assume he isn't interested?"

Tabitha's gaze softened. "Amanda, you are a good woman with so much to offer—"

"I'm not asking you to stroke my ego," Amanda said, shaking her head. "I just want to be realistic. If he doesn't come—"

"The next step needs to be his," Tabitha said. "It *must* be his. If he's interested, even if he doesn't come to the social, he has to make the next move. You can't chase him all the way to the vows."

Amanda held the empty Tupperware container in her lap, and her earlier elated, hopeful feelings drained away. Was she just being silly? She'd made it this far without any of the men showing any interest at all. What made her think that Menno would be any different?

But one little spark kept her hope alive. Tabitha had said that every man had something attractive about him . . . and it stood to reason that every woman had something attractive about her too. She knew what her own attractive quality was. She could cook very well, and her baking was impressive. She looked down at her hands—fingernails short, fingers on the stubby side. She folded her hands up into fists on top of that Tupperware container.

But would Menno appreciate what she had to offer?

17

Menno did not come by with any excuse to see Amanda, and for the next two days, Amanda tried not to think too much about it. She even went along with her sister to the clinic in town, and after she got a tour of the place, she stood back and watched while her sister inspected a dog's hurt paw.

But when they started a spay surgery on a cat, Amanda had to step out. Her stomach could take a lot, but the surgery was a little too much. So she headed out to the farm supply store to look around, and her breath caught when she spotted Menno inside, his arms crossed and his lips pursed as he looked over some mouse traps. She was both happy and embarrassed. It almost felt like she was following him around at this point. But she wasn't. Menno looked up then, and he startled when he spotted her.

"Hi," she said shyly.

"Hi." He picked up a package of mouse traps and circled around the bin, stopping in front of her. "I'm getting traps."

"Oh." She smiled timidly. "Those are good ones."

"Are they?" His warm gaze met hers, and she felt herself

melting just a little. He dropped his gaze to the package of traps.

"We use them in the barn." She took a step closer to get a better look at the brand. *Yah*, it was the same.

"A cat is better," Menno said. "I have four barn cats, but these are for the house. I don't want a house cat."

"A cat is always better," she agreed. "Why don't you want a house cat?"

"I'm not inside enough. I don't want to clean out a litter box either. It's just more work."

"We don't have a house cat either," she said. But she liked the thought of a cat keeping her company when she was cooking and cleaning and waiting on her husband to come home. This chitchat was almost painful. She shifted her feet and dropped her gaze to her running shoes.

"What are you shopping for?" Menno asked.

"I'm avoiding a surgery in the vet clinic," she said, laughing softly. "So I'm not really shopping."

"Surgery?"

"A cat spay."

"Oh. *Yah*, those are important if you don't want a hundred cats." He smiled. "Are you helping your sister?"

She nodded. "I enjoy it. It's nice to get out and see people. And I like helping the animals. I'd just rather feed baby piglets than hold an oxygen mask during a surgery."

"That's fair. Baby piglets are pretty cute."

They were silent for a couple of beats, and Amanda glanced over her shoulder as the door opened to let an *Englischer* into the shop. She was in blue jeans and had her graying hair pulled back into a pony tail. She headed right for the dog food aisle.

"How's Zeke?" Amanda asked.

"Growing." Menno's eyes lit up, and Amanda wondered if he'd ask her to come back and see the piglet. "Your sister's vitamin shot seemed to do the trick. He's finishing his bottles now."

"That's good."

"Can I help you pay for that?" the teenaged cashier asked, giving Menno a friendly smile.

"*Yah, danke.*" Menno turned toward the checkout, but then he stopped and looked back at Amanda. He looked stuck, uncertain of which direction to move, and an Amish teenager looked at them curiously from the end of an aisle. They were drawing attention now.

"I should go back to the clinic," Amanda said. "I'm supposed to be helping."

"Okay . . . see you later?" Menno asked, and Amanda nodded.

"*Yah.* Bye."

But if she did see him later, that would be because he came to the shortcake social. So was he planning on coming? What did that mean? Oh, how she wished she didn't get knotted up into a ball when she talked to him!

She walked briskly down the sidewalk toward the veterinarian clinic. She should have asked. Or maybe not. That might have come across as desperate. . . . Why, oh why, did this have to be so difficult?

When Amanda and Tabitha pulled into their own drive late that afternoon, Amanda noticed Rose's buggy parked beside the house. The side door opened, and Rose appeared, her face blotchy. She held a wadded up handkerchief in one hand and dabbed it under her nose. Her pink dress and white apron had gotten some streaks of dirt on them. A tendril of hair had come loose from her *kapp* too. Their normally impeccable sister looked mussed. Amanda's heart skipped a panicked beat.

"Oh no . . ." Tabitha breathed. "I wonder what's happened?"

"Is Daet okay?" Amanda called as she hopped down from the buggy.

"*Yah*, he's fine," Rose replied.

Amanda heaved a grateful sigh. "What's wrong, then?"

"I just needed to get away." Rose sniffled.

"It's Aaron, no doubt," Tabitha said, her voice low enough for Amanda's ears alone. Tabitha worked quickly to unhitch the horse, and Amanda joined her in unbuckling the other side.

"Why do you say that?" Amanda asked.

"Because a married woman doesn't come home in tears to her *daet*'s house for many other reasons," Tabitha replied.

But then, Rose hadn't come by with any complaints before Tabitha's return. She'd been fine . . . or she'd at least appeared fine. Had Tabitha coming home tapped into a well of unhappiness that Rose had kept hidden away?

They sent the horse into the corral and then headed up toward the house. Rose had disappeared inside, and when they got in, they found her at the table, her shoulders hunched up and an untouched glass of meadow tea in front of her.

"What happened?" Amanda asked.

Rose shook her head. "I do not understand my husband. At all. He's a complete mystery to me."

"At least Daet's not home," Tabitha said, her gaze flicking toward the door. "I remember his rule about us discussing our husbands."

Amanda knew the rule well enough, although it didn't

apply to her. Daet said that they were not to say anything disrespectful or unflattering about their husbands under his roof. He said that a wife should speak well of her husband to others and take care of her problems privately.

"I'm the only one it applies to right now," Rose said bitterly.

"What happened?" Tabitha asked. "It isn't complaining. You can't just keep all of that inside of you."

"He won't talk to me," Rose said. "I hardly know him, and we've been married two years! What does he dream about? I don't know, but he has nightmares and thrashes around and then claims he didn't dream anything. What is he thinking about when he gets that faraway look in his eyes? I don't know that either, because when I ask, he says it isn't fair to ask a man what he's thinking about."

"He won't tell you anything?" Amanda asked.

"Nothing that matters," Rose replied.

"Maybe it isn't anything interesting," Amanda suggested.

"Amanda, you don't understand marriage," Rose said. "I cook for that man, clean up after him, plan his meals, shop for his groceries, wash his clothes. . . . It's more intimate than it sounds. It's housework, but it's housework for *him*."

Actually, Amanda could understand that rather well. Wasn't it what she was longing to be able to do for a husband of her own? But now wasn't the time to argue with Rose about how much she understood.

"He's neglecting you," Tabitha said.

"I didn't say that."

"Well . . . if he does everything else but doesn't give you affection, that is emotional neglect."

"Don't make more out of it than it is," Rose said curtly.

Amanda glanced between her sisters. Tabitha pressed her lips together, and Rose looked downright defiant.

"I'm not making more of it. I know that from some therapy sessions I took after the divorce. I learned a few helpful words: *neglect*, *gaslighting*, *infidelity*. There are names for all of it, and somehow it's not so overwhelming and baffling when you can name what's going on."

"Well, that doesn't help me," Rose said. "My husband is not cheating on me."

"Okay, maybe not. But knowing what to call these things does help," Tabitha said. "It makes you feel less crazy."

"Did it help you? Did it help other *Englischer* women? Or does all that therapy and *Englischer* sympathy just end a marriage?" Rose snapped back.

"That's not fair, Rose," Amanda cut in. "You came to us, and Tabitha is only trying to help. She's gone through more than any of us, and it might help you to hear her out."

Rose heaved a shaky sigh. "I don't need you to tell me I'm right in my worries. I need you to tell me that this is normal, and I'll be fine."

Amanda shook her head. "I'm not married."

"And I'm divorced," Tabitha said. "I have little idea of what normal looks like. I'm full of warnings about what something going terribly wrong looks like, but I don't know the other side of it. You'll have to talk to one of our *aents* or someone else."

"I'm not telling an *aent*. That's how gossip starts," Rose muttered.

She wasn't wrong. That was how gossip got started, and the story of Rose and Aaron fighting could be repeated all over their community. That would be embarrassing for Rose, but she'd also have to explain herself to Aaron.

"When I married Michael, I meant it just as much as you did when you married Aaron," Tabitha said quietly. "But you have something going for you that I didn't. You're both Amish. He understands the basics of what a husband is supposed to do and how he is supposed to take care of you. Having the shared faith and understanding in common is actually a step ahead for the two of you. Running a farm on his own is hard work. Maybe he's still trying to find a balance. Or maybe it's harder for him than he thought, and he's upset about that and doesn't want to admit to it."

"And running a home isn't hard work? This is the thing—he should know how hard a woman works. He watched what his *mamm* did in the home. I cook, clean, garden, preserve the food, sew the clothes, but I still have some heart left over for my marriage. Why doesn't he?" Tears rose in Rose's eyes again. "Unless he's realized he doesn't love me, after all. Maybe he's realized that I'm . . . boring."

Boring? Well, that wasn't a possibility. Rose was also pretty and energetic and full of ideals about serving Gott through her housework and through loving her husband well. The question seemed to be, Why wouldn't Aaron let her love him? Who knew him well enough to even answer that question?

"Have you asked his mother?" Amanda asked.

"I don't want to do that," she said. "I know she'd give me advice, and she might even sit her son down for a heart-to-heart talk, but it would also be admitting that we're fighting."

"Are you actually fighting?" Tabitha asked. "I mean, outright?"

"Like cats and dogs!" Rose said. "Everything seems to spark an argument. I can ask how his day went, and he'll argue about it. Or I'll come inside and see his dirty boots on the floor making a mess for me to clean up, and I'll be so angry that I just erupt. I know it's silly. I know it's just a little thing, but all I can think is that he doesn't appreciate how hard I'm working to keep our home clean. And if I tell his *mamm* that we're fighting, I'll have to admit to my part of it, too, and I'm thoroughly embarrassed about it. I know I'm not being a sweet, kind wife. I can't do it!"

"Your feelings matter too," Tabitha said. "You can only push them down for so long."

"I'm not pushing them down as well as I'd hoped," Rose said.

"Then tell him how you feel," Tabitha said. "He needs to know. You're miserable, and that isn't fair. You deserve to feel happy in your own home as much as he does."

"I just don't want to fight with him more." Rose sighed.

"That seems rather convenient for him." Tabitha shook her head. "You can't say anything because it might start an argument? So what does that mean—you can't talk?"

"That's a good point," Rose said. "It's my life too."

"It is," Tabitha agreed.

"And I'm frustrated. That should matter!"

"It should."

"I'm tired of him being so emotionally distant. I need affection and for him to open up to me. I need to know what goes on inside of him. I feel like I'm nothing more than a maid and a cook half the time. He marches in, eats the meal, and marches back out again. He talks about cattle and weather, and that's it."

"Maybe it's what he's thinking about," Amanda said. "I mean, he's a farmer."

Rose cast her a tired look. "There has to be more, Amanda. We're married. What about love and tenderness?"

That question brought some heat to Amanda's cheeks. She didn't know about that side of marriage, and if Rose wanted her to butt out, she'd made her point.

"Do you know what it is that's bugging you so much?" Tabitha asked. "It's more than dirty boots. I know you hate the idea of therapy, but that's something I learned from those sessions. It's not about the boots. It's something deeper."

"It's also the way he breathes when he eats," Rose muttered, but then she and Tabitha shared a little smile, and Tabitha laughed.

"Maybe just stop reacting to his annoying things," Amanda said. "Let the floor be dirty. Let him breathe like an ox when he eats, if he wants to. Just stop reacting."

Both of her sisters turned to look at her, and Amanda could feel the silent skepticism between the two of them.

"Amanda, can I just talk to Tabitha about this?" Rose asked. "I don't have a lot of time, and Tabitha has been married before. She gets it."

So now Tabitha was the expert—after Rose had just told Tabitha that she was less than helpful. This didn't seem so delicate to Amanda at all, but apparently, just because she wasn't married, she couldn't have a logical thought to contribute. Two months ago, before Tabitha had come back, Rose would have been talking this out with Amanda, and she would have given her advice some thought too.

Amanda pushed back her chair with a noisy scrape and headed over to the counter, where half a pie waited. She got herself a plate and dished up a piece, listening to the conversation between her sisters—the quiet sympathy from Tabitha and the teary complaints from Rose.

If Rose just wanted someone to pat her hand and tell her how awful marriage was, she shouldn't have come here.

Amanda would love to have those problems, because it would mean she had her own home. And she wouldn't take it for granted either.

But marriage wasn't any easier on the other side of the vows, it seemed. Rose had all the characteristics that Amanda lacked. She was sweet, fun, beautiful, charming, and an excellent quilter. She had everything that would keep a man's heart, or so Amanda had always thought. And Aaron was a sober, decent Amish man. His dirty boots and breathing shouldn't be that irritating. . . . There was more to it. There had to be. So what was going wrong over there?

Daet's boots sounded on the steps outside. The door opened, and Tabitha and Rose fell silent as their *daet* appeared at the mudroom door.

"Rose, you came by for a visit?" Daet asked. "That meadow tea looks good. Can I get a glass? I'm parched. It's a warm day out there."

Rose stood up and poured her father a glass of cold meadow tea. He took it and chugged it back, then held out the glass to be refilled.

"What's wrong?" he asked.

"Nothing, Daet," Rose said quickly. "I'm fine."

"You've been crying," he countered.

"I'm emotional sometimes," Rose said. "It's just a woman thing."

"Ah." Daet put a hand up and nodded. "Understood. But don't be too long away from home. When a man comes in thirsty, looking for a drink, he likes to find his wife there too. Take it from a man who knows."

"Very true," Rose said, forcing some cheer. "I'd best get back home. I'm sure you have clients to see still today, Tabitha."

Amanda seemed to be entirely forgotten by both of her sisters. She took a bite of pie, chewing slowly as she watched Rose head for the door. Tabitha went with her, and they talked in low tones that Amanda couldn't overhear and then headed outside together.

"Amanda, you are my level-headed daughter," Daet said. "I'm glad of that. I don't think I could handle three of you being emotional."

Amanda gave her father a slight smile. Her *daet* thought she was wonderful just as she was. He might be the only one who did.

"That pie looks good," he added.

"I'm level-headed enough to remind you about your diet, Daet," Amanda replied.

"Fine . . ." Daet pulled out the last of the apple crumble. "I'll have this, I suppose. Where did the muffins go? Weren't there cinnamon rolls here the other day?"

Those had been given to Menno.

Amanda felt some heat touch her cheeks. "Diet, Daet!"

Daet muttered under his breath, and Amanda scraped her plate and licked the fork. Tabitha had warned Amanda to be careful, and while Amanda was inclined to brush off her sister's worries as excessive, seeing Rose's misery today left her feeling less certain of her goal of finding a husband.

A good husband was a gift from Gott. But what about a bad one?

18

Tabitha watched as Rose's buggy turned out of the shade-dappled drive and onto the sun-splashed road with a creak. The clop of hooves rang from the road, mingling with the whisper of wind through the trees and the twitter of birdsong. Despite the soothing scene, Tabitha's chest felt tight. She glanced back toward the house and then up the drive again. She wasn't ready to go back in.

The look on Rose's face had knotted up her stomach and chest. She'd seen that helpless heartbreak, the bewildered look of a woman who couldn't understand why everything was going wrong. And Tabitha had felt that way before. She'd blamed herself, too, thinking that maybe it was her fault that her husband was pulling away from her. She'd tried everything she knew to show him she loved him—cooking his favorite meals, wearing the dresses he complimented, trying to talk to him about his day. . . . It turned out there was another woman doing all those things for him too.

Gott, why can't men just appreciate the wife they have?

Tabitha started up the drive at a brisk walk. She needed just a few minutes alone. She'd come back to Shepherd's

Hill thinking that she could start over, but she'd dragged her heartbreak along with her. There was no turning back the clock to less complicated times, and she was still trying to unravel everything that had gone wrong in her marriage. She and Michael had had good times too. She used to like bringing him home with her for a visit—showing him Amish life and shocking him with things he didn't know about it. They used to go for long drives together and talk about all of their plans for the future. Back then, she'd been talking about when she was a veterinarian, and he'd been talking about opening his own mechanics shop. They said they'd have children later, once she finished school. She hadn't been entirely sure how she'd work and have little ones at home, but she thought maybe she could work part time and have the best of both worlds. And Michael had been supportive of that. Whenever she started to wonder if it was too much, he'd remind her that *Englischer* women did it all the time, and she'd felt better.

Then, close to the end of her veterinarian schooling, he'd started getting critical. She spoke with a Pennsylvania Dutch accent. She didn't use her cell phone properly. She forgot to check her texts. She didn't understand his friends' jokes. She tended to dress a little awkwardly—she'd never fully gotten the hang of dressing in *Englischer* styles without looking like she was in a costume. And he'd gone from being a generally supportive husband to being annoyed with everything she did. That was when the affair had started. But she hadn't known that then. She'd thought maybe she needed to behave better, be more patient, love him more deeply. She'd thought that she was the problem.

Tabitha reached the top of the drive and headed down the gravel road in the opposite direction than her sister had

139

gone. Tabitha was heading for the phone hut. It was a perfectly good destination, and the more often she checked her answering service, the better.

The sun was comfortingly warm on her shoulders, and as she crunched along the gravel road, she could feel those knots loosening.

Gott, why didn't you stop me from marrying him?

It was an old, scarred prayer, and she'd prayed it often. But Tabitha had been swept up in the flush of new love and the arrogance of youth. She hadn't been listening to anyone, let alone her own Maker. Oh, she'd prayed before she married Michael, but those prayers had been requests for blessing on her plans, not requests for guidance. She couldn't blame Gott for her mistakes. But all the same, she wished Gott had thrown some wrench in her plans—sent the car into a ditch, stopped Michael from meeting her at the truck stop, something! Instead, Gott had given her exactly what she'd asked for—a straight, clear road right into Michael's arms.

And Tabitha could only hope that Amanda didn't make the same mistake she had. Just because a woman could marry a man didn't mean she should.

The phone hut was deserted. Just a little A-frame building with a small window for light and a door that could be shut for privacy and to block out cold in the winter. There was a little wooden table, a telephone on top, and a three-legged stool to sit on. From that seat, she could see the trees out the window and a squirrel sitting on a tree branch. She picked up the phone and called her answering service. There was one message waiting.

"Hello, Tabitha. This is Jared Blank. I've got cows with some extreme stomach bloat. It looks bad. I need help quick—my remedies aren't working. Please come as soon as you can. It's Jared Blank. My farm is out by the skating pond, if you recall."

Tabitha knew the way to the Blank farm. In fact, this was the family hosting the strawberry shortcake social that weekend, and Tabitha knew his wife, Katherine, from school days. Jared and Katherine had seven kids all under the age of ten. So while the oldest of the children could do chores, they weren't a lot of help with the big jobs.

There were no other messages, so Tabitha hung up the phone and headed back down the road at a brisk walk. With cattle bloat, things could go badly very quickly, and it wasn't unheard of to lose cows that way, so time was of the essence.

When Tabitha turned down the drive, she spotted Amanda on the porch.

"Amanda! Let's hitch up!" Tabitha called. "We have an emergency call!"

Her sister broke into a jog and headed for the corral, and Tabitha felt a rush of relief. Amanda was a good helper. There was no flapping and theatrics with her, and Tabitha had been able to count on her to remain calm and collected. If Tabitha had a choice in which sister assisted her on this call, she'd choose Amanda, hands down.

They hitched up the buggy and then headed up the drive. Once they hit the road, she let the horse open up into a trot, a dry breeze pushing at Tabitha's *kapp* as they headed in the direction of the Blank farm.

"What's happening?" Amanda asked as she settled into her seat.

"Stomach bloat," Tabitha said. "I'll have to move fast, and you'll need to hand me tools when I ask for them."

"Of course," Amanda said.

"It will be invasive," Tabitha said. "I hope you don't get queasy."

Her sister cast her a brave grin. "I'll do my best."

"I'm the one who does all the invasive stuff. I just need you to hand me supplies," Tabitha said. "You're good at this, Amanda."

And hopefully the pep talk would help Amanda push through any nausea, because Tabitha would have to work quickly.

"I guess I'm better at assisting with veterinarian duties than I am at giving Rose advice," Amanda said.

"What?" Tabitha reined in the horse at a four-way stop, leaned forward to look both ways, and then flicked the reins again.

"Rose used to ask me what I thought before you came back, you know," Amanda said. "Not anymore, though."

Tabitha shot her sister a quizzical look. "Did we offend you today?"

"No."

"It sounds like we did," Tabitha said. "Oh, Amanda, I'm sorry if we pushed you out. It's just that some things look different on the other side of those vows. Having been married before, I think she should just confront him. Get it out into the open. I regret how much time I spent pussyfooting around Michael."

"She won't do that," Amanda said.

"He's her husband. She can't talk to him?"

"You know it's different here," Amanda said. "She's supposed to love and support him. Not upset him."

"They're married. Behind closed doors, it's very different than the appearances couples keep up," Tabitha replied.

Amanda shrugged. "You'll see. She won't do it."

Tabitha was tempted to argue with Amanda, but Amanda might know more than Tabitha gave her credit for. She'd been the one Rose used to talk to, and Amanda had been living in their community all the time that Tabitha had been away. She might understand these dynamics better than Tabitha, marriage experience or not.

Rose's problems were forgotten as they finally turned down the drive to the Blank farm. Katherine sat on a chair in the shade of a cherry tree, shucking peas into a metal bowl on her lap. Her four littlest ones played nearby. One boy was still a toddler in diapers, and he wore a baby dress—simpler for diaper changes. A baby slept on a blanket beside her. It was a sweet domestic scene, but the worry was clear on Katherine's face. She spotted them and waved urgently.

Beyond the shady yard was a small field of strawberries, their ripe scent sweetening the air. Tabitha and Katherine had worked picking fruit together for several summers in their teenage years, but ten years had changed a lot. Where Katherine used to be rail thin, she was now rounder and more authoritative. That was motherhood shining through. Katherine put two fingers in her mouth and whistled loud and shrill. Jared appeared at the barn door just as they reined in.

"Hi, Katherine!" Tabitha called. "We're going to run over there and see what we can do for the cows, okay?"

"*Yah, yah!* Jared's in the barn."

Tabitha grabbed her bag, and Amanda hoisted the second bag of supplies. They left the buggy hitched up, tied the horse to the hitching post, and headed briskly across the yard toward the gate that led to the barn beyond. Amanda was breathing hard next to her, but she didn't slow down a bit.

Jared held the barn door open for them as they hurried inside. The farmer's hair was awry under his straw hat, and he had a full, reddish-blond married beard, his upper lip properly shaved. He gave them each a quick nod. He had his two oldest boys with him, Matthias who was ten, and Jakey who was eight. The *kinner* stood soberly next to their father, both standing with their weight on one leg like their *daet* stood.

"I came as fast as I could," Tabitha said. "Where are they?"

"In stalls. I got them inside." Jared gestured into the dim barn, and Tabitha had to let her eyes adjust for a moment before she spotted them. Four cows occupied separate stalls. Their heads were hanging, their bellies dangerously distended, and one was moaning softly.

"How long have they been like this?" Tabitha asked.

"I don't know. I found them a couple of hours ago, and I drove them back to the barn. Then I went to the phone hut to call you and came back. So several hours by now."

The closest cow staggered and fell to her knees. If a cow was going down, it was near death, and Tabitha sprinted toward that animal first. She'd arrived just in time.

"Amanda, hand me the stomach tube." Tabitha let herself into the stall and wrapped an arm firmly around the cow's head. If she didn't move fast, this animal would die. Amanda unzipped her bag and pulled out the long sanitized tube and handed it over.

Tabitha lifted the cow's head up—the animal was too tired to fight—and fed the plastic tube down the cow's throat, aiming past the windpipe to get the tube down into the animal's stomach. That was where the foam would be, preventing the cow from being able to belch up the extra gas in her belly. She pushed the tube gently at first, then harder, pushing past sphincters that wanted to stop the foreign tube from passing. Then she felt the release as the tube made it into the stomach, and she stopped quickly so as not to go too far. Perforating the stomach lining would only make the animal sicker. Immediately, a foul-smelling gas started to whoosh out of the tube.

"The defoamer," Tabitha said, and her sister passed her the mineral oil. "And the funnel."

Just as the gas stopped escaping, she used the funnel to pour the correct dose of mineral oil down the tube and directly into the stomach. That would help the froth and foam to collapse and let the animals digest properly once more. She pulled the tube out in one smooth tug, and the cow stumbled to her feet. A good sign.

"Can you hose this off?" Tabitha said, and Amanda grabbed the hose tube and proceeded to spray it down from a water hose next to a drain.

The next animal was painfully distended on the left side, but it was a calf, so a smaller animal to handle.

"This is a feeding issue," Tabitha told Jared as she entered the next stall. "Are they grazing or getting silage?"

Tabitha was very familiar with feeding issues—especially when it came to Fritz. Horses were more closely supervised so an uncomfortable bloat could be caught quickly. When cattle were out in the field, they could be dead before a busy farmer caught the problem.

"This time of year it's all grazing," Jared said.

"You'll need to check your pasture for weeds and plants that cause bloat," she said, accepting the hose from her sister again. She wrapped her arm around the calf's head. She slid her fingers under the calf's lip and behind his teeth, applying pressure on the roof of his mouth until he opened his mouth and she could slide the tube down his throat in the same procedure she'd done on the last cow. He stomped

145

and tried to back up, but she moved with him, keeping his head high.

"Come on, friend," she said. "You'll be glad we did this."

The tube made it down to his stomach, and that familiar hiss of escaping stomach gas hit the air. The calf stopped struggling as the painful distension started to go down.

"There you are . . ." Tabitha murmured. "We want a quarter dose of the defoamer," she added to Amanda.

They continued that way until all four of the cows had been treated. The children stood back and watched in silence as they worked.

"She's a lady," Tabitha heard the older boy whisper. "And she's the vet."

"She doesn't have a husband, right, Daet?" Another whisper that was loud enough for Tabitha to hear.

"Hush. We'll discuss it later."

Obviously, she'd been a topic of discussion around this home. What did Katherine think of Tabitha's return—really? What did she think of Tabitha working a man's job? There were opinions, for sure and certain.

Tabitha came out of the last stall, and she held the hose out to be washed off over the drain in the concrete floor. Amanda sprayed it thoroughly.

"I'm grateful," Jared said. "*Danke* for coming so quickly."

"I'm glad I got the message soon enough," Tabitha said, looking back over her shoulder at the last cow. It was doing better already, the distension gone, as well as the pain.

"You're . . . a good vet," Jared said. "A very good vet."

The boys' gazes bounced between their father and her.

"*Danke*, Jared. If you'd let your neighbors know that, I'd appreciate it."

Jared's face colored. "Have you been getting flak?" But he knew the answer to that. She could see it in his face.

"A little, *yah*," she replied. "People don't like a woman doing this job, especially an Amish woman."

"I'll tell them you're good," Jared said. "You have my word on that."

"*Danke*," Tabitha said. "I have the bishop's blessing, and as you know, I need to support myself. I've got the education and the skills, and I can help our community. It's a solution for my . . . delicate situation."

Jared met her gaze for the first time and smiled faintly. "I can appreciate that."

She wouldn't have a provider once her *daet* passed away. If she could provide for herself, she wouldn't be a drain on the community either.

Tabitha and Amanda gathered up their supplies and headed back out of the barn. Katherine sat in the yard with her big metal bowl. Instead of playing now, the *kinner* were helping her shuck the peas. The younger ones were simply opening pods and shoving fresh peas into their mouths, but the two older ones seemed to be getting peas into the bowl, even if there was some snacking going on. For a moment, Katherine just watched Tabitha and Amanda as they walked across the field, and then she waved.

"*Danke* for helping," she called.

"My pleasure, Katherine," Tabitha called back.

But something had changed between her and her girlhood friend. Tabitha was not a regular Amish woman, because if she were, she'd be shucking peas and chatting with Katherine, not saving the family's cattle from a deadly bloat. Tabitha was back home again, but she hadn't settled into a regular Amish life. She'd slipped into a space all her own, and she could feel the uncertainty in the other woman's gaze.

How did the Amish women know how to relate to a divorcée veterinarian? Even if they'd picked fruit with her for several summers . . . even if they'd attended each other's birthday parties and sat in the same group at hymn sings?

They didn't. That was the challenge. They simply didn't relate to her at all.

The space between regular Amish life and being a complete outcast was chilly, and when she looked over at Amanda, she felt a wellspring of gratitude for her sister's loyalty. Coming home might be lonely in a lot of ways, but having her sisters back in her life made up the difference. They had each other, for better or for worse, for a lifetime.

And suddenly she knew that she wasn't going to leave Rose alone in her unhappiness. She knew what it felt like, and Rose was sitting in the cold right now. She was miserable, trying to hide it, and feeling like a failure for not pleasing Aaron. Maybe Tabitha could be a shoulder to lean on and a listening ear.

They were sisters. If they didn't support each other, who would?

19

Jonas heaved a bale of hay out of the loft. It dropped to the wagon below and hit the empty bed with a dusty thunk. The horse—their newest purchase—didn't even flinch. He swished his tail, and Jonas aimed the second bale to land next to the first.

"Hey, watch it!"

Jonas looked down to see Aaron standing below with his thumbs stuck in his suspenders, squinting up at him. Aaron's married beard was still short and a bit wispy, but Jonas could still see his old friend in the lazy grin. He and Aaron had been best friends since the first grade when they discovered they both liked digging up worms and throwing them at Susan. For six-year-old boys, this was a solid foundation, and they'd stoically done their time in the second recess with their heads down on their desks for all the worm flinging.

"Hi, Aaron," Jonas said. "One last bale."

Jonas tossed the third bale, and it landed on top of the other two, rocking and almost falling off, but Aaron put a hand up to stabilize it. The horse remained unflappable, and Jonas was impressed. This was fast becoming his favorite workhorse, and he'd been giving him some extra treats for his hard work too. Jonas headed down the ladder and out the barn door to where his friend waited for him.

"How are you doing?" Jonas asked.

"Pretty good," Aaron replied. "I was wondering if I could borrow your post-hole digger. Mine is rusted up tight."

"*Yah*, of course," Jonas replied. "Hop up, and we'll drive over to the other barn before I head out to fill the feeders."

Both men took a seat at the front of the wagon, and Jonas loosened the reins. The sun shone warm on his shoulders, and it glistened off the horse's glossy hind quarters. Jonas had started to call the horse Rocky because he was as solid as a stone foundation. It suited him.

"New horse?" Aaron asked.

"*Yah*, Daet got him at auction."

"Nice animal."

"*Danke*. Good disposition and knows the work already. He was a great deal."

The horse pulled the wagon at an easy pace, responding to the lightest touch on the reins and heading up the dirt road toward the main barn.

"Oh, my wife has been baking," Aaron said. "We've got more bread than we can eat. I'll bring you some, if you want."

"My *mamm* wouldn't turn it down," Jonas replied. "She's been helping my *aent* at the nursery in town, so we'll eat it."

Jonas's aunt and uncle owned a nursery in town that did very well this time of year, so they always hired extra workers. This year, Mamm had asked if she could pitch in. She was saving up some money to buy a second propane-fueled freezer for the basement.

"I saw Rose the other day," Jonas added.

"Oh?" Aaron cast him a sidelong look.

150

"She came with Tabitha to do the cattle vaccinations."

"*Yah*, she's been helping her sister," Aaron said. "I didn't know she was here, though."

"Tabitha wants to set me up with Amanda."

That was something that Jonas hadn't even mentioned to his parents, because they wouldn't see the obvious mismatch there. They'd probably get on board with it. Aaron was a friend that Jonas could count on to see things his way.

"Amanda?" Aaron's eyebrows went up. "Are you considering her? Because if you are, you and I would be family."

Jonas shook his head. "That would be nice, but no. She's a great cook and has a good head on her shoulders, but I'm not getting married just because a woman can cook. I want love—the real thing."

The wagon bumped over a hole in the road, and Jonas braced his feet as they jostled past it.

"What is the real thing?" Aaron asked. "I mean, do you want a woman who makes you think about her all day and turns your head inside out?"

"Yeah, pretty much," Jonas replied. "A lifetime is a long time to spend with one woman. I want her to be the one who makes everything worth it."

"I married a woman I felt like that about," Aaron said. "Rose is beautiful and funny and sweet, and she can bake up a storm. . . . I thought it was a matter of choosing a woman who'd make me happy, but you've got to ask yourself if you'll actually make her happy too."

"Are you two still butting heads?" Jonas asked.

"Yep."

His tone said enough. Jonas wouldn't ask more about that. It wasn't his business.

"She seemed happy to me when I saw her," Jonas said.

"She and Tabitha make quite a team. Have you seen Rose when she's assisting her sister?"

"No," Aaron said. "She talks about it, though. I don't know if I like having my wife hopping around from farm to farm."

"She's not hopping," Jonas countered. "She's working. They got the vaccinations done in record time, and Tabitha is a good vet."

"I've heard that she's really good," Aaron said. "And I know her situation is a unique one. She's got all the qualifications, and the bishop gave his blessing on it, so I'm not complaining that Tabitha is working as a vet. I mean, it'll only benefit me when I can call on my sister-in-law when I need her services. But I hoped my wife would be happy at home, taking care of the house. I'm half afraid she'll end up like her sister and wanting more than an Amish life offers."

That was a valid worry. Tabitha's career might be sanctioned by the bishop, but it was far from the life a regular Amish wife could expect.

"Maybe when the *kinner* come she'll be more focused on the home life," Jonas said.

"*Yah*, maybe."

"There's nothing wrong with a woman making some extra money," Jonas added. "My *mamm* is making some money at the nursery. Most wives find some way to bring in extra money."

"Most wives sell eggs or sew quilts. They don't act as veterinarian assistants," Aaron said. "And I take care of the money. She doesn't have to worry about it. Our farm is profitable."

So it was Aaron's pride that had taken a hit. Men liked to think that it was about their duty to provide or the care their work showed for their families. But it came down to their pride, and Jonas might not have any marital experience, but every Amish man knew that pride went before a fall.

"Maybe she wants to do it," Jonas said.

Aaron nodded. "*Yah*. And I do want her to be happy. Forget I said anything."

They came up to the main barn, and Jonas reined in the horse in the shade of the building. A breeze whispered past Jonas's neck, cooling him momentarily, and from across the farm yard, the clucking of the chickens underscored the songbirds in the trees. Beyond, by the house, he could see Aaron's buggy, still hitched up.

"Let me get you that post-hole digger," Jonas said.

"*Danke*." Aaron jumped down, and he eyed the horse for a moment.

"What?" Jonas asked.

"The horse is familiar," he said. "He looks like one my father-in-law has. Maybe from the same brood mare."

"*Yah*, you never know," Jonas replied, and he headed into the barn to find the tool.

"You sure you don't want to be my brother-in-law?" Aaron called jokingly after him.

If Aaron joined the ranks of everyone trying to get Jonas married, he might just head for the hills. Besides, he'd been serious about not marrying a woman until he was boots over hat in love with her, and her with him. In fact, he'd been praying one very specific prayer for years—that Gott would show him the woman for him and that Gott would stall any relationship efforts if the woman wasn't Gott's will. So far, Gott had stalled everything.

Besides, Amanda Schrock deserved someone who was smitten with her too. And that wasn't Jonas.

153

20

Amanda didn't see Rose the next couple of days. She didn't come by or offer to help with any veterinarian calls. By Saturday, Amanda noticed Tabitha perking up at any sound that might be a buggy. Once it was a buggy pulling in, but it was one of Daet's friends coming to say hello and talk about a friend's health issues.

Normally, Rose came by, but Amanda had to wonder what had happened after she'd gone home. Had she and Aaron sorted things out?

"Do you think Rose is okay?" Amanda asked her sister.

Tabitha shrugged. "I think she's busy. She's got a home of her own to keep up. I'm sure we'll see her tonight at the strawberry shortcake social."

Her sister's presence at the shortcake social wasn't the one that Amanda was hoping for, though. Amanda was more anxious to see if Menno came to the social that evening.

Let him come, she silently prayed. *Please, let him come.*

If Amanda were praying fairly, she'd ask Gott to let Menno come if it was Gott's will and if Menno was the husband for her. But she'd been thinking about what Menno had said about seeing Gott as a friend, and in a moment like this one, where she longed for something this much, she needed not only a Gott who guided their community but a Gott who intervened on her behalf.

Gott, I want to get married. I want a husband and a home, and I see something sweet in Menno. I think the others overlook him, just like I've been overlooked. I feel something special between us. I don't think I'm imagining it, but I might be. Please give me a husband.

It was a different prayer from the one she'd prayed the last few years. A couple of years ago, Amanda had given up on being chosen by some nice man, and she'd started praying for Gott to give her some other meaningful occupation to fill her time. She'd asked for Gott to take away her jealousy of her married friends and to fill her heart when she felt lonesome. Good prayers. Practical prayers. But then Tabitha came back, and with Tabitha came a very meaningful occupation in helping her sister in her veterinarian duties. Gott had provided! But Tabitha was also back in the family home, and Tabitha could help take care of Daet.

So now Amanda was tearing aside all those well-crafted, well-intended requests for a reasonable future, and she was dumping her heart out in front of her Maker.

Please give me my turn at marriage and a family. Please.

What Amanda really wanted in the deepest part of herself was a husband to love. And whenever she thought about marriage lately, the husband at her side was a not–overly tall Amish man with kind eyes. She thought she could be very happy with a man like Menno. And she would work hard to make him happy too. If only she could have an opportunity.

The day crept by, and by the time Amanda and Tabitha

were on their way to the Blank farm for the shortcake social, Amanda was already feeling tired from the stress of waiting.

Eight buggies were already parked in the side field when they drove up, identical black buggies standing out against the green grass. The horses were in a corralled area beyond, munching on a feeder full of sweet hay. There were folding tables set up outside in the yard and large metal bowls lined up on the tables. They'd be filled with washed and sliced strawberries, picked from the small strawberry field beyond. Children were playing and laughing, and some older ladies sat in folding chairs in the shade of fruit trees. Their white *kapps* seemed to glow a tad brighter against their white hair.

Their *aent* Dina had her knitting with her, like she always did. A young girl came running up to her, leaning onto the arm of the chair and looking up into her face. Aent Dina didn't have grandchildren, but the children in the community loved her all the same. She kept peppermints in her purse, and she crocheted little frogs for them to play with if they asked her.

"Help me unhitch?" Tabitha asked.

"*Yah*, of course." Amanda hopped down.

It didn't take them long to unhitch their horse and send him into the corral with the others. But as they turned back toward the house, Amanda saw the hesitant look on her sister's face.

"Are you all right?" Amanda asked.

"*Yah*. I'm fine."

"You look nervous."

Tabitha seemed ready to disagree, then she shrugged. "I used to be good friends with Katherine. She's polite now. Kind, even. But I don't think we're friends anymore."

The farmhouse side door opened, and Katherine came

out with a platter covered in a tea towel. She was careful going down the steps, and she didn't look in their direction.

"A lot has changed," Amanda said softly.

"*Yah.*" Tabitha forced a smile. "But I'll be fine. There's a price to pay for having left, too, right?"

It struck Amanda how big that cost was for her sister. She'd given up more than just a chance at marriage again when she returned. She'd come back with stigma attached to her, and she'd never be accepted back in the same way. When Tabitha left, she and her friends would have been on the same footing. But everything was different now. Katherine was a married mother of seven.

"Why don't you and I sit together?" Amanda asked. "I might not be your old friend, but I am your sister."

Tabitha shot her a smile. "You're sweet, Amanda."

"I mean it, though," she said. "The others might take some time to warm up, but if you and I stick together, they'll see that not so much has changed. We're still family, and you're still a good person."

The sound of another buggy approaching drew Amanda's gaze. The buggy shone clean in the evening sunlight, and the man with the reins made her heart skip a beat.

He'd come!

Menno was alone in the buggy. He spotted her immediately and reached up and touched the brim of his straw hat in a hello. She couldn't help the smile that sprang to her lips.

"So he came after all." Her sister fell in beside her.

"*Yah* . . . What do I do?" Amanda whirled around to face her sister, her heart pounding. Suddenly, all of this felt very important, and she realized that she hadn't made a plan for how to respond if Menno did come to the social. "Do I wait for him to come to me or . . . ?"

Tabitha's gaze followed his buggy as he parked next to theirs. Tabitha did know more about these things than Amanda did, and Amanda needed answers rather quickly.

"He's not been spending time in the community much," Tabitha said, her voice low. "I imagine you can't expect him to know what to do either."

"So we're both clueless?" Amanda's heart hammered harder in her chest. Was this where she played coy? Was she supposed to walk away and let him come find her? What was she supposed to do?

"Do you want to just go talk to him?" Tabitha asked.

"Is that the right thing? Will I look desperate?" Amanda asked. "I'm not very good at this either. I have no idea what to do!"

"That makes two of you, then. Go talk to him," Tabitha said, bumping Amanda's hip with her own to get her moving in the right direction.

Amanda could hear her sister's soft laugh as she started in the direction of Menno's buggy. She was making a spectacle of herself, she was sure, and she felt heat in her face as she slowed to a stop a few paces from where Menno had parked. He walked his horse to the corral, his head down.

Amanda was just about to turn around before she made a fool of herself when Menno turned and looked over his shoulder. Those soft brown eyes met hers, and a relieved smile touched his lips.

It didn't take him long to put the horse in the corral, and when Menno reached her, he stopped a few feet shy of her.

"I'm glad you came," Amanda said. "I wasn't sure if you would."

"I wasn't planning on it," Menno said. "But then you asked, and . . ." His face reddened.

"Menno, did you come for me?" As the words came out, she wished she could take them back. It was too forward! Who asked that sort of thing?

"Well . . ." Menno licked his lips. "*Yah*. If you hadn't asked, I'd be at home with Zeke. You know . . . feeding a baby pig."

His lips turned up. Was he thinking about their meeting in the farm supply store?

"I'm glad you came," she repeated.

"*Yah*."

Amanda wasn't sure what to say to him, and for a moment, they just stood there, the sunlight warming her shoulders. He dug the toe of his boot into the grass.

"Why have you stayed away from community events?" she blurted out.

He blinked at her.

"You and I could talk about nothing and comment on the weather and point out calves in the field," Amanda said, "but I think it's probably better if we talk straight."

Menno nodded. "*Yah*. It might be better."

"So why have you stayed away all this time?" Amanda asked. "This is your community."

"People talk about me," he replied. "About my family. About . . . my *daet*."

"Then give them something new to say," she replied.

Menno met her gaze. "When Tabitha left, and people were talking about her running off with an *Englischer*, did you find it hard to face people?"

"*Yah*, but I did face them." She'd even argued with them, to her own detriment. "It wasn't me who had done wrong. It was my sister. I loved her, and I wanted her to come home, and . . . It wasn't me."

159

"Well, for a while I was just as bad as the rest of my family," Menno said. "So maybe I was ashamed of myself too."

"But not anymore," Amanda said.

"No, not anymore," he replied. "I've worked really hard to put all of that behind me, and I believe that Gott can give me strength."

They started to walk slowly toward the fence line, and Amanda could see the younger women looking at her pointedly. The older folks were still focused on their own conversation. Amanda angled her face away to avoid making eye contact with those who were watching her.

"You know about how my *mamm* left, right?" Menno asked. His tone deepened, tugging her a little closer. She found them walking only a few inches apart now.

Amanda began to nod, then shook her head. "I heard she ran away. I don't know why. We guessed."

"I was fifteen, and I'd started drinking with my older brothers already. We boys weren't mean, but we were out of control. I'll admit to that. My *daet* was mean, though, and he drank all the time. He hit her sometimes and said biting things. I could see her giving up. I actually watched her pack her bags. She made me promise not to say anything until Daet noticed she was gone. She needed some time to get away. She went to my grandparents' place in Indiana. I thought she'd come back. I waited and waited, but when I sent her a letter a couple of months later, my grandmother answered it. She said Mamm had had a nervous breakdown, that she'd just been a shell of herself. Then one day she packed her bags up again and left, and they didn't know where she'd gone."

"She left you all behind?" Amanda whispered.

"*Yah.*" He was silent a moment. "That nervous breakdown that my grandmother mentioned—I think I saw the start of it when I watched her packing her bags at home. Something had changed in her. She wasn't the *mamm* I knew anymore. She was . . . desperate. Panicked."

"Has she ever sent you a letter or come to see you?" Amanda asked.

"No."

"Oh, Menno . . ."

"Maybe I understand why she snapped. We were a houseful of drinking men—she'd had enough of us. And I've since learned that people all have a limit to what they can endure. And when they reach that limit, something happens. For my *mamm*, something inside of her broke. She couldn't take it anymore."

"She'd had enough of your father, but you weren't a man yet," Amanda countered. She'd seen fifteen-year-old boys. They were still a bit gangly and had goofy senses of humor. They were *kinner*, even if they thought they were ever so grown up.

"No, I wasn't a man. I know that. But . . . we weren't listening to her either. She'd gotten worn down, I suppose. Then after Mamm left and Daet died from liver failure, I realized that I'd better change something. But stopping drinking turned out to be harder than I thought. I'd declare myself done, and a few hours later I'd be pouring myself another drink."

"Did you know about Alcoholics Anonymous then?" she asked.

"Not yet. I was praying for strength, and then I saw a sign in a men's bathroom for some meetings in town. I took it as a sign from Gott, and I went. I took a drink before I stepped in the door. But those meetings gave me what I needed to stop drinking completely. I knew I could be a better man than my brothers or my *daet*."

"Did you worry that no one could forgive you for your mistakes?" Amanda asked.

Menno stopped walking, and for a moment he looked off toward the fields of cattle.

"I knew they could forgive me," he said at last. "I didn't think they'd trust me, though. And somehow that was worse."

That was why he'd stayed away. He'd been a rowdy boy abandoned by his *mamm* and left with an unfit father. And all this time, he'd been dealing with it alone. How much bravery had it taken for Menno to go visit Elder Yoder and tell him he wanted a wife?

"Are you angry with her for leaving you?" Amanda asked.

Menno didn't answer, and Amanda heard someone calling her name. She turned to see Katherine beckoning to her. She stood in a group of women, her baby girl on her hip.

The last thing Amanda wanted was to go chat with the women. Not now!

"They're trying to help you," Menno said.

Menno wasn't wrong. Amanda knew what Katherine was doing—trying to get her away from Menno so that they could set her straight about his family, or perhaps just provide a polite escape.

"I don't need rescuing," Amanda said curtly, and she turned her back on them.

For all their good intentions, they'd protect her right into becoming an established spinster. They'd go out of their way to keep her away from a questionable man, but would they give equal energy to finding her one they'd approve of?

"Amanda!" Katherine came up, breathing hard. Her baby girl balanced on her hip, and Katherine's cheeks were red from the exertion. "Take the baby, would you?"

162

Katherine passed the chubby infant over to Amanda, and Amanda kissed baby Lily's cheek.

"She's getting so big," Amanda said. "You remember Menno Weaver, don't you, Katherine?"

"Of course." Katherine's tone cooled just a little. "It's nice to see you, Menno. How is everyone?"

"Everyone meaning my brothers?" he asked.

Katherine's cheeks deepened in color. "Oh, well . . . I suppose, *yah*. That's what I meant."

It hadn't been. It was just a polite question posed by someone who'd forgotten that Menno had very few people connected to him who were up to any good.

"My brother Simon got fired last week from his job at the canning plant," Menno said. "Daniel is still living with my *onkle* in Huntington, and I haven't heard from him in months. And Emmanuel is living with some *Englischer* girl in town."

Katherine's smile faltered and then fell. "Oh."

"That's my family, I'm afraid." Menno's gaze sparked with irritation, and then he shook his head. "I'm sorry. I shouldn't have said all that."

"Your brothers aren't you," Amanda said firmly. "I don't think Katherine meant anything by it."

"No, of course I didn't," Katherine said, and she reached to take her baby back. "Amanda, I could use your help. Do you mind?"

"I'll be right there," Amanda said. "Can you give me a minute?"

Katherine nodded and headed back toward the cluster of chatting women, Lily held just a little closer, leaving Amanda and Menno alone.

Amanda bit her lip uncomfortably.

"This is why I stayed away," Menno said, his voice low. "I'm sorry. I told myself I'd do better than this. She didn't mean anything. I shouldn't have gotten sensitive."

"It's been a long time since you've done something with the rest of us," Amanda said. "Maybe you're just out of practice."

"For the record, I hate the way my brothers behave too," he said. "But they'll be the first ones to point out that I can't think I'm better than they are."

"I dare say you are better than them, Menno."

Menno's gaze slid over her shoulder, and she turned to see what he was looking at. Katherine and a few other married women were watching them. Whatever privacy she'd hoped to get in talking with Menno appeared to be at an end.

"You'd better go," Menno said. "They want to warn you away from me."

Amanda laughed. "I like you anyway, Menno."

And for the first time, Menno's granite face broke into an actual, open smile.

"Do you really?"

"*Yah*. I do."

"Go on, then," Menno said. "I'll try and make nice with the men."

As Amanda headed back toward the women, her heart was tumbling around inside of her. They'd give her all sorts of warnings, she had no doubt. But Menno wasn't the danger they thought. He'd been hurt, and she could tell that he longed for something better.

She looked over her shoulder and saw Menno watching her still.

Yah, she liked him very much.

21

Tabitha stood next to a folding table, arranging little round cakes on the trays. Two large bowls of velvety whipped cream sat next to the cakes, but Tabitha's attention wasn't on the food. She was watching as her sister came back toward the women. There was a little smile on Amanda's face that looked downright mutinous, and she had to wonder who Amanda's back was up against—Katherine or Menno?

Some men were chatting in a large group, joking about something that made them all shout with laughter. Jared slapped his knee as he hooted, and Tabitha wished she could hear what the joke was. It looked like it was a good one. Jonas Peachy was in the group, too, and he was shaking his head and laughing, but then he raised his eyes, and he saw her. For a split second, their gazes locked, and Tabitha looked away quickly, embarrassed to be caught trying to listen in.

With the *Englischers*, men and women would chat together, and there would be no impropriety. In college, she had a group of friends that included men and women—some married, some dating, some single. And she'd enjoyed those groups of people—their shared experiences being what cemented the friendship, not their gender.

But the Amish world was different, so even though Tabitha had more in common with the farmers right now, she stayed back with the women, as was only proper. She'd better find something to have in common with the women, or she'd be very lonely indeed.

Katherine, her baby snugged onto her hip, came over to the table and scanned the food.

"It looks ready, right?" Katherine asked.

"I think so," Tabitha agreed. "How are the cattle doing?"

"Oh, they're all better now," Katherine said. "Thanks to you, of course."

She wasn't asking to draw attention to herself, and she felt some heat in her face.

"I was just wondering if there were any others that were showing signs of bloat," Tabitha said. "It's the veterinarian in me. I can't help but worry about herds that don't belong to me."

"No," Katherine said. "And my husband rooted some weeds out of the field. He and his brother went around all afternoon pulling them up." She put a little extra emphasis on the words *my husband*, and Tabitha smiled faintly. The women didn't know how to relate to her, and they certainly didn't want her bonding with their husbands. These strict gender lines were practical and were meant to protect marriages. So the message was received. Jared was a taken man. Tabitha would never try to overstep those lines, but she understood that she occupied a different social position now.

"I'm glad they went over the field," she said. "How's Lily?"

166

She reached out and touched the baby's fingers, who instantly latched onto hers with a damp little grip.

"Lily's been growing faster than any of my other babies did," Katherine said. "She was ten pounds when she was born, and she just keeps growing!"

"She's healthy and strong," Tabitha said, and Katherine smiled at that.

"*Yah*, she is." She glanced around. "I think we're ready to eat, *yah*?"

Katherine gave her husband a little unobtrusive wave, and the couple exchanged a small smile.

"Is there something going on between your sister and Menno Weaver?" Katherine asked, adjusting Lily up a little higher.

"They've gotten to be friends," Tabitha replied.

That was a coy response, because *friends* could be used to describe the growing romantic feelings between single men and women who were looking for marriage or a simple sibling-like comradery between young teenagers. A couple could be courting for years and their families would introduce them as friends until an official engagement. After marriage, though, friendships changed. Men were friendly with men, and women were friendly with women.

Katherine shook her head. "Do you remember his *daet*? I remember when the elders asked him to leave Sunday service because he smelled so strongly of alcohol and was stumbling around."

"*Yah*, but you can't make someone pay for what their family member did," Tabitha said. "People deserve another chance, don't you think?"

Katherine dropped her gaze. "I suppose they do, if they really, truly want to start over."

This was beginning to feel a lot more personal, and Tabitha sucked in a wavery breath. She could feel perfectly confident pushing a hose down the throat of a bloated cow, but facing her school friend made her hands shake.

"Katherine, we used to be friends," Tabitha blurted out. "We used to walk to school together, and we made those handkerchiefs with our initials in the corner, and we exchanged them so we'd always remember each other."

Katherine's blue eyes rose again. "*Yah*, I remember that. And the sleepover at my place when my brothers set a mouse loose on our bed."

Tabitha started to laugh, remembering how they'd shrieked. They'd had their revenge the next morning when they put salt in the sugar bowl.

"I know I've been away," Tabitha said. "And I'll never be a married woman like you are. I'm going to be single, and I'm going to be working with the herds. But I'd hoped that we could find some friendship again. When I come by for professional reasons, I'd love to be able to stop in and have a tea with you."

"I might be a bit boring to you now," Katherine said. "You've got your big career, and we've all heard how smart you are."

What had they heard exactly? This was precisely why the Amish strove to keep everyone the same. Jealousy or insecurity could damage relationships faster than anything else.

"That's just a skill like harvesting a garden," Tabitha said. "And you're very interesting! You keep up with seven *kinner*, Katherine. No amount of schooling teaches that."

Katherine smiled at that. "You learn as you go."

"I know when I was *Englische* and visited things were awkward. I was a little high on myself then, and I'm sorry for it. I'm a little wiser now."

"You didn't visit me," Katherine said, lowering her voice. "After you were married, when you'd come back to visit, you never came by."

"I was . . . scared," Tabitha said. "I thought I wouldn't be welcome because I'd jumped the fence. And you were so proper and had your *kinner* and your good Amish ways . . ."

"I missed you, though," Katherine said. "I thought you didn't care anymore."

"I cared!" Tabitha reached out and caught her hand. "I did. I was overwhelmed and distracted and thought I was doing the right thing by going *Englische* back then, but I did care. I just wasn't being a good friend."

"You know, I told my *mamm* you'd come back," Katherine said with a nod. "I told her that you'd see what you'd left behind. And everyone said I was silly."

"You were right, though," Tabitha said. "I did see what I left behind."

"You should come by for a visit when you have time," Katherine said. "We can catch up properly over some tea."

Tabitha's heart swelled, and she nodded. "I'd like that. *Danke.*"

Just then, Katherine's toddler broke into a wail. They both turned to see his little straw hat on the ground, and he sat next to it, cradling his foot.

"Oh dear," Katherine said, and she cast Tabitha an apologetic look before she headed off to help him, leaving Tabitha alone. Katherine's sister, Sarah, jogged over to help, too, and she scooped Lily from Katherine's arms so the young mother could attend to her son.

Amanda came up to the table and glanced in Katherine's direction.

"What did Katherine want?" Amanda asked.

The little boy had stopped crying now that he had his *mamm*'s attention. Somehow sympathy was an effective pain reliever.

"Just to chat," Tabitha said, and she exhaled a pent up breath. "She invited me to come for some tea one of these days to catch up."

"*Yah?*" Amanda smiled. "About time too. You two used to be such good friends. Maybe you'll be grown women who whisper and tell secrets now."

Tabitha chuckled. "We're grown, Amanda, so I certainly hope we're more mature than that. But maybe we can connect again and start over. She used to be a lot of fun."

"She's still quite fun," Amanda said.

"Everyone, it's time to eat!" Jared called. "Let's gather around and ask Gott to bless the food."

The older ladies began to stand up, pushing themselves up from those creaking lawn chairs—a longer process since they weren't as mobile as they used to be. Aent Dina's gaze rested on Tabitha, and she gave her a warm smile. The older men who'd been sitting on a couple of benches hoisted themselves up too. Everyone came around, and Tabitha noticed that Menno came up behind the younger men. He stood there, no one quite noticing him, and seeming almost more alone for his proximity to the rest.

Everyone bowed their heads, and in her heart, Tabitha prayed for the food, but also for the people here. For Amanda, who longed for marriage, and for Menno, who seemed to just want to belong in some way. They were all just doing their best to live right, and it wasn't always easy.

Jared cleared his throat loudly, the sign that the prayer was over, and the women who'd agreed to serve quickly stepped up to their places behind the table, and Tabitha stepped back

170

to let the others start eating first. But as she backed up, she collided with someone solid, and she turned to see Jonas.

"Sorry," she said. "I didn't see you there."

"It's okay." Jonas made room for Tabitha next to him. "Did your *daet* come?"

"Not today," Tabitha replied. "I think he was looking forward to having the house to himself for a few hours. He doesn't get that too often anymore. Did yours?"

"*Yah*. He's—" Jonas looked around. "He's around somewhere."

So much for encouraging some friendship between their fathers today.

"How is your new horse?" Tabitha asked.

"He was doing really great," he replied. "He's a well-trained, hardworking horse. But this afternoon he started slowing down a bit. I think he must miss his old barn or something."

Slowing down. That wasn't a good sign. That normally preceded a bout of illness in Fritz.

"Slowing down how?" Tabitha asked.

"Oh, just seeming a bit tired and sad. Horses are highly emotional. They—" He stopped and smiled. "But look who I'm telling. You know that."

Tabitha was about to ask more about the horse when Jonas nodded over toward the far apple tree. Amanda had brought Menno a plate of strawberry shortcake, and Menno's face was ablaze as he accepted it.

"Menno Weaver came," Jonas said. "I'm shocked. I don't think I've ever seen him outside of Service Sunday."

"It's a good thing that he's getting more involved, isn't it?" Tabitha asked.

"I suppose, *yah*," he agreed. "But will it last?"

171

"It will if we're friendly and make space for him," Tabitha said. "He deserves some credit. He stayed Amish. It would have been easier for him to leave."

Jonas eyed her uncertainly. "You think he'll jump the fence?"

"No, I think he's trying to find a way back into the community, though," she replied. And she could understand that—so was she.

Jonas's gaze moved toward Menno thoughtfully.

"If you think his efforts won't last, what about me?" Tabitha asked. "Are you waiting for me to go *Englische* again?"

Jonas blinked—he didn't look like he'd been ready for that question—and she could see the moderate friendliness in his expression slipping away. She was doing it again, being too bold and honest.

Jonas sighed. "All right. *Yah*. Sometimes I wonder if you'll bother staying."

"I was born here," she reminded him. "I was raised here."

"But if you stay, you can never marry again," Jonas countered. "We all know it. And you're young still, and beautiful and talented and . . ."

Tabitha felt her face warm ever so little. "I didn't ask to be flattered, Jonas Peachy."

"Flattery?" He chuckled dryly. "I mean it as a weakness. You're young enough to have a family of your own, and you know you can attract male attention. Do you really want to stay Amish badly enough to give up a chance at a family of your own? That's what people are wondering."

People had lined up for their dessert, and Jonas moved farther away from curious eavesdroppers, and Tabitha followed him. She didn't want to give them something to gossip about over the next quilting session.

"Are you wondering that, Jonas?" She crossed her arms tightly over her chest.

Jonas shrugged. "It crossed my mind. I figure I'll wait and see what you do. Not that it's my business, I suppose."

No one believed she'd stay. Somehow that stung more than it should. She knew the community was hesitant, but did they not trust her vows at all?

"I made my vow to Gott and the church," she said.

Jonas pressed his lips together but didn't answer, and she felt her irritation spark. It was one thing to hear what people were murmuring behind her back, but quite another to have Jonas Peachy tell her that he was thinking the very same thing. He'd seen her at work. Somehow, she'd hoped he'd see a little more of who she really was—the strength of her resolve and the meaning she was trying to find in her life.

"Why do you think I came back, then?" she demanded. "Why would I uproot my life to return to my father's house, make my vows to the church, try to find a way to fit in with the community . . . Why do all of that if I had no intention of staying?"

"Because you got your heart broken," he replied. "You're licking your wounds. You had all of this before—community, faith, people who'd known you all your life—and it wasn't enough for you. Why is it enough now?"

That was a bold question, but it was likely one that everyone else was asking too—those women who used to be her friends, the family members who had endured the stigma of her leaving the way she had, and even those who had known her nominally and were simply observing to see what she did. What made Shepherd's Hill her final destination?

"Because I realized that my happiness isn't found out there somewhere," she said. "It doesn't come from a man or even from a job. Men will let me down. Jobs will too. But real, true, deep happiness comes from the place inside of me that connects to Gott. And when I am in the center of Gott's will, I am satisfied. It's truly as simple as that."

Jonas met her gaze. "Are you happy now?"

"I'm satisfied," she replied. "And that lasts longer."

But was she happy? That was a more complicated question. She would be happy—she could feel it. But there was still a climb to get there while she found her place back in her community again. The Amish were right that community was the center of everything. Without her community, she'd been an individual fighting a current that had been much too strong for her alone. There was safety and contentment in people working together. She'd learned that the hardest way possible.

Jonas jutted his chin in the direction of Amanda and Menno. They were talking, standing a proper two feet apart. Amanda had her ankles pressed together, and she was looking down at her feet. "What's happening between them?"

Tabitha was a little startled by the sudden change in subject, and her gaze followed his toward her sister.

"They're just talking," Tabitha said.

"He seems to like her."

"Why shouldn't he? Amanda is lovely, and I don't think anyone really gave her a chance. She's sweet and hardworking. She's loyal too."

"All true."

"If you know that, I'm surprised you haven't given her a chance," Tabitha said. "She's just as single as you are, and she's a loyal woman. I know your sweetheart broke your heart, but Amanda isn't the kind of woman to do that. When she loves, it's honestly and truly."

Jonas shot her a wry look. "Another man is angling for her, and you're still going to try and encourage a match between us?"

"So Menno's angling," Tabitha replied with an exaggerated shrug. "Are you afraid of a little competition?"

"Tabitha . . ."

She sighed. "You aren't interested."

"I'm sorry. I'm not."

Tabitha felt the sting on her sister's behalf. For all of the benefits of community, it was hard for a woman to find a good match in a place that knew her too well. Sometimes romance required some mystery.

"It's not easy being an Amish woman, you know," Tabitha said. "She has to wait to be chosen. And she's got to have something that sparks a man's interest from afar, because no one gets close enough to get to know her real strengths otherwise. What use is a beautiful smile or elegant hands if she's short-tempered or selfish? Who do you want by your side—a rare beauty or a woman with rare character?"

"I'm not the right man, Tabitha," he said gently. "Look, I know you want to find your place here, but it isn't going to be as a matchmaker. Sometimes you just have to step back . . . let people sort themselves out."

Her intentions were pure, but maybe Jonas was right that this wasn't the way to settle back into Shepherd's Hill.

"Okay. I'll leave it alone," she said. "I don't mean to be a busybody. I just . . . care."

"I know you do," he said. "But it can be too much sometimes."

She could feel heat in her face at his direct words. Well, she was direct with others, wasn't she? This was what it felt like to be on the receiving end.

Jonas nudged her arm with his elbow. "I'll tell you what I will do, though."

"What's that?"

"I'll make Menno feel welcome," he said. "We all deserve a second chance, right?"

Tabitha looked up at Jonas, and a conciliatory smile touched his lips. He was trying to make up.

"*Yah*," she agreed. "I think we do."

Jonas headed over in Menno and Amanda's direction. Amanda couldn't stand there all afternoon, obviously mooning after a man. It would be bad for her reputation. So Tabitha waved at her sister with a big smile.

Jonas was a fool if he wanted a loyal woman with character and refused to look in Amanda's direction. But Menno obviously saw what Amanda offered. Menno wasn't blind—credit to him.

22

Jonas shouldn't let Tabitha provoke him like that. He'd told himself that he'd keep his opinions to himself when it came to their veterinarian, but here he was telling her exactly what he thought of her.

That morning during his own personal devotions, he'd come across a Proverb that seemed to apply right now: "Even a fool, when he holdeth his peace, is counted wise: and he that shutteth his lips is esteemed a man of understanding."

He really should have shut his mouth and kept his opinions to himself. Somehow, it just made him feel exposed. Tabitha made him feel things he didn't want to feel. She made him look closer at what he wanted out of life, and she made him wonder if he was really happy. Because while he hadn't jumped the fence, he had locked himself away from any other possibilities of marriage and romance of his own.

When Miriam left him, she'd broken his trust, and he didn't want to start planning a life with a woman again without true, honest love. He'd been completely in love with Miriam—for whatever that was worth. But more than that, even if he found a woman he was interested in, he wasn't sure that he'd be willing to take that leap again. When Miriam had dumped him, it had hurt worse than anything else in his life, and it had shaken his confidence more than he liked to show. He'd given his whole heart to Miriam, and she'd handed it right back without so much as a second thought.

So Jonas was actually rather impressed with Tabitha for coming home and owning the pain of her mistakes. She'd married the wrong guy. He'd broken her heart, and she'd been forced to leave him. She was home again—not as *Englischers* defined success but as a newly baptized repentant. She didn't defend herself. She didn't explain beyond her church confession. She didn't berate the guy who'd ruined her future. That had taken guts.

And Tabitha was right. Everyone deserved a second chance, at least when it came to being part of the faith community.

The men stood in small groups talking—older men together, some middle-aged married men talking more seriously, arms crossed over their chests, and the younger men laughing at each other's jokes, enjoying some socializing time before everyone was back to work again. Beyond them, the buggies were parked in their neat rows, black canvas tops contrasting with the green pasture beyond. The horses were corralled in a space too small to allow them all to graze, and a round feeder sat in the middle for the animals to eat at their leisure.

It was a quiet Saturday afternoon in June, the time of year when it was difficult to feel anything but satisfaction, and yet Jonas felt a stirring of discontent. It was ironic that talking with Tabitha, who was now convinced that her deepest joy was found here in their community, could spark his own frustration. Maybe he wasn't as satisfied as he thought with things just as they were. Maybe he did want more.

Jonas stopped next to Menno. The shorter man stood rather uncomfortably a few yards away from the other men, who were laughing and chatting while they ate their shortcake.

"So how's the hog farm?" Jonas asked.

"Uh, pretty good." Menno looked surprised at being spoken to. "How's the farm?"

"Not bad." Jonas nodded, and they both turned forward and let their gazes move over the women, who were chatting in small groups, and the older folks, who had started singing a hymn together.

"The market price for pork?" Jonas asked.

"Going up. Beef is good?"

"*Yah, yah.* Can't complain."

They both nodded.

"How's Simon?" Jonas asked. "He and I were in the same class in school. I haven't seen him in years."

"He got fired from his job in town," Menno replied. "He's pretty upset about that. He was accused of stealing."

"Did he do it?" Jonas asked, lowering his voice. From what he remembered of Simon in their youth, he'd had a habit of taking things that weren't his and then lying passionately about it.

"Probably," Menno said. "Still, he's out of work now. He's staying with my brother Emmanuel."

"Sorry about that," Jonas said.

Menno shrugged. "That's family, right?"

It wasn't Jonas's experience of family, but he understood that Menno had it different. Stories about the Weavers had whipped through town on a regular basis when Jonas was growing up. There was always something.

"So you run the hog farm on your own?" Jonas asked. "Your brother doesn't help?"

"No, he doesn't like the work," Menno replied. "Besides, I'd rather do it myself. At least I know it's done right that way. I have a good reputation for quality hogs, and I don't want that ruined. Worse, I don't want the hogs to suffer because I didn't see something that Simon didn't do."

"You've put some thought into this."

"I have to." Menno's gaze flicked in his direction.

Jonas didn't have to run a farm alone for more than a week or two when Daet got sick or traveled to see his brother in Indiana, but that was enough to know how much work it would be. Menno handled a lot on his own.

"Do you ever hire laborers?" Jonas turned toward the other man, his interest piqued.

"I haven't yet. I might need to as the farm grows, though. Have you hired seasonal laborers?"

The men settled into a conversation about farming, reliable seasonal help, and the logistics of running a small farm. Jonas couldn't help but respect Menno. He was a hard worker, and he had put a lot of planning into his operation. Jonas found himself glad that Menno had come out this afternoon.

It wasn't that the other Amish men didn't take farming seriously, because they did. But Menno treated his farm with the serious focus of a man twice his age.

And when Jonas happened to look up, he saw Tabitha's gaze on them, a smile turning up her lips. He felt a little surge of satisfaction at pleasing her. She hadn't been back long, but she was influencing things around here—bringing out his own better instincts, at the very least.

And Jonas had to admit that he was glad she'd returned, and he truly hoped she found what she'd been looking for here at home. And maybe he'd find what he needed too.

23

Ellen Troyer's daughter lay in Amanda's arms, one little arm flung out as the toddler breathed slowly and deeply. With all the little *kinner* running about, there was always someone in want of some cuddles, and Amanda often found herself holding a child during these social gatherings. The little girl's name was Naomi, and she had a thumb in her mouth and was resting her white-bonneted head on Amanda's shoulder, breathing warm, strawberry-scented breath onto Amanda's neck.

There was a time when the women used to joke meaningfully with Amanda, saying that babies looked good on her and she might want to look into getting married so she could have a few of her own. But that joking had stopped about a year ago, and no one mentioned Amanda getting married now. The community had seemed to come to silent agreement that Amanda was to be a spinster.

Amanda looked over the girl's crisp white bonnet toward the men. Jonas was chatting with Menno, and Menno gestured as he answered a question. Whatever they were talking about, it seemed like a subject they were both passionate about. She found herself wishing she could be part of the conversation, see what stirred him up like that.

Menno had come to see her, but they couldn't spend the whole time together either.

Ellen, who was roundly pregnant with her second child, came up and said, "*Danke*, Amanda. You're a lifesaver. My back is killing me."

"She's getting so big," Amanda said.

"Tabitha, are you really working with the men?" Ellen asked, turning her attention to Tabitha.

"I'm working with the animals," Tabitha said with a short laugh. "It's not like I'm out raising a barn or something."

"Do you ever cook anymore? Or knit? Cross-stitch?" Ellen asked. "Do you have time?"

Amanda looked over at her sister, interested to hear her response.

"No, not really," Tabitha said. "I cook sometimes, but I'm always out on calls and working. You know the time it takes to do a good job on a meal or when baking. Sometimes I wish I could sit down and work on a quilt, decide on the canning schedule, or sew a dress. But I'm never going to be a wife again. And I won't have babies. So . . . I make the best of it."

"Do you ever think of getting your husband back?" a younger woman asked. Her name was Mary, and all eyes turned toward her. She squirmed with discomfort and looked at the other women. "What?"

"He's married to someone else," Tabitha said quietly. "He married the woman he was cheating on me with. I can't get him back. And I don't want to."

Amanda saw the slight tremble in her sister's chin. This might be a story she was used to telling, but it still stabbed deeply for her. It was an intriguing story to others and a personal heartbreak for Tabitha. Her sister swallowed hard.

"It isn't worth it," Amanda spoke up before Tabitha had a chance. "He hid things from her before they married, and he was flagrantly sleeping with another woman and expecting Tabitha to just accept it. If you get a bad man, you can't just love him until he's good. We want to, and trust me, my sister tried. But it doesn't work like that. She didn't have a choice in this."

Tabitha shot her a grateful look.

"How do you know if a husband will be bad?" Mary asked.

That was a wise question from an unmarried woman, and Amanda had no idea. How were they supposed to know when a man would make their lives miserable?

"He was *Englische* to start with," Katherine said.

"*Yah*, that's true," Ellen agreed. "He wasn't one of us, right, Tabitha?"

That was an easy excuse, though, and even Amanda knew that. Michael had been a terrible husband, but back when Tabitha had run off with him, Amanda thought he was handsome and dashing. Amanda hadn't seen the warning signs any better than Tabitha had.

"True," Tabitha said. "He wasn't one of us. But we've all heard the stories of women in Amish communities who have experienced something similar. It happens with the Plain people too."

"The woman in Bird-in-Hand . . ."

"And the one in Bountiful, Indiana."

"Was she the one whose husband left her for the *Englischer* woman?"

They batted around a few more examples of women

they'd heard of, and Amanda exchanged a pale look with Mary. Mary was significantly younger than Amanda—about nineteen—but they were both single. These stories were warnings for them.

"The man in Bird-in-Hand was a gambler and a drunk," Katherine said. "So for a warning sign, I'd say watch how much he drinks."

"Oh yes! Men who drink are problem husbands. My *mamm* warned me about that since I was little."

Amanda's heartbeat sped up. She'd been warned about the same things, and Menno used to drink. But he'd stopped. She glanced toward the men again. Menno was standing apart from the rest now, and Jonas was telling a story to the group. Somehow he looked very much alone over there.

"What was the warning sign you missed, Tabby?" Katherine asked.

Amanda looked over at her sister. She wanted to know the answer too. What had been the big flaw that Tabitha hadn't noticed in time?

"He had a lot of private things," Tabitha said. "Little secrets. Big secrets. I thought it was normal because our men take care of the money and business. We Amish women don't ask a lot of questions surrounding those things. So I didn't ask Michael. But I've since learned that his habit of keeping everything private from me—his phone, bank finances, mail, conversations, friendships—that was the big warning sign I missed."

The women fell silent, and Amanda could feel them all internally rolling this information over. How much did they all fail to question because it wasn't what Amish women did? How much did they simply leave to their husbands without ever asking a follow-up question?

PATRICIA JOHNS

Women were supposed to be meek. They were supposed to
be supportive and trusting. A good woman didn't question
a man. . . . So how were good Amish women supposed to
know if the men who courted them were hiding anything?

A woman waited to be courted. She waited to be chosen.
She waited for a proposal, and she waited for her husband
to provide her a home. Her home was her domain—nothing
further. So how on earth was she supposed to *know*?

It was a very wise question, but Amanda feared that in
proper Amish behavior, there wasn't a good answer. A woman's gentleness and trusting nature could be a husband's
greatest blessing or a woman's most dangerous weakness.

Little Naomi had fallen asleep. She lay limp across
Amanda's chest, and Amanda's arm started to ache from
the weight.

"Mary, do you want to hold her?" Amanda asked.

"Sure." Mary smiled down at the pink-cheeked toddler,
and Amanda eased her into Mary's arms.

"Oh, a little one to cuddle, Mary . . ." Ellen said with a
smile. "A baby looks good on you. We need to find you that
good Amish husband."

Mary still had hope in their eyes, so she'd get the good-
natured teasing. But after that conversation, Mary didn't
look excited at the prospect.

Amanda's dress felt a little damp where the toddler had
been against her body, and a warm breeze was a cooling relief. She looked toward the men again, and this time, Menno
was gone. She turned all the way around and spotted him
walking toward the buggies. Tabitha had moved over to talk
with Aent Dina, and the women had turned their attention
toward Mary, talking about finding her husband, so when
Amanda slipped away, no one noticed.

185

Menno strode briskly ahead of her, and Amanda broke into a jog to catch up. She refused to look back. If they were staring, then let them stare. But she'd seen Menno's discomfort, and she felt partially responsible for it since she'd asked him to come.

"Menno?"

Menno's step hitched, and he turned around just as he reached where the buggies were parked.

"Are you leaving?" she asked.

"*Yah*. I'm—" He looked toward the horses, and she could almost feel his desire to get away from there.

"We're going to join the older folks in singing," she said feebly. "And they'll put up a volleyball net."

"I don't like volleyball."

"Oh." Amanda liked it. She was rather good at the game.

"Look, I don't really fit in here," Menno said. "I talked to Jonas a bit, and that was nice, but that's one man out of twenty I can say anything to. They're trying, but I just don't feel comfortable. I'm sorry."

"It's okay," she said. "If you started coming to these events more often, you'd get more comfortable, and you'd get to know people better."

Menno looked at her mutely. He had no intention of coming to another social event, did he? She could see it written all over his face.

"It's not always fun for me either," Amanda went on. "My friends are all married. I hold their babies and listen to them talking about family life. It's hard being the single one—for women at least. I'm not sure what it's like for men. But it's not fun for me, either, all the time. But I keep going. I keep trying. I do things that are uncomfortable in hopes that one day I'll be one of the married ones with my own babies."

That had been blunt, but she didn't care anymore. He'd asked Elder Yoder to help him find a wife, hadn't he? He was doing uncomfortable things too.

"They think I'm a danger, you know," Menno said.

"And they'll always think it if you don't prove otherwise."

Menno tipped his head to one side in silent acceptance of that statement.

"I wish you'd stay," she said.

"They'll only rush you off and keep you away from me," he replied. "And I will have to listen to the men make small talk."

"Then let's see each other again—away from here," she suggested.

"*Yah?*" He smiled faintly. "I'm supposed to ask that, you know. It's the man's place to ask to see each other more."

As if Amanda were any good at these games.

"You didn't get around to it yet," she replied.

"I was getting there." His warm gaze met hers, and his smile warmed too. "I was also going to ask your sister to come check on a sow for me. She farrowed, and I think there's a problem."

"Okay," Amanda said. "I'll bring Tabitha by as soon as I can. How serious is it?"

"Tomorrow is Visiting Sunday. It can wait until Monday, I think. The sow isn't too bad, but I see some worrying symptoms." They fell silent, and Menno shrugged. "Would you come with her?"

"I normally do."

"But would you . . . make sure you came with her to my farm this time?"

Amanda smiled and nodded. "*Yah.*"

Menno pulled off his hat and bent it in his hands, then replaced it on his head once more.

"I'm looking forward to seeing you, Amanda," he said. "It'll be easier for me without all these people watching us have a simple conversation. I don't mind your sister."

"I suppose I understand that," she said. "But they mean well."

These people were their community. Sometimes it took some work to get past the jostling and imperfections of human beings, but it was worth it in the end. Ultimately, they took care of each other. This community was the church to which they belonged and to which they'd vowed their loyalty at baptism.

"They mean to stop this between us," Menno said. "That's their intention."

He wasn't wrong. "We're both grown, though. We're both members of the church. We can spend time together, if we like."

"*Yah*, we are." That warm gaze locked onto hers again. "And I like you very much."

Her heartbeat thundered in her ears, and she nodded quickly. "I feel the same."

"So . . . Monday, then," Menno said.

"*Yah*." She wished she had something better to say, but her mouth was dry, and her pulse was racing.

Menno headed to the corral for his horse. Amanda turned back to the gathering, and as she walked toward the chatting women—some of whom had joined the older folks in singing a hymn together, heads pressed together over a hymn book— she realized that Menno had not offered to drive her home.

That was how courting worked. The man asked the woman if he could drive her back. He hadn't asked. But he also hadn't stayed the whole time, so maybe that was why.

She looked over her shoulder to find Menno hitching up.

He looked in her direction, and their eyes met. Her stomach flipped in response. He'd said he liked her. He'd said he wanted to see her. What had he said exactly? Oh, her brain was a muddle. But something was certainly happening between them, even if it wasn't following the normal path.

Menno had not asked to drive her home, which would be the signal to everyone here that he was interested in her romantically. But he had made himself very clear to her.

24

Y ou caused quite a stir," Tabitha said to Amanda when they were finally hitched up and plodding up the drive toward the road. The sun hung low over the rolling Pennsylvania hillside. The air had started to cool, too, and the chirp of crickets rose up from the grassy ditch and the fields beyond. Behind them, laughter and a shriek from a volleyball game made Tabitha smile.

A verse ran through her mind: *"Thou annointest my head with oil; my cup runneth over."*

It felt applicable tonight. She'd returned for moments like this one—soft wind, golden light, and a peace that surpassed understanding settling around her. There was something about Amish country that seemed to be nestled under Gott's own hand, and she'd never quite felt this way in her *Englischer* life—not even in the quiet of an evening, on a hike in a park, or sitting on a chair on her apartment balcony. This particular kind of peace seemed reserved for Shepherd's Hill.

Amanda smiled. "I don't mind causing a stir. It's high time I shook things up a little bit."

Tabitha chuckled. She didn't have it in her to lecture her

younger sister. She was a grown woman, and she knew exactly how much she had to risk.

"Did Menno enjoy himself?" Tabitha asked.

"Sort of." Amanda looked out the buggy window, then she sighed. "No, actually. He hated it."

"Oh . . . I'm sorry."

"He liked seeing me," Amanda explained. "He's just not used to spending time with the men anymore. It's awkward for him. Maybe it's awkward for all of them."

"I can understand that," Tabitha admitted. Time would loosen the bolts, and eventually, those relationships would feel more natural. She was happy that she'd been able to reconnect with Katherine a little more tonight too. The men would know that Tabitha was a good veterinarian, and they'd trust her advice and instincts. The women would figure out that Tabitha was moral and trustworthy too. But it all took time. She'd settle in, and this evening she could feel it.

"Didn't he talk to Jonas, though?"

"*Yah*, and they seemed to have a good chat," Amanda agreed. "It looked that way, at least."

"It's a good start," Tabitha said. "And we all have to start somewhere."

"Menno did ask if we could go by and look at one of his sows that he thinks is sick," Amanda said. "He said Monday would be soon enough."

"*Yah*. Of course. Is this an excuse to see you?"

"Yes. I mean, he did especially ask me to come along, but he does need a veterinarian."

"What were the symptoms?"

"A sick pig."

"Right." Tabitha shook her head. "You said he liked seeing you, though? What does that mean?"

"I wish I knew. But I like him, and he likes me."

Tabitha shot her sister a smile. "I'm glad. You deserve a nice boyfriend."

"I don't want a boyfriend. I want a husband."

"First things first." Like with settling into a community, these things took time. Amanda looked out the window again, and Tabitha sighed. "He does seem to like you a lot. I saw the way he was looking at you when you were walking away from him. I dare say everyone saw that."

"Looking at me how?" she asked, turning back.

"Like he was halfway in love with you," Tabitha replied. "He's got a crush, that's for sure. I'd say your baking worked."

Amanda smiled coyly and turned back to the window again. Let her enjoy it. Amanda hadn't had the easiest time these last few years, and if she found a man she liked, and he liked her, too, maybe it was time for Tabitha to leave well enough alone.

"I'm just going to drop off these canning lids for Rose on our way back," Tabitha said, lifting a cloth bag at her side. "Katherine asked if we'd return them for her. It won't take long."

Rose was weeding the garden in the last of the daylight when they arrived. She knelt in a row of leafy plants, and when they pulled in, she pushed herself to her feet and brushed her hands off, then planted them on her hips. Tabitha couldn't make out her expression.

Tabitha reined the horse in and handed the reins to her sister.

"I'll just be a minute," she said to Amanda.

Tabitha took the bag of lids and hopped down from the

buggy. Rose crossed out of the garden and dropped a bucket of weeds onto the grass.

"Hi," Tabitha said. "We missed you at the strawberry shortcake social."

"I didn't go," Rose said shortly.

"*Yah* . . . that's why we missed you." Tabitha gave her a small smile. "Katherine sent your lids back."

"*Danke.*" Rose accepted the bag. There was an obvious chilliness in her demeanor, and Tabitha paused uncertainly.

"Rose, are you okay?" Tabitha asked.

"Not really," Rose said.

"What's wrong?" Tabitha stepped closer and lowered her voice. "What happened?"

"I took your advice. That's what happened," Rose replied. "And it didn't go well, I'll tell you that. I never should have listened to the advice you got from *Englischer* therapists. Having it out with my husband did not clear the air or reveal what the problem was, and only ended in me sleeping in the guest room."

"Why are you doing that?" Tabitha asked.

"Things are getting out of hand, and I'm not even sure my husband is glad he married me anymore!" Rose said, tears welling in her eyes.

"I didn't mean to give bad advice," Tabitha said. "I'm so sorry, Rose. Can I help? Is there anything I can do?"

Rose wound the cloth bag handle around her hand. "No, just leave my marriage alone. You have been away for a long time, and it's almost like you don't even know how to be Amish anymore."

That stung.

"Rose . . . you should be able to talk to Aaron. That's not cultural."

"It isn't your business."

No, but Rose had come to them in tears.

"You're right, of course," Tabitha said. "I just wanted to help. I didn't want you to experience what I did."

"I won't. If you're worried that I'm going to divorce him and cast him aside, you can put your mind at ease. I'm Amish!" Rose said.

As if Tabitha had had any choice in her own failed marriage. As if Tabitha was divorced because she somehow hadn't loved her husband enough or hadn't been devoted enough. The thing that Rose didn't understand was that not all divorced women were callous, angry women who didn't love enough. Many times, like in Tabitha's situation, they were heartbroken women who'd loved with everything they had, and it hadn't been enough.

"That wasn't fair," Tabitha said, her voice shaking.

Rose dashed a tear off her cheek. "I'm sorry—that was going too far."

But there wasn't any warmth in Rose's brown eyes, and she took a step back.

"Are we okay?" Tabitha asked. When they'd been girls who'd sometimes shared bedrooms, buggies, and long, lazy summer afternoons, they'd been able to forgive all sorts of infractions, but they were grown women now, and the stakes were so much higher.

"We'll get there," Rose replied.

Rose turned around and headed back out into the garden, and Tabitha watched her go, hoping Rose would turn back. But she didn't. She knelt down in the row again and continued her weeding. Tabitha turned back toward the buggy. Amanda was frozen in place, wide eyes fixed on Tabitha as she climbed back up into the buggy seat next to her.

Tears welled in Tabitha's eyes, but she stubbornly blinked them back. She had overstepped in a moment when she'd thought they were sisters sharing wisdom and insight. Apparently that wisdom was not one-size-fits-all. Thinking back on that conversation, Tabitha realized Amanda's advice to simply stop reacting to things that were irritating seemed more prudent by far.

Rose didn't turn again, and Tabitha flicked the reins, swallowing against the lump rising in her throat.

"Are you okay?" Amanda asked gently.

"*Yah*. I'm fine. It's been a long day. I'm just being emotional."

At the very least, Tabitha had thought that her painful life experience would give her some wisdom to impart. She might not be anyone's wife or mother, but at least she could be a discerning woman with advice.

Although, it seemed that the wisest thing was to keep that advice to herself. Here was her own pride pushing up its ugly head again. She thought she knew better. She thought she was experienced and could guide her sister. But she'd been wrong about that.

So if she wasn't here as a source of hard-won wisdom, what did Tabitha offer besides her veterinarian skills? Or was that where her contributions ended?

25

꧁꧂

"Menno! Menno, open up!"

Thumping on the door downstairs roused Menno Weaver from his sleep. He'd been dreaming of strawberries and warm breezes. He'd been watching Amanda talking with other women, and whenever he tried to get her attention, his voice had evaporated. He couldn't raise a hand to wave to her. He couldn't call out her name. It was a dream that mingled longing with a strange acceptance of the situation, and the more he struggled, the farther away Amanda seemed to slide until there was a field of waving grass between them.

A voice popped the dream, and he groggily blinked his eyes open.

The bedroom was dark, his blind drawn. In the dimness, he could just make out the softly ticking clock on his bedside table. The dream was slipping away now, and he couldn't quite remember what it had been about. The feeling of frustrated longing remained, though. He looked at the clock more closely. It was two in the morning. There was another thump on the door downstairs, and he rolled over and threw back his covers.

Someone whooped, and an engine revved, then the sound of tires retreating up the drive.

"Menno! Open the door! Why's it locked? Menno!"

He knew that voice. His brother's words were slurred, and Menno could hear him stumbling around on the porch outside. There was a creak and then the sound of breaking wood. That sped Menno up, and he headed to his window and pushed up the blind. He heaved his window open a little farther than it already was and leaned outside. The retreating car's brake lights shone up at the road, then disappeared from view.

"Simon, what did you break?" Menno demanded.

His brother lay on his back on the grass, laughing, his arms flung out wide. The post that held up the clothesline was bent at a precarious angle. Menno would have to fix that, and anger simmered inside of him. Simon never stopped to think what work he caused others, or what money he cost them either with his drinking and carelessness. But that was some thick irony, because a few years ago, Menno hadn't been much better.

"What are you doing here?" Menno called.

"What do you mean?" Simon rolled over. "I live here."

"No, you don't. You're staying with Emmanuel."

Emmanuel and his girlfriend lived in town, and Simon had been sleeping on their couch for the last few months. He'd been evicted from his own apartment for various infractions of the rules and late rent payments. Emmanuel had let him stay with him and Alanna for the short term, which had bled into something significantly longer.

"What?" Simon lay there on his side, his legs scissored out across the grass.

"You don't remember?" Menno sighed. "You're staying with Emmanuel and Alanna. You don't live here."

"This is my house too!" Simon pushed himself up to a seated position. "Ugh, my stomach . . ." He slid back down to the grass again.

This farm was the family home, and Menno had been living in it alone for the last couple of years. When their father died and left the farm to all four of them, Menno had bought them out for this very reason. So now Menno ran the family farm, and his brothers did whatever they felt like doing, but all of them had grown up here. They'd all worked this pig farm, done the chores, and done their best to avoid their *daet*'s attention. If Mamm ever came looking for her sons, this was where she'd come.

Menno muttered something bitter under his breath, and he pushed himself away from the window. He'd better let his brother inside, or else he'd just lie on the grass out there bellowing all night—what was left of the night, anyway. Menno normally got up at four to start chores.

Menno pulled on a pair of pants and a set of suspenders to hold them, then headed down the dark, creaking staircase. He stopped to light the kerosene lamp over the kitchen table with a match, the soft glow assaulting his sleepy eyes as the light flared up. Zeke snuffled from his crate as Menno shook out the match.

"It's not morning yet, Zeke," Menno said. The last thing he needed was a hungry piglet on top of his drunken brother. Menno headed over to the side door and hauled it open.

"You've got to stop coming here when you're drunk, Simon," Menno said, coming down the stairs. The night air was chillier than he expected, and he shivered.

"I'm not drunk."

"*Yah*, you are." Menno bent down, caught his brother's arm, and hoisted him to his feet.

From inside the house, Zeke squealed. He was awake now, and he'd want milk. Menno would have to check on the sow soon too. This was going to be one early morning.

His heart hammered to a stop.

Amanda and Tabitha were coming in the morning. As his brother tripped on a step and fell heavily against him, he wondered if he could get Simon back in a taxi before the women arrived. Not very likely.

Oh, Gott, I don't want her to see this! It was a complaint to the Almighty more than a request. He wasn't even sure what to ask of Gott.

"Mamm called Emmanuel," Simon said as Menno dumped him onto a kitchen chair.

"You're drunk, Simon. Stop talking."

"She did. Daniel found her. He gave her Emmanuel's number."

Menno's heart lodged in his throat. "Did you . . . talk to her?"

"*Yah.*"

"What did she say?" he breathed.

"She was sorry. She hoped we were happy." Simon laughed bitterly. "She had no idea Daet was dead."

Menno sank to a chair next to his brother, Zeke's plaintive oinks fading into the background of his own shock. Mamm had reached out. . . . He'd dreamed of this day ever since she'd left, and now he felt like the wind had been crushed out of his lungs.

"Where is she now?" Menno asked.

Simon leaned his forehead onto his arms.

"Simon! Wake up! Where is she now?" Menno said, jostling his brother's shoulder.

"Cut it out," Simon muttered. "I don't know. She said she'd come to the farm. Something like that."

In that moment, Menno wanted to laugh and cry and rage all at the same time. She was coming to the farm after all, was she? She was coming back to the home she abandoned, to the sons she'd left to fend for themselves with a drunken brute of a father. He'd missed her desperately all those years and made up excuses for her absence. He'd blamed himself for being just like his *daet* and chasing her away. He'd wholeheartedly forgiven her—or he thought he had until this moment when he was filled with so much fury that he could hardly breathe.

In times past, he used to drown these emotions in alcohol, blur them out, melt them away . . . And he had such a sudden thirst for a drink that it nearly rocked him. Just one stiff drink . . . He wanted it so badly his hands started to shake. But he would not crack. Not tonight.

Gott, give me strength.

Menno pushed himself to his feet and went to prepare a bottle of formula for Zeke. There was still work to do, hogs to care for, a piglet to feed. It was the only thing that Menno knew how to do, besides drink his feelings away.

What would he say when Mamm came home?

26

That morning, Amanda looked out the side window of the buggy, trying to calm her nerves. Some clouds blocked out the sun, everything around them suddenly dimming, but then they moved on just as quickly, and the sun's rays burst out again, the countryside breaking back into sunny glory.

Tabitha had been quiet since her attempt to apologize to Rose, and she didn't say anything more about it, but Amanda had no doubt that Rose and Tabitha would sort things out, as would Rose and Aaron. Her mind was on Menno, and she was remembering the things he'd said—how he liked her so much, and how he wanted to find ways to see her more often. A pleasant shiver went up her arms.

People changed. They learned and grew, and if Tabitha's return home after her ten-year absence wasn't proof of that, she didn't know what was. And maybe that was why she and Menno felt such an easy connection—of all the people in their community, Amanda understood the best.

Could this be her chance at marriage at long last? Was this what that path to a husband and family felt like? She'd

certainly never experienced anything quite like this before
. . . and she'd watched her friends being courted and seen
how they'd fallen in love.

*Are you answering my prayers, Gott? Is Menno the man
you have for me? I wish you'd tell me plainly.*

The horse plodded along, up the hilly road that led to
the Weaver farm, and Amanda watched the bees hovering
around the wild flowers that grew up from the ditch on the
side of the road. Tabitha turned the horse onto Menno's
drive, and Amanda smoothed her hands down the front of
her dress, attempting to look calm and collected.

Tabitha reined in by the hitching post, then hopped down
and tied the horse up. Amanda went around to the back of
the buggy. She'd help carry her sister's bags, as usual.

The side door to the house opened, and a man Amanda
didn't recognize squinted in the sunlight. His hair was standing up in tufts as if he'd just woken up, and he wore a T-shirt
with some *Englischer* band on the front with a pair of blue
jeans.

"Is that . . . Simon Weaver?" Amanda murmured.

Simon Weaver was known for his bad behavior. He'd been
a drunk and a rebel ever since his early teens. The community
hadn't known what to do with him. His mother had left,
and his father wouldn't take him in hand. When Simon had
jumped the fence like his other brothers, there had been a
collective, albeit guilty, sigh of relief. He was someone else's
problem now. Except he seemed to be back at the Weaver farm.

Tabitha stopped at Amanda's side. "You'd know better
than me. I remember Simon as a boy who stole candy from
the farm supply store."

Simon grimaced and shaded his eyes. "Is the sun always
this bright?"

The sour smell of booze was strong enough that it floated over to where Amanda stood, and her stomach curdled in response. She remembered boys just like Simon at the old ice house parties that had gone on for a few years when Amanda was a teenager. The elders had caught wind of it and had held a meeting with the unwitting parents and put a stop to it. But before they did, Amanda's friends had tugged her along with them to a pretty wild party with Amish and *Englischer* teens. She could still remember a boy who had been out of control, groping girls and vomiting on the barn floor. It had terrified her, and she'd never gone to another one. And Simon had that same look about him—bleary, nauseated, and disrespectful.

"We're here for Menno," Tabitha said, all brisk professionalism. "I'm the veterinarian. Is he inside?"

"*Yah*, he's in there." Simon stifled a yawn. "I remember you, Tabitha Schrock. Look at you, dressed like a nice Amish girl again. I heard you came back."

Tabitha gave him a dry look. "I heard you were up to no good, Simon."

"That's a matter of opinion." He gave her a slow smile. "I heard the same about you."

Tabitha's spine straightened, and Amanda put a hand on her sister's arm.

"Don't spar with him," Amanda said. No good could come from arguing with the likes of Simon Weaver, anyway.

"Menno said he had a girlfriend," Simon said, turning his attention to Amanda. "Told me to steer clear of her. That's not you, by any chance, is it?"

Amanda blinked at him. Was Menno telling his family that she was his girlfriend?

The door opened, and Menno appeared behind his brother.

Menno muttered something under his breath and came outside, the piglet in one arm, and he shook a bottle of formula in the other hand.

"Ignore him," Menno growled. "He talks nonsense when he's drunk."

"If I were still drunk, my head wouldn't be pounding," Simon retorted.

Menno came down the steps and glanced between Amanda and Tabitha with a steely eyed stare. Amanda shivered, but this time, it wasn't in some foolish, girlish anticipation of romance.

Amanda waited for Menno to soften, for that gaze to turn familiar again, for him to say something nice to her, but he didn't. He marched past them, scooped up a beer bottle by the neck and threw it with a crash into a garbage bin.

This was nothing like the home she'd seen in previous visits. This felt like a completely different place, and her earlier optimism drained away. Why was Simon here? She didn't think he lived here anymore, but he'd certainly made himself at home. He smelled like a man who'd been drinking for days, and Menno just looked tired.

"The sow is in the barn," Menno said.

"How is Zeke doing?" Amanda asked. She was still hoping to chip past this cold shell of his and get back the warm man she'd seen at the shortcake social.

"He's eating every two hours," Menno said. "He's growing."

Menno slowed his pace, and for the first time he met Amanda's gaze. His eyes were filled with unnameable currents, and he sighed.

"Do you mind feeding Zeke while I show Tabitha the sow?" Menno asked.

"Sure."

Menno looked like he wanted to say more, but his gaze went over Amanda's shoulder, back toward the house. She looked back and saw Simon outside again, an open brown bottle in one hand.

Amanda took the piglet and the baby bottle, and Menno gave her a nod of thanks that was so distanced she might have been a stranger, and then he turned back toward the path that led to the barn. Tabitha shot her a sympathetic look as she hoisted up her bags.

They'd warned her, hadn't they?

So this was the life that Menno lived—one of anger, irritation, and with at least one vice-addicted brother. This was the home he wanted to hand over to a wife. And looking back at Simon, she wondered when he was going to leave . . . and how long he normally stayed when he showed up like this.

Did Menno still drink? He said he didn't, but he'd also said that he lived alone. Sometimes men said the things they wished were true.

Amanda held the piglet up and popped the bottle nipple into his searching mouth. He latched on, and bubbles immediately started rising in the bottle of formula.

Menno opened the barn door, allowing Tabitha to go inside first, and his eyes met Amanda's once more. She had a stew of questions boiling up inside of her. All of this felt wrong. Even Menno. He was distanced, and his emotions seemed to be behind a brick wall. She couldn't see the Menno she knew in those steely eyes. He was like a different man.

"Does Simon live here?" Amanda asked.

"He seems to think so," Menno said. "I'm sorry. He arrived last night. I don't know when I'll be able to get rid of him again. I'm doing my best."

And that was her fear—that Menno's best effort wouldn't be enough to turn him into a good Amish man who could maintain a good Amish home. But all she could think about now was the smell of booze and his rude brother. Menno's hopes for a good, clean life were real, but so was his family.

This was what Tabitha had been talking about, wasn't it? This was the risk.

"Should I not have come?" she asked hesitantly.

Menno's expression melted. "I'm sorry, Amanda. I thought I was ready for this, but everything is crashing around me right now. I don't have a lot to offer. I'm sorry."

Amanda swallowed hard, and Menno passed into the barn ahead of her. The piglet wriggled, and she adjusted her grip on the little guy, her heartbeat pattering in her throat.

Was it over, then? Had whatever this was started and ended as quickly as that?

27

The sows oinked softly—a truly maternal sound. Tiny piglets oinked back, and as Tabitha crouched down next to the sick sow, she had to pull three piglets off her teats, leaving a dribble of milk on their chins. Even with a sick *mamm*, these little piglets just wanted more milk.

"In a minute," she murmured, settling them an arm's reach away in the hay. They squealed their annoyance.

"Amanda, could you put the piglets under the heat lamp?" Tabitha asked without turning. They'd be quiet then, enjoying the warmth.

Tabitha took her time with an examination of the sow and saw that she had the beginning signs of posterior paralysis from a deficiency in calcium. That was easily treated with some calcium supplements in her diet, thankfully. Motherhood was not an easy feat for any species. It took everything a female had to give—her body, her time, her hormones, her affection, and her bodily calcium stores too. The sow would be fine, though, thanks to Menno noticing that something was wrong quickly.

As Tabitha gathered up her supplies again, she watched

her sister and Menno out of the corner of her eye. Amanda stood with Zeke in her arms, looking slightly spooked, and Menno stood a few feet away from her, his expression granite.

Was this the end of Amanda's infatuation? The whole community would hope so, but Tabitha wasn't sure what she thought now.

Simon had gone back into the house, and Tabitha was glad to see the back of him. He was an unlikeable man, but he could not shame her. Returning to home meant a full confession in front of her whole church. There were no secrets. Everyone knew the worst, and they knew that Gott had forgiven her, and so must they. That was part of the Amish faith too.

All the same, Simon made her uncomfortable, and she'd be glad if she never had to see him again. She knew it was wrong to be glad someone had jumped the fence, but Simon was no longer Amish, and if this was the way he treated women, it was just as well. But he was back at the Weaver farm—something no one would notice if it weren't for a sick sow and Amanda's determination with Menno.

"Are you ready?" Tabitha asked her sister.

Amanda nodded. She handed the piglet back to Menno and took one of Tabitha's bags over her shoulder.

"Can I help?" Menno asked, gesturing to Amanda's bag.

"I'm fine," Amanda replied stiffly.

Something had certainly cooled in Amanda, and Tabitha tried to pretend she hadn't noticed as they headed back toward the buggy. She glanced toward the house and saw Simon in the open doorway, leaning against the frame. He was watching her, and she felt a shiver slide down her spine. He held a brown liquor bottle loosely between two fingers, like he knew his way around a bottle.

"*Danke* for helping with the sow," Menno said. "I appre-

ciate it. I'll pay both bills—this one and the one from your
visit—at the same time, if you're okay with that."

"That's fine," Tabitha said, eager to get away from the
farm. "Take care now."

"Will do."

All very professional, except for Menno's brother in the
doorway, staring at her like some long-lost enemy. Maybe
Simon was the kind of man who needed someone to pit
himself against just to feel alive. She'd come across that sort
before. All the same, she'd rather he find someone else to
fixate on. Maybe someone closer to his own size.

Tabitha put her bags into the back of the buggy, including
the one Amanda had been carrying, and she and her sister
got up into the seat.

"*Danke*, Menno," Tabitha said. "We'll see you again, I'm
sure."

"Good-bye," he replied. He turned to Amanda, and
even Tabitha could see something crack in the man, then.
"Amanda—"

"Good-bye, Menno," Amanda said quickly.

Tabitha eyed her sister, and when she didn't look again
at Menno, Tabitha flicked the reins. They were five minutes
down the road before either of them broke the silence.

"I don't like Simon Weaver one bit," Tabitha said. "He's
not a good man."

Amanda didn't answer.

"What happened with Menno?" she asked.

"I don't know. His brother being here makes Menno different. I knew his family was problematic, but seeing his
brother . . ." Amanda shook her head.

"Are you feeling differently about him now?" Tabitha
asked.

"I need to think. Maybe I was being a bit naïve after all."

Romance was such a fragile thing, but so was a woman's spirit. Tabitha had believed that she could endure anything for the sake of love, but she'd been proven wrong. There were things a woman could not bear for a lifetime, no matter how pure her ideals were. And seeing the warning signs early was important. It was better to think things through now.

"No family is perfect," Amanda said after a moment. "Every family has their complicated rebel."

"That's true, but when you marry a man, he comes with a family. And the Weavers are more than just a family with one complicated person. They're all . . . complicated." That was a gentle way of saying it. None of the Weaver boys had turned into well-adjusted Amish men, and their father had been worse than the sons. Menno's uncles had been as bad as his father, and their *kinner* had grown up and left the Amish faith or moved away. The Weavers had left the whole community flabbergasted. What to do with a family like that?

"What was Michael's family like?"

Tabitha shrugged. "Wonderful. His mom adored me. His dad said I was the smartest choice Michael ever made. They were supportive and helpful. Sunday dinners at their place were a love fest."

Amanda was silent, her face turned toward the window.

"I know that doesn't help. The family isn't always the problem," Tabitha added.

Sometimes a man couldn't be redeemed no matter how well-intentioned the family. That had been Tabitha's experience, and Michael had been far from an introverted Amish farmer with difficult kin.

"Everyone says Menno is trouble waiting to happen," Amanda said quietly. "Everyone."

"People care about you."

"They do . . . when they want to keep me from doing something they think is dangerous. But do they care enough to help me move my life forward? No, then they just mind their own business."

Her sister wasn't wrong. People seldom meddled where a woman wanted them to, and Tabitha was no exception there. Rose was angry with her for just that. She had a sneaking suspicion that Amanda wouldn't be pleased to know that Tabitha had been trying to nudge Jonas in her direction either.

All the same, Tabitha had all sorts of advice welling up inside of her—warnings against men who drank, against intrusive in-laws, against those first flushes of love that couldn't hold up the weight of a marriage. Advice was useless unless asked for, though. Did she want to be like everyone else, holding Amanda back from any chance at romance at all?

Gott, give my sister wisdom, Tabitha prayed. He was the source of it, after all. And only Gott knew the future.

When they turned into the drive, Tabitha spotted a buggy parked by the house, and Jonas Peachy was leaning against the side of it, arms crossed over his chest. It was hard to tell how long he'd been waiting. Was this a veterinarian call? Or was it something else?

"I wonder what Jonas wants," Amanda said.

"Not sure . . ." Tabitha reined in, and Jonas pushed himself off the side of his buggy and headed in her direction.

"Your *daet* said you'd be back soon enough," Jonas said.

"Were you waiting long?" Tabitha asked.

"About ten minutes," Jonas replied. "We've got a sick horse. Belly bloat and lethargic."

That sounded rather familiar, and her heart dropped.

"The one you bought recently?" Tabitha asked cautiously. But she knew the answer already.

"*Yah*, that's the one. We aren't sure if it's the feed we're giving him or something else, but I came by to see if you'd take a look at him."

Tabitha knew exactly what was wrong with this animal, and it wasn't something she could cure. But she could make Fritz more comfortable. Did she have to tell Nathaniel who had sold this horse? Full Christian honesty seemed to require it, but it would upset her *daet*.

Gott, what do I do?

She looked toward the house. If Daet was inside, he'd made himself scarce.

"Do you mind if I don't come along for this call?" Amanda asked.

Tabitha could almost see her sister's heart all balled up into a knot. She needed time alone to unravel everything she was feeling right now.

"Of course," Tabitha said. "I completely understand."

No Amish family was perfect, but they didn't have to have the Weavers' dysfunction for every member of that family to reflect upon the others. Daet had sold a sick horse, and the community's ability to trust Tabitha would be shaken when that fact came out. Everyone saw them as a unit—a family that shared a moral fiber. She knew it was wrong to be worried so much about herself, but she couldn't help the anger stewing deep inside of her. It was hypocritical to judge the *Englischers* for their bad behavior when the Amish were selling unhealthy horses and drinking themselves into oblivion.

Tabitha might have reflected badly upon the family in times past, but she was walking the straight and narrow now, and her *daet* should be too. Abram Schrock should be better than this.

Tabitha leaned forward to meet Jonas's gaze. "I can come now, if you want."

Jonas nodded his thanks.

This secret was not going to keep, not with a clean conscience, at least.

28

꠸꠸꠸

Amanda knelt down in front of the stove, a big metal scraper in hand. If she was going to be frustrated, she might as well make use of her extra energy and clean out the large woodstove in the kitchen. She'd do the laundry a little later, or maybe she'd be a complete rebel and wait to do the laundry until Tuesday. She put on a pair of work gloves and adjusted the ash bucket beneath the main firebox. Then she plunged the hand trowel into the cold ash and started to fill the bucket.

She needed Gott right now. She needed some reassurance, and she needed it close to her heart, not far away in heaven but right here next to her.

Normally, Amanda would pray with the words that she thought Gott wanted to hear, the humility she ought to express or the forgiveness she believed was only right. She said the right words and hoped that her heart would follow. And truthfully, it usually worked. Gott provided when she stepped out in faith. But she didn't have any right words right now. And she didn't know the right step to take. She was like a rain barrel filled with dirt and leaves and twigs. . . . There was nothing presentable inside there. And yet she craved answers from the only source she trusted.

I thought Menno was different. But I saw something today that scared me. Gott, I thought I knew what I wanted, but now I don't know.

What had happened this morning? Had she seen the inside of Menno's real life? Was their flirtation at an end this soon? Tears blurred her vision. It was hardly fair. There'd been one man who'd seen her as more than just the plain sister in the Schrock family, and this was going to be the end of it?

Gott, is Menno a good man or not? And if he isn't . . . if he isn't, I'm going to be very sad and a little angry too. I shouldn't be. I should trust you. I should meekly accept what is. But I can't anymore! Will I ever be loved? Will I ever be a wife?

That was Amanda's deepest fear, that Gott's will for her was a single life. That she was beating with her fists against a solid, locked door.

Will you give me the love I long for, or am I throwing a tantrum like a child, making a fool of myself like Aent Linda did? And why won't you tell me anything, Gott? Why won't you give me any clear guidance? I can make my peace with being alone, so long as I know to give up hope.

She shoved the trowel deeper into the ash again, filling the bucket with a steady rhythm. Creosote coated the inside of the door, flaking off onto her sleeve each time she reached inside. Normally she'd be more careful with her dress. This one would take a lot of scrubbing to get clean now. But it was either throw herself into the work or let the rising tears out of her.

She heard the side door open and the tramp of her father's boots.

"Amanda, you're back?"

"*Yah.*" Her voice was choked, and she didn't turn around.

"Are you all right?" he asked.

Amanda scraped up the last of the ash that she could scoop up, then looked over her shoulder at her father. Her eyes stung.

"What happened?" he asked.

Her throat closed off, and a tear leaked down her cheek. "It was nothing, really."

"Then tell me about this nothing," Daet said gently, and he pulled up a kitchen chair and perched on the edge of it. "What happened?"

"Menno's brother Simon was there. He was drunk, and he stank. Even the pigs smelled better."

"Ah." Her father nodded. "And you've never seen that before. You've certainly never seen it here."

"I have, actually."

"When?" Daet straightened.

"When I was a teenager, Sarah took me to a party at the ice house before it was renovated," she said. "It doesn't matter. I hated every second of it, but I've seen drunk boys before, and it made my skin crawl to see Simon."

"Was Menno drinking too?"

She shook her head. "No, but his brother was, and he was there in the house. Menno can't seem to kick him out either. And he's looking for a wife. But how can he bring a woman back to that? He said as much himself. Will his brothers stay away or just push their way in? Would a wife have to cook and clean for all of them—his drunken brutes of brothers too?"

Daet was silent, and he chewed on the side of his cheek, his gaze hardening. Her father was angry—well, maybe she was too!

Amanda turned around again and reached into the main firebox with the wire brush, sweeping the ash from the corners. She swallowed hard against the lump in her throat.

"A man can't try and bring a woman into that," Daet said, his voice quiet but sharp. "That's no home, Amanda. That's just being a servant for a bunch of louts, and Gott did not create women for that. You deserve to be a treasured wife who is appreciated, not someone's cook and maid."

Amanda shoveled the last of the ash out, then pulled open the ash drawer beneath. It would have to wait. She needed to empty the ash bucket first. She pushed herself to her feet. It wasn't like anyone was lining up to treasure her either.

"That Weaver family—they were a complicated situation," her father went on. "And it wasn't like we didn't try with them. Schoolteachers kept reporting them to the bishop when the boys showed signs of neglect or abuse. And the bishop and elders would march on up to that pig farm, and they'd sit Eli down and tell him that Gott would judge him severely for how he treated his family. Somehow Eli would convince them that he was a reformed man, and they'd leave him alone again. Maybe it's us—maybe we should have done more. Maybe we should have demanded more of him, because no matter how the church tried to reach out to those boys, they still went wrong."

"Except for Menno," Amanda qualified.

"I saw him drinking like a fish, Amanda," Daet said, shaking his head. "He was just as bad as his brothers. Mark my words, just as bad."

"He stopped drinking years ago, Daet."

Somehow she felt the need to defend that point. Maybe she'd stop this friendship with Menno, but they owed it to him to tell the truth, and Menno had been working hard to stay sober.

"He's a Weaver, Amanda. He was raised in that half-civilized mess by a father who tormented him and a mother who eventually abandoned him to that fate. He wasn't raised with gentleness and love like the rest of the *kinner* in our community. We let that boy down, I won't say we didn't. But he's no longer a child we can try to rescue. He's a grown man with inclinations that you have no idea about."

"What kind of inclinations?" she asked.

"Well, I don't know, either, but I'm saying there's things you don't know about that man—guaranteed."

In her mind's eye she saw that bottle of booze dangling between Simon's fingers. How much more alcohol did Simon have in the house? And how much willpower did Menno have around bottles like that? Her father was right. There was a lot she didn't know.

"I have a lot to think on," Amanda said.

"And to pray on," her father added with a meaningful nod.

"*Yah* . . . and to pray on." That was the most important thing she needed to do.

She'd been reading and rereading the twenty-third Psalm for the last few mornings in her own personal devotions, and she just kept coming back to that first verse: "The Lord is my shepherd, I shall not want."

It meant she wouldn't lack anything. And yet she felt like an aching hole of want these days. She didn't have all she needed. She was a grown woman, and she needed more than to be the daughter in her father's home. Maybe if she continued to work as Tabitha's assistant, the meaningful job could fill some of those holes, but she would still grieve the loss of her hopes for a family of her own. Were her own green pastures and quiet waters to be found in her work with her sister?

Gott, I know you don't tend to just boom from heaven. Not these days, at least. But I would do just about anything to get an answer from you. Yours is the only answer that matters right now.

Amanda hoisted up the ash bucket and carried it out the side door to the ash heap. As she was heading back toward the house, she heard the rattle of a buggy turning down the drive, and she paused, expecting to see one of her sisters arrive.

When she spotted Menno behind the reins, her heart skipped a beat and pattered hard to catch up. He spotted her at the same time, and his dark, warm gaze met hers.

There he is. She finally recognized him again. The softness was back, and he reined in next to her.

"Amanda, I'm glad you're here. I have to talk to you."

"What about?" she asked.

"I need to explain myself." He hopped down to the gravel drive next to her. "I wasn't at my best. My brother showed up on my doorstep in the middle of the night, and I'm frustrated that he's there. I don't want him in my home, but that's the problem. This is the house we all grew up in. There's what's mine on paper, and what's ours because we were all raised there. It's not easy."

"So . . . he's there to stay?" Amanda asked.

"No. I'll find a solution," he replied. "I need to get him out, obviously, but I don't think I can manage it alone. We've always relied on each other. And my brothers have a hard time seeing how I might want to put my own plans ahead of rescuing them all the time."

"And it's the family home," she murmured.

"*Yah*. So you see the problem?"

"I do."

Menno was silent for a beat. "I'm sorry you witnessed that."

Amanda struggled for words that could somehow fix all of this.

"He's part of your life," she said. "It was only right that I see your life as it is. I needed to know the truth."

"It's not how I want it to be, though," Menno said. "And I think I can fix it, but it will take me sitting down with the elders and the bishop and getting some advice. I'm sure there are solutions that I haven't thought of."

"That's wise, Menno."

"I can't take the credit for it. That's something you learn in the Presbyterian AA meetings—that just because something feels impossible and overwhelming, it doesn't mean that's the truth."

That Presbyterian belief in a power from an ever so personal Gott. . . . Gott had helped Menno so far, hadn't he?

The house door opened, and Daet came out onto the step.

"What are you doing here, Menno?" Daet called brusquely. "My daughter is busy right now."

Amanda looked back at her father pleadingly. Maybe she shouldn't have told him what she'd seen . . . but she had. And now her father was bent on getting rid of Menno for her.

"Daet—" she started.

"Amanda, go back inside," her father said curtly.

She took a step toward the house and realized that she'd obeyed upon instinct. She was a grown woman now, and she had the right to talk to a young man if she wanted to. She didn't need permission.

"Daet, I want to talk to him," she said firmly.

"I hope that's okay with you, Abram," Menno said, his tone more conciliatory.

"No, it is not," Daet snapped. "My daughter came home a shaken mess after being at your farm, and I don't take kindly to that."

"Daet, I want to hear what he has to say," Amanda said.

"I apologize," Menno said. "My brother arrived late last night—"

"It sounds like your hands are full with your brother, then," Daet said. "Kindly leave."

Amanda stared at her father in shock. He'd never cast anyone off their property before. Menno glanced toward Amanda, and then he nodded quickly.

"I'll take my leave, then," Menno said.

"No!" Amanda turned back toward Menno. "You are my guest, and if you aren't welcome here, then take me with you."

She didn't wait for an answer. She went around to the other side of the buggy and hoisted herself up. Her father glared at her, bristling with anger, and she turned purposefully away.

"*Danke*, Menno," she murmured. "But I'm a grown woman, and I won't be ordered about like a girl."

Menno looked at her uncomfortably, and Daet went inside the house, slamming the door after him.

"We can go now," Amanda said.

Menno flicked the reins, but he still looked uncomfortable.

"Amanda, I can't just take you to my house. Your *daet* will think—"

"I know," she said. "I'm sorry to put you in this situation, but I was angry, and I won't be fenced in either. We need to talk, don't we?"

"*Yah*, I'd say we do," he agreed.

"Then let's talk. And then you can drop me off at my sister Rose's house. I'll get home again easily enough."

Menno's jaw loosened, and his shoulders lowered. He gave her a faint smile. "You're gutsier than you look."

"I didn't mean to be," she admitted. "My father is just upset right now. He'll calm down. I couldn't let him throw you off our property, so I . . ." She'd openly defied her father—that was what she'd done—but she couldn't quite bring herself to say the words.

Her father who was worried about her and who hated the thought of her being around brutish men for any reason. Her father who was only trying to do his job in protecting his unmarried daughter . . . She pushed back the tickle of guilt and leaned against the buggy seat. Her reserve seemed to have shattered. She was boldly baring her heart to Gott, and to her father, too, it seemed. But there were lines . . .

Her *daet* wanted to protect her, but Menno was not Simon, and while there still might be no future between them, they both deserved the chance to at least talk about it.

Fledgling romances needed time, but so did good-byes. Whichever way this one went, Amanda did not want to live with the regrets of what remained unsaid or chances she hadn't taken because she'd been too shy to open her mouth. The rest of a lifetime could feel like an eternity.

29

The Peachy horse barn was newly built with a fresh concrete floor and a lofty open roof. Rafters were the only thing between them and the high curved roof overhead. The cross beams, posts, and other wood inside the barn were all polished to a deep glow. It was the kind of barn that hit Tabitha right in the pleasure center of her brain. This was downright luxurious compared to other Amish barns she worked in. The large windows along the top let in ample light to work by, and on the roof were solar panels that would collect enough energy to run some heaters in times of emergency.

They even had their own telephone in the barn—also for times of emergency. But most Amish folk made do with the telephone huts set up along the roads. It spoke to their affluence that they had a phone of their own out here. The Peachys were obviously doing well for themselves.

Tabitha ran a hand down Fritz's bloated abdomen. The gelding was in pain. He shuffled his hooves and huffed a breath out through his nose at her touch. This wasn't the same situation as the cattle bloat, but then, she'd had the

223

better part of eight months treating this particular horse. Even before she'd returned to the community, she'd been giving her father instructions on Fritz's care and feeding.

"What he has is something akin to irritable bowel syndrome," Tabitha said.

"You've hardly looked at him," Jonas replied.

"I don't have to. He's got a bad gut, and you didn't do anything wrong, exactly, but I'm guessing you were giving him high roughage silage?"

"*Yah.*" Jonas nodded. "You've seen this before, I take it?"

That was almost too on the nose. Was Gott teasing her or tipping her right into utter honesty?

"I have." She stroked a hand down the horse's long nose. "Put him on regular hay. I've got a mineral oil that will settle his stomach for now and get his digestion moving. But stay away from the back end of him for a while—it's effective."

Jonas chuckled at her blunt directions. "I'll take your advice on that."

"You can't make his feed too rich," she said. "Even putting him out to pasture and letting him graze on fresh grass might be too much until his stomach settles down again. He needs plain hay. "

She filled a large plastic syringe and eased it between the horse's gums behind his back teeth so she could shoot a steady stream of the mineral oil toward the back of the horse's throat. She held on tightly to his bridle when he tried to pull back and emptied the syringe. Fritz hated the taste, but he seemed to remember that it helped his belly, so he didn't fight too hard.

"This should take care of it?" Jonas asked.

This was it—the point of truth or falsehood. Her *daet*

would be upset at the betrayal of her telling the Peachys about the horse, but she had her own reputation to worry about too. As well as her own conscience.

"No," she said.

"No?" Jonas frowned. "What are you saying? I thought it was just a bad gut?"

"It's a chronically bad gut," she said. "I know this horse. I've been treating him for months."

Jonas blinked at her. "My *daet* just bought this horse at auction. Are you telling me that someone knowingly sold a sick horse? Who was the previous owner?"

Tabitha licked her dry lips. "We said we'd work to get our fathers to stop this feud between them, didn't we?" she said. "Well, this isn't going to help matters."

Jonas's gaze clouded. She saw when her hint landed and that uncertain gaze cleared, slamming into hers.

"This was your father's horse?" Jonas demanded.

"*Yah.* I'm afraid he was, but just let me explain." Her heartbeat sped up. "First of all, my father never told me he was selling Fritz. It was news to me. I would have stopped him. Second, my *daet* truly believed this horse was healed."

"Healed?" Jonas shook his head.

"He'd been praying for Fritz's full healing," Tabitha said, "and I was treating the horse's symptoms, and I had them pretty well under control. But Fritz wasn't healed, he was simply being maintained. My *daet* didn't understand that. He thought his prayers were answered, and he'd gotten a miracle. So he sold the horse."

"So now we're stuck with a sick horse?" Jonas pulled off his hat and slapped it against his thigh.

Jonas was understandably angry, but her father wasn't trying to inflict harm on Nathaniel Peachy. Not with this horse, at least. He hadn't chosen the buyer—that was all done at auction.

"No, you won't be," Tabitha said. "But this will be delicate. Let me talk to my father about it. I'll let him know that Fritz is still sick, and I'm sure he'll do the right thing and return the money to your father and take him back."

"Do you think he will?" Jonas asked. "There's also the cut that the auction house takes."

"We'll return the full amount your *daet* paid," she said firmly. "But you have to give me time. It isn't my place to fix this. It's my father's."

"And if your father refuses?"

Tabitha studied Jonas. What exactly did he think of her *daet*? She was being generous in her view of his family. He could do the same in return.

"Jonas, he's a good man. He's a Christian man. Have a little faith in him. He'll make this right."

Jonas didn't answer, but he put a soothing hand on the horse's long nose.

"Do you really think that badly of us?" she asked.

"You?" He shook his head. "You've been gone for a decade. I don't know enough about you yet." He shrugged. "Your *daet*, though, has made my father's life miserable all that time you were gone."

From what her father said at home, it went both ways.

"I see a different side to him," she said.

"You would."

"Every person has more than one or two sides to them," Tabitha said. "Even you, I dare say."

"This just got personal?" Jonas asked, but after a beat of tense silence, he smiled faintly, taking the edge off the words. "How do I come off to you?"

Tabitha exhaled a shaky breath. "I don't think I dare tell you."

"Come on," he said. "What's your impression?"

"I think you're decent," Tabitha said. "But I think you're scared."

"Of what?"

"Marriage? Commitment? I don't know. But here you are with no wife or *kinner*, helping your *daet* run the family farm, and you're almost thirty."

"And you were foolhardy," he retorted. "You took the leap and got married, all right, but you lived to regret it."

"I won't argue that," she replied. "I'm not saying I did it right, but I don't think you are either."

Jonas shook his head, but before he could respond, the barn door opened, and Nathaniel came inside. He pulled off his straw hat and rubbed a hand over his salt-and-pepper hair. He was a slim man with deep lines in his face and a sparse white beard.

"Well?" Nathaniel called as he headed in their direction. His voice echoed through the barn.

Tabitha looked over at Jonas. How much should she tell? She'd already told Jonas the worst of it.

"Tabitha thinks it's a chronic gut issue," Jonas said.

"What? I just bought a sick horse?" Nathaniel demanded. "Of all the—"

"It's treatable," Tabitha said. "I can tell you what to feed him and what signs to watch for. I gave him some mineral oil that should—" On cue, the horse released some of that tension in his gut onto the floor in a powerful evacuation. "It's working."

"You can tell me how to feed him for the time being?" Jonas asked, giving her a meaningful gaze.

"Of course."

"He's going to be expensive if there are too many vet visits just to feed him." Nathaniel sighed. "A horse is supposed to be a tool, not a liability."

"This visit is free," Tabitha said.

"Free?" Nathaniel eyed her uncertainly. "Why?"

"Because I didn't do much," Tabitha said. "Besides, as I've been telling your son, I think our families have been at odds for too long, and I want to do my part to mend fences."

"You do." It wasn't a question. And it didn't sound like he believed her either.

"*Yah*, I do." Tabitha hoisted her bag onto her shoulder. Who knew how Nathaniel saw her? Maybe he distrusted her just as much as he distrusted her *daet*. She was his daughter, after all.

"Does your father know you're working at our farm today?" the older man asked.

"Yes," she replied. "Jonas told him he was waiting for me to see about a sick horse, and he knows I've been here before, and there are no hard feelings."

Nathaniel grunted. "That's not what he told me a few weeks back. He told me I'd better not stiff you on your payments. You're the veterinarian, and I'd better respect you as such."

"My *daet* said that?"

"*Yah*, he did. So you'd better write my bill. I won't have Abram Schrock telling the community at large that I take advantage of people. I pay my way."

"Well, I am the veterinarian, and I say this visit is on the house," she said.

Nathaniel's eyebrows went up threateningly, and she had to fight the instinct to take a step back.

"You're also someone's daughter, and in this community the people you belong to count more than your employment," Nathaniel said. "Write the bill, young woman."

The order in his tone was unmistakable, and something inside of Tabitha reared up in defiance. She was trying to do the right thing here and trying to prove herself as a veterinarian at the same time. This was a long-standing feud between two men who should both know better, and the next generation shouldn't have to fix it.

Gott, please intervene here. Work this out for the good, she prayed.

"All right, then," Tabitha said. "If you insist."

If the man wanted to pay, let him pay. But he'd have to remember that she tried to spare him this cost.

30

Amanda stole a look at Menno. He sat straight with the reins held in one hand and one hand flat against his thigh. His straw hat was slightly askew, a tuft of brown hair sticking out the side. He looked a little rumpled, and those warm, brown eyes were filled with uncertainty. He glanced over at her, then back at the road.

Her father would be furious, and under the anger, he'd be hurt. She'd never defied him before. What would happen now? She was feeling equally uncertain, but she was the one who'd just defied her *daet*.

Amanda needed this chance to talk to Menno, and she'd risked quite enough to get it, so she'd best not squander this opportunity.

"What did you want to tell me?" Amanda asked as the horse hit her stride.

"Your father thinks I'm some kind of monster."

"No . . ."

"I saw the look on his face. He thinks I'm a danger to you. But I'm not. And I need you to know that too."

She nodded. Her father did think that Menno was a danger, and after seeing Menno so different with his brother around, Amanda's nerves hadn't quite settled yet either.

"Why were you like that?" she asked.

"What do you mean?"

"At the farm, with your brother there, you were so different. You were . . . hard."

"Was I?"

"*Yah.* I didn't like it."

"I'm sorry. I didn't mean to be. I was angry with my brother and trying to keep that under control," Menno said. "I did tell him that I had a girlfriend. I said that he'd better clear out, or he'd ruin my chances with her."

"With me?" she breathed.

Menno cast her an apologetic look. "I'm sorry if I was overstating things, but you're someone I care about, and a woman I wanted to show my best side to. I thought my brother might understand and leave, but he just got angry. It was frustrating, and I spend a lot of time with pigs, so I guess I'm not very good in situations where I feel frustrated or awkward."

"Oh. I see. . . ." It did make sense now that he was explaining it.

"But I was upset about more than Simon," he went on slowly. "Simon said that he heard from our *mamm.* Daniel found her, and he put her in contact with Emmanuel and Simon."

"Your *mamm*?" Amanda's heart slammed to a stop. "She's . . . back?"

"Not quite. She's made contact. Apparently, she's apologized. I haven't spoken to her yet, but Simon says she's got plans to come to the farm and see me."

This woman had become something of a fable over time

. . . the woman who had been abused and crushed, and had finally fled. The woman who'd left her *kinner* behind to save her own skin. *Yah*, Amanda could definitely see why Menno had been closed off.

"I can see why you were shaken," she said softly.

"Do you?" Menno asked hopefully. He reached over and closed his hand over hers. "Because that about covers it. You seem to be able to give words to what I'm feeling. I am pretty shaken. I haven't seen my *mamm* since the day she left, and my *aent* tried to tell me that my mother loved me, but that she just couldn't face her life anymore. Now she's going to come see me, and . . . and I don't know how I feel about it."

"Do you want to see her?" Amanda asked.

"I do, and I don't. I thought I'd forgiven her, but I'm not sure I have."

"Do you know if she's okay?" Amanda asked. "Do you know what kept her away?"

He shook his head.

"I'm glad you could tell me this, Menno. *Danke.*"

"You're the only person I've told," he said, and she warmed at that. "You were safe, you know," he added. "I know my brother was being obnoxious, but I wouldn't have let anything happen to you. And while he has a big mouth, that is where it stops for Simon."

"I'm not used to being around that sort of thing," she said.

Menno reached up and touched her cheek with the back of one finger. "Good. Let's keep it that way."

"Is that what things are like at your home?"

"Not anymore. Not for a long time." Menno dropped his hand. "Watching my *daet* be cruel to my *mamm* . . . First, I vowed that when I was older, I would beat my father for what he did. Then, after I got sober, I vowed that when I had a wife, I would always make her smile, and I'd take care of her the way a woman deserved. I know I come from a dysfunctional family, but I want a better life than that. And I'll never, ever be the kind of man my father and brothers are. Never."

"Did you ever beat your father?" she asked hesitantly.

"No. I'm not a violent man. I was just a very angry boy. Boys who feel helpless often fantasize about the day when they'll be big enough to do something about it."

He'd been an angry and helpless boy—stuck up at a farm on the very edge of the district, out of eyesight of anyone who might have helped. Even her father felt some guilt over things that could have been done to help those boys that hadn't been.

"I know my family is a problem," he went on. "I'm not blind to that."

"What will you do about Simon?" she asked.

"I've been thinking that I will tell him he can stay so long as he attends AA meetings with me and so long as he doesn't bring a drop of drink into the house or on the property."

"Will he do that?" she asked.

He shook his head slowly. "I don't know. Probably not."

"Why not just make him leave?" she asked.

"I'll have to eventually, but I have a childhood bond with him," Menno replied. "We grew up together. We hid from our *daet* together when he would come home in a drunken rage. We used to sit outside by the road, close enough to see the house, but far enough away to run if we had to. We almost froze to death out there one winter, and I got frostbite on my fingers."

"Menno, that's terrible."

"It is," he agreed. "I remember Simon when he was my

older brother who used to protect me from bigger boys at school. He'd stand between me and Daet when Daet got into one of his darker moods. And Simon used to be funny. He'd make us all laugh until our sides ached."

"What changed him?" she asked.

"Anger, alcohol . . . I was no better for a while. We had to find some sort of emotional escape. If I'd known where my mother went, I would have followed her, but I had no idea where to look. So we escaped into the bottom of a bottle—a whole lot like our father. We forgot about our troubles for a little while. And Simon is still forgetting."

"I can't go to your home while Simon is there," Amanda said.

"I know. I understand." He looked over at her with a tender smile. "I even admire that about you. You should never be around a man like that, but I wanted you to know that he wasn't always like that."

"Were you tempted to drink again when Simon came?"

Menno nodded slowly. "Tempted? *Yah.* Mightily. But I didn't do it."

Amanda felt a flood of relief. "Good. That's so good, Menno. What stopped you?"

"I wanted to maintain my sobriety more than I wanted the relief," he replied. "I wanted to stay a good man."

Amanda squeezed his hand, and a smile touched his lips. She was proud of him. He *was* a good man.

Menno slowed the horse to a walk, then reined in a few paces away from Aaron and Rose's drive. They both stared at the mailbox for a moment or two, and then Menno turned toward Amanda.

"I'm looking for a wife," he said, his voice low and deep.

"I know."

"I told you before how unprepared I am." He reached out and touched her fingers gently, then pulled back. "I think I need to fix a few things before I can ask a woman to marry me."

Amanda's heart stuttered in her chest. "Are you—" She swallowed. "Are you calling off whatever this is between us?"

"No," Menno said. "I just feel like I need to explain myself. I drove down here to see you because I care so much. But I've got a drunken brother in my house, and no trust around the community. Your father thinks you aren't safe with me, and I'm sure he's not the only one to come to that conclusion. Marriage is about more than just the couple. It's about our families too. I might not like my brothers most of the time, and I might not want them around, especially when inebriated, but they are my brothers. They don't stop being my family."

"So you need to figure out your family first?" she asked uncertainly.

"I think I'd better."

Why did this feel like a good-bye, then? They certainly weren't moving forward. Perhaps this was Menno's way of letting her down easily, because his family wasn't going to be easily resolved either. Like he said, a family was a family, and right now, he had a brother in his house who was defiantly refusing to leave.

"If you've changed your mind about me," Amanda said, "I'd rather you just tell me that. Perhaps you see that you need a tougher woman than I am, or maybe you're seeing that you don't care as much as you should, or—"

"Amanda, stop," Menno said, and he caught her fingers. "I haven't changed my mind about you. If I had, I would have let you hate me and left well enough alone, okay?"

Green Pastures

She smiled hesitantly. "That makes sense."

"I want a beautiful wife in my kitchen, and I want to drive to Service Sunday with her at my side. I want people to see that she is cared for and protected and respected. I want to take long drives together, and I want to spend cold winter evenings in front of our stove together."

"This wife of yours," Amanda said. "Have you narrowed down your choices?" She needed him to be clear.

"When we were teens, I remember being at a youth event, and one of the younger girls fell into some mud. I watched you help her clean up, and you gave her your own apron to cover her muddy dress."

Amanda's breath caught. "I hardly remember that."

"I remember it," he said. "You were kind to everyone. You would notice when someone was embarrassed and try to help if you could. That takes a good heart."

"I didn't think you even noticed the rest of us," she said. "You kept to yourself so much."

"I always noticed," he said. "I think sometimes you made me a better man too. When you were in your *rumspringa*, there was a big ice house party going on. My brothers were going to it, and I was going to tag along, just to be with them. But then I saw some girls ask you about it, and you just shook your head. There was something in the way you could say no to something that was wrong that gave me pause. I didn't go to the party that night. If you could refuse, so could I."

"You remember more of me than I do of you," she said.

Menno dropped his gaze.

"I liked you then," he said, his attention on his hands now. "I really liked you. But you were better than I was, and I wasn't foolish enough to go court rejection."

"I wish you would have tried," she whispered. Because

if she'd known earlier than he felt this way, she might have started to look for his goodness too.

"I'm trying now." Menno met her gaze uncertainly.

Amanda sucked in a breath.

"Can I kiss you?" he asked softly.

Amanda's breath caught in her throat. "*Yah.* Okay."

There had to be a better response to his question, but he didn't seem to mind. Menno leaned closer, and she blinked as his breath tickled against her lips.

"Close your eyes, Amanda."

She did as he said, and his lips pressed gently against hers. This was the first time she'd ever been kissed, so she didn't know what to do. She held her breath, and he kissed her twice, then pulled back. Her eyes fluttered open, and she felt heat in her face.

"Was that okay?" he asked.

She nodded, feeling embarrassed still. She wished she'd asked Tabitha about how to kiss a man—or one of her married friends. But there hadn't seemed to be any threat of her being caught in a kissing situation before today.

Menno picked up the reins again, and the horse pulled them down the drive to Rose's house.

"I'll come see you again," Menno said. "I have a feeling I'll need to talk to your *daet* a bit and let him see the kind of man I am."

"Okay." She couldn't help the smile that came to her lips. "That would be nice."

He reined in at the house, and Amanda slid down to the ground. The door was propped open with a rock, and she saw her brother-in-law pass a window.

"They're home," Amanda said. "It'll be fine. *Danke* for coming to talk to me, Menno. I'll sort things out with my *daet* too. I won't let you take the blame for me running off like I did."

Menno smiled and flicked the reins, the buggy rolling forward and around, then back up the drive again. Then she turned toward her sister's house.

Menno had kissed her. Goosebumps ran up her arms at the memory. He'd kissed her, and he said he'd come back and talk to her father. It might be complicated, but Menno was serious.

And she had a feeling that Rose might understand.

31

The sound of scraping could be heard coming from the house while Tabitha unhitched her buggy and brought the horse to the corral. It echoed across the yard and up through the chimney, making a flock of sparrows flap up in a black sheet, wheel around, and head away. It sounded like Amanda was cleaning the indoor cookstove—a chore that didn't need to be completed until fall when they moved the cooking back inside again.

The clothesline was empty. Monday was laundry day, and Tabitha could get started on getting the clothes washed and hung out to dry.

Tabitha had always hated stove cleaning. It was labor intensive and filthy work. But a stove needed to be completely cleaned at least once every two months when it was in regular use, and back when Tabitha was living at home, Tabitha had been the oldest daughter, and the chore had fallen to her most often.

Tabitha headed up the steps, and when she entered the kitchen, it wasn't Amanda on her knees in front of the big stove after all. She found her father using a long-handled tool to scrub the stove's interior, the hollow scraping sound filling the kitchen. He was crouched back behind the stove, flakes of creosote falling onto the tiled part of the floor that surrounded the stove for safety. Daet grunted and eased himself back to his feet.

Tabitha glanced around. There was no sign of her sister.

"Daet, what are you doing?" Tabitha asked.

"I'm cleaning out the stove."

"Why?" That was firmly in the realm of women's duties, and since Amanda and Tabitha lived here, there was no reason why her *daet* would be doing this particular chore.

"Because I didn't want to leave it half done." He tossed the brush into a bucket.

"Where is Amanda?" Tabitha asked more pointedly.

"Menno came by. I told him to leave, and Amanda left with him."

That was a concise story, and Tabitha shook her head. "You're going to have to explain this one, Daet."

"Menno wanted to talk to her, and your sister was incredibly upset already by what she saw up at that hog farm. I can only imagine how bad it was. I told him he wasn't welcome here, and Amanda took issue with that. So she left with him." Daet sighed. "I know I shouldn't have been so rash, but . . . if you'd seen how shaken that girl was when she told me about Simon Weaver. He's a bigger pig than the ones they farm."

"True. Simon is awful," Tabitha agreed. "But she sees just how awful that man is. And she's twenty-seven, Daet. She's grown, and you can't just tell her what to do anymore."

"I'm very clear on that," he replied. "But she's still my daughter, and I can stand between her and a man who I think has the potential to hurt her. That's my Gott-given responsibility."

So Daet had gotten protective, and Amanda had left with Menno. But for the grace of Gott, that could have been her. She'd been overstepping everywhere lately. Tabitha put her bags down on the kitchen table.

"I've been scrubbing out the stove and trying to decide how long to wait before I go up to that farm and fetch her," Daet went on. "If I go too soon, she'll just be angry, and no good will be done. If I wait too long, anything could happen. But I once came down hard on my eighteen-year-old daughter and her *Englischer* boyfriend. I've had a decade to look at all the things I did wrong, and I don't want to repeat it with your sister."

Daet's lips trembled, and then he picked up the wire brush and turned back to the stove. Tabitha stood motionless as his words settled.

"Daet, do you think my marrying Michael was your fault?" she asked.

"Whose else was it?" her father replied gruffly. "If your mother had been alive, she would have handled it differently, I'm sure." He didn't lift his head, though, his attention on the stove. "From the very start I told you to stay away from Michael. He was trouble, and I could see it. But every time I pushed against him, I pushed you further into his arms."

"Daet, I made my own choices," Tabitha said. "I didn't marry him out of rebellion. I honestly loved him. I saw all his potential. I saw the way he looked at me, and I wanted to be his. That's why I married him."

The scrubbing slowed, then stopped. "If I'd pushed less?"

"I still would have married him, Daet. It wasn't your fault."

If only she could blame her terrible choice in husband on someone else, but the truth was that Tabitha had loved the wrong man. And maybe Michael was a better man at the time of their wedding. They'd had two relatively happy years together before he started to get antsy and subtly cruel. Michael had made choices too.

"How long has it been since Amanda left?" Tabitha asked.

Daet looked at the clock ticking loudly from the kitchen wall. "Twenty-two minutes."

"We should give it another ten minutes," Tabitha said.

"And then?" he asked.

"Then I'll drive up and get her. It won't come off as so aggressive if it's me. I'm just her sister."

"Not by yourself, you won't. You might be a well-respected veterinarian in these parts now, but you're still a woman, and there are things that are still dangerous. I'll go with you."

"All right." There was very little chance of talking her father out of it, and it wasn't like they wanted to let anyone else know about this. Amanda might be considered an old maid at this point, but dashing off with a man—especially a Weaver—would ruin her reputation beyond repair.

Her father eyed the clock again. "I'll go hitch up the buggy."

"Daet?"

Her father paused at the door.

"Fritz is sick again."

"Jonas mentioned."

He chewed the side of his cheek, then he turned and headed outside without another word.

Tabitha's gaze strayed over to the embroidered psalm hanging on the wall. If Mamm were still alive, what would she say? Would she have some deep wisdom, some innate understanding of Amanda's heart?

Or would her mother have been able to catch this early

and talk Amanda out of it more effectively than Tabitha had done? Would she have talked Daet out of selling that horse in time?

Surely goodness and mercy shall follow me all the days of my life.

So lovingly stitched by a woman who'd thought she'd see her girls grow up, and who thought she'd grow old with her husband. Life was not easy, and it came with pain, but there was truth in that verse. Even with the mistakes Tabitha had made, there was goodness and mercy waiting for her too. And there would be for Amanda.

But here was hoping they could spare Amanda the pain.

32

〜〜〜〜

Amanda knocked on Rose and Aaron's side door as Menno's buggy disappeared up the drive. She held the screen open with her hip as she waited for someone to answer. Normally, Rose would have heard her arrive and opened the door by now. But she'd spotted Aaron inside, so she knocked all the same.

Silence.

"Hello?" Amanda called, knocking louder. Maybe he'd gone upstairs. She stepped off the stairs, letting the screen fall shut, and shaded her eyes to look up at the windows, then she headed around the back of the house to the large garden.

There were rows upon rows of leafy vegetables. Tomato plants, weighed down by clusters of green tomatoes, twined their way up stakes. The pea plants looked like they'd been picked recently, but there were still flat pods growing and a few white blossoms—another crop of peas in a few weeks, and then a few last peapods later. The potato plants were thick, green, and tall. Carrot tops rose above the well-weeded dirt, but they'd need more growing time to become big orange carrots. They'd be small and extra sweet right now.

Rose had a talent when it came to making plants grow,

but she wasn't in her garden. Amanda headed back around to the side of the house, and the door opened then. Aaron stood there in a clean shirt, his head hatless, and his loose blond curls refusing to be restrained by the Amish haircut.

"Hi, Amanda," he said. He rubbed a palm down the side of his pants. "Can I help you?"

"Hi, Aaron," she said with a smile. "I came to see my sister. I just got dropped off. I hope that's okay?"

"Uh . . ." He rubbed a hand through his hair and glanced over his shoulder, back into the house. "She's not in right now."

Somehow Amanda hadn't anticipated that possibility, and she shuffled her feet uncomfortably.

"My ride just left," she said. "I'm sorry. I guess I can walk home from here. . . ."

It would be an hour walk, but maybe it would be good for her anyway—an hour to set her heart right before she apologized to her father for speaking to him the way she had earlier. An hour to think over the things Menno had said and to relive his kiss.

"That's probably best," Aaron said, and he started to close the door.

"Could I just get a drink first?" Amanda asked. Aaron stopped, seemed to deflate just a little, then pulled the door open all the way.

"Come in," Aaron said, stepping back. "Of course you can have a drink."

"It's nice to see you, Aaron," Amanda said, following him into the house. "It's been a while since you and I got to chat."

"*Yah*, it's nice to see you too. Sorry, I've been really busy lately, but I know Rose has been working with you and Tabitha quite a bit."

"We're enjoying it," Amanda said, casting her brother-in-law another smile.

"She says the same." He looked away.

Amanda's gaze moved around the kitchen. It was clean, and some bread was cooling on the counter with a white dish towel covering the loaves. Rose was a good homemaker—better than Amanda was.

Then her gaze landed on a kitchen chair, and sitting on that chair, almost out of sight underneath the table, was an open duffel bag. Some clothes were stuffed inside—men's clothes by the fabric, and by the balled up black tube socks. Aaron saw the direction of her gaze, and he stepped quickly in front of her and pushed the chair under the table so that she could no longer see the bag.

Amanda's pulse sped up, and she sucked in a breath. There might be a perfectly innocent explanation for that bag . . . if he hadn't just tried to hide it.

"Aaron?" she said.

Aaron handed her the glass of water and cleared his throat.

"What's that bag?" Amanda asked, setting the untasted water onto the table.

Aaron's jaw set, and he was silent for a couple of beats. Then he sighed. "I'm just going away for a few days."

"Where?"

"Away." He shot her an annoyed look.

"Is Rose going with you?" Amanda asked.

"No."

"Rose didn't mention it," Amanda said. "Does she . . . know?"

Aaron pulled the chair out and zipped shut the bag. "I guess it's no surprise that we haven't been getting along."

"You've been married such a short time—" Amanda began.

"Two years in the fall," he said.

"Less than two years, then," she said. "It isn't very long. We all love you, though. Especially Rose."

"I don't make her happy," Aaron said, his voice shaking. "I try. I do. I don't know what she wants from me, but hard work, providing for her, and coming home to her every night doesn't seem to be enough for her."

"I'm not married, Aaron, so I don't actually have advice," Amanda replied. "But I know my sister loves you."

"I love her too."

"Then . . . why are you leaving?" Amanda asked.

"I just need some space for a few days," Aaron said. "I'll come back and do chores, so she doesn't need to worry about that."

Aaron was leaving. . . . She felt she'd taken a kick to the stomach. Aaron was actually leaving!

"Please don't do this," Amanda said. "Stay and talk to her."

"I don't think there is much to say," Aaron replied. "All I know is that she's not happy, and I'm miserable, and this isn't working—"

"So you're just going to leave her?" Amanda asked breathlessly.

"No. I'm leaving for a little while to get my head on straight."

It didn't matter that it was for a little while. That might only be what he was telling himself now.

"When is Rose due home?" Amanda asked.

"She said she'd be home by three." He glanced toward the clock. It was a little after two.

Rose would be coming home to start supper, no doubt. That was the time everyone seemed to start supper. It took at least two to three hours to make dinner—build up the fire, get the meat in the oven, start the side dishes . . . and she'd find her husband gone.

Amanda's head started to spin. The couple had been having some difficulties. Had it really gone so far between them? What they needed was some intervention from the elders or the bishop. Someone with some experience needed to sit them down and talk some sense into both of them! But Amanda wasn't that person. She was just a sister . . . an unmarried one, at that.

Aaron took a note out of his bag and put it on the table. "That should explain it for her. You don't have to stay."

The envelope had been licked shut, and on the front Rose's name was written in bold block letters. No flourishes. No endearments.

"Do you mind if I do stay?" Amanda asked. "I think she'll be upset, and I don't want her to be alone when she finds that note."

"Sure. You're a good sister."

"Can I tell her anything from you?" Amanda asked helplessly. "That you love her? That you want to talk to her, maybe?"

"The note will explain it," Aaron said. "I don't need a messenger."

Right. He was being very clear about that.

"Where are you going, exactly?" she blurted out. Amanda owed her sister that much.

"My parents' place."

Amanda pressed a hand against her stomach. Rose was going to be both heartbroken and humiliated. Their unhappiness was about to become common knowledge.

Aaron shouldered his duffel bag and headed for the door.

The screen bounced shut after him, and Amanda sank into one of the kitchen chairs.

Things had gone very, very wrong, and she wasn't sure what she was supposed to do about it. Her sister was due home in less than an hour, and Aaron seemed determined to put some space between himself and his wife.

Amanda lowered her face into her hands.

"Oh, Gott, what do I do?"

There was no answer, only the slow, steady tick of the clock on the wall. Her own sweet kisses with Menno paled in the shadow of a real, troubled marriage. She'd always thought that being unmarried would be the most difficult cross to bear, but anticipating her sister's arrival, she changed her mind about that. This would be worse. Marrying a man and having that marriage fall apart would truly hurt more.

33

D aet kept the horse moving at a brisk trot as they headed up toward the Weaver hog farm. The wind coming in through the open windows was cool, but it wasn't quite enough to really cool the buggy down. The black canvas top absorbed the sunlight and heated up the interior like an oven. Her father had been silent during the drive, and Tabitha eyed him warily.

"Daet, we need to talk about that horse," she said.

"Later," he replied. "Right now, we're picking up your sister."

"Daet—"

Her father kept his eyes on the road, and Tabitha sighed.

"Fine, then I'll talk about the horse," she said.

"You seem to have lost any kind of respect for your father," Daet said irritably.

"I'm almost thirty, Daet," she said. "I'm a grown woman, and I have a reputation around here I need to protect too. I know that horse is Fritz. I know his medical history too. I can't keep that to myself. If you don't do something, I'm going to be forced to."

"You wouldn't," he said, casting a scandalized look at her.

"I would have to, Daet. It's not that I want to."

"I prayed about that horse. He was better," he said. "I prayed, and I prayed. I say this was an off day. That's it."

"And if it isn't?" she asked.

"I have faith."

"So do I, Daet, but sometimes Gott has other plans. His ways are not our ways."

"Don't you preach at me, young lady."

"Daet, why won't you just do the right thing?"

The scenery whisked past them, the horse's hooves clopping a ringing rhythm of metal shoes against asphalt.

"I had no choice in who bought the horse," he said. "That was out of my hands. I didn't even know it was Nathaniel. This was not intentional, but Nathaniel Peachy is a bad apple."

"I don't see evidence of that," she replied. "He's an Amish brother."

"And now you're an expert on Amish brethren?" he demanded.

"What did he do that was so terrible?" she asked. "I don't understand this feud, and quite frankly, Daet, you're the one coming off as the unchristianly man with a grudge."

"Is that what you think of your father?"

"No, it isn't," she said. "But it's how this is going to look to people on the outside. So tell me what started all of this, because I need to understand."

He was silent.

"Daet, I'm not a child anymore. I need to understand the problem so I can back you up. Of course I'll be on your side. But I have to understand."

Her father sighed. "It's awkward to tell this to my own daughter."

How bad could it be?

"I'm your grown daughter. That should make a difference."

There were a few hoofbeats of silence as the buggy rattled forward, and then her father began to talk in a low tone. "It was a long time ago. Your *mamm* and I were courting, and we were planning a wedding for the fall. Nathaniel had been nursing a crush on your *mamm* for a long time. I knew it, but she'd chosen me, so I thought it didn't matter. Well, we got into some silly argument—about what, I don't even remember—but Nathaniel went over to your *mamm*'s home, and he sat her down and told her that she shouldn't marry me because I wasn't a good man, and I'd only make her miserable."

"Ouch," Tabitha murmured. "But obviously she did marry you, and Nathaniel married Mary."

"That's not the part that makes me angry," he replied. "The first couple of years of marriage can be really tough. The vows are there for a reason. Feelings aren't always enough to keep two spirited people united. I think you can understand that."

It was a harsh statement, but not one made without love. Tabitha knew that. Life could be punishing and unforgiving. Feelings hadn't been enough for Tabitha to keep her husband's affection, and it hadn't been enough to keep him faithful. Although vows hadn't been enough for him either.

Tabitha nodded. "I can agree there."

"Well, your *mamm* and I were struggling through some differences between us, and she was so upset. I'd let her down somehow, and I didn't even really understand how. Newly married husbands can be a little oblivious sometimes. I tried to talk to your mother, but she just kept getting angrier and angrier. I'd think we had it resolved, and then she'd go off on another tangent. She said I didn't really love her—that is the part I still remember clearly. She looked me square in the face and told me I didn't know what love was. It wasn't like her at all. She was ready to move back in with her parents, and I was so confused as to what was going on. I was crushed."

"What was happening?" Tabitha asked.

"I decided to find out. So I followed her one evening. She met up with Nathaniel on that little stone bridge three miles south of here."

"Mamm and Nathaniel?" Tabitha gasped.

"He wasn't married yet at that point. And, no, they weren't having an affair. But she was crying on his shoulder, and he'd been pouring poison in her ear. He'd been the one telling her that I didn't really love her, and that she'd better stand up for herself now, or I'd crush her completely. He was the one tearing us apart."

"What did you do?" she asked.

"First of all, I talked it out with your *mamm* and broke that spell. She saw that she'd been wrong to confide in anyone outside our marriage, and she saw that Nathaniel had been causing grief. She promised not to talk to him again."

"Good," Tabitha said.

"And as for Nathaniel, I met him in his barn one afternoon, and I punched him in the nose."

"Daet!"

"Judge me if you will—the community certainly would—but it resettled a few boundaries between men."

"So it's settled, then. Why the anger still?" Tabitha asked. "Mamm is gone now. Nathaniel is married with adult *kinner* and *kinnskind*."

"After that, it was one thing or another," Daet explained.

"He reported me for some infraction to the bishop, and he spread rumors about the quality of my beef. I confess, I had my own little ways to get back at him, and we've pestered each other for the rest of our lives. But it all started with one spiteful man who tried to ruin our marriage. I haven't forgotten that."

Daet's rule that his daughters weren't allowed to say anything unflattering about their husbands in his presence suddenly made a lot more sense.

"Is that why you won't let Rose say anything about what's going on in her home?" Tabitha asked.

"If Rose wants to fix problems in her marriage, putting her family in the middle of it isn't going to help anything," he said. "She'd best talk to Aaron, not to us. And that is the best marriage advice I can provide."

Tabitha fell into silence as they swept along the road that led toward the district boundary. Tabitha hadn't meant to meddle in her sister's marriage, but she'd caused trouble. Another finger of guilt wormed its way through her middle.

When they arrived at the Weaver farm, they bumped down the gravel drive. Menno's buggy was already unhitched and parked under a shelter. The pigs looked happy enough— some lying in the sun, some in the shade of a little shelter, and a few rooting around in a big mud puddle with the running hose.

At the house, Simon sat on the front porch rocking chair, his jean-clad legs stretched out and his cowboy boots crossed at the ankles. He didn't move, but his head followed them as they drove up, and Daet reined in the horse.

Daet glanced over at Tabitha questioningly. There was no sign of Amanda.

"She must be in the house," Tabitha said.

They both hopped out of the buggy, and Daet tied the horse at the hitching post.

"Is my sister here?" Tabitha asked, raising her voice so that Simon could hear her.

Simon pulled his legs in and sat up. "Who?"

"Amanda," Tabitha replied. He was going to play games now, was he? As if he had no idea who she was talking about.

"Haven't seen her." Simon stretched his legs out again and leaned back in the chair.

"I'll find her, Daet. He's just being difficult," Tabitha said softly. Then she raised her voice again. "Is your brother here?"

"Yup."

"Where is he?"

"I don't know . . . around the farm somewhere," Simon said. He reached down and picked up a beer bottle and slurped noisily from it.

"And why are you here?" Daet asked, crossing his arms over his chest.

Simon squinted at them. "I live here."

"You used to," Daet retorted. "When your father died, Menno bought you all out. He owns this farm. I know that because the bishop made it plain to all of us so that there'd be no confusion."

"Who cares who got it on paper?" Simon snapped. "I was born here."

Tabitha left her father and Simon to their verbal sparring and headed around the side of the house. Menno was coming out of the stable, and he picked up his pace when he saw her.

"Is there a problem?" Menno asked.

"I'm looking for Amanda."

"She's not here," he replied. "Look, I would never drive

off with a woman who isn't my wife and just take her home with me against her family's wishes. That is something I will not do. Ever."

"Then where is she?" Tabitha asked.

"I dropped her off at Aaron and Rose's place."

"Oh." Tabitha heaved a sigh. "Okay."

"I wouldn't just drive off with her and take her up here," Menno repeated. "She should be home by now. Or maybe she went out with Rose. I don't know. But I left her at Rose and Aaron's place."

"I'm sure she's fine," Tabitha said. "We thought—" She felt her face heat, and she glanced around the farmyard.

"Well, whatever you thought—no," he replied, and then his gaze slipped past her toward the house. "Is that your *daet*?"

"*Yah*. We came together." She knew how this looked—like a family rescuing their daughter. Let it look that way. Amanda had a family behind her. "I see Simon is still here."

"*Yah*, he's not willing to budge," Menno said. "I promised your sister I'd deal with him, and I intend to."

"Do you want help?" Tabitha asked, and when he gave her a quizzical look, she put her hands up. "Not mine. From the men, I mean."

Menno's eyebrows went up, and she could see him considering that. He headed past Tabitha toward the house, and she had no choice but to follow him back.

". . . so you have no job, no money in savings, and no desire to find work?" Daet was saying. "Is that what you're telling me?"

"I don't see how it's your business, old man," Simon growled.

"Not my business, huh?" Daet pursed his lips and inhaled

a deep breath that puffed out his broad chest. He glanced over at Menno. "Do you want Simon here?"

"Not especially," Menno said.

"It's my home as much as yours," Simon said icily. "I'm not leaving here. What makes you so special, huh? What makes you more of a Weaver than me?"

"It's not being a Weaver that makes Menno special," Daet replied evenly. "It's being Amish. And when you were but boys, we didn't do enough to help you as a faith-abiding community. At first we kept shunning your *daet*, and then we realized that despite his apologies and promises to do better, he wasn't making any lasting changes, so all that happened by shunning him was that you *kinner* and your poor *mamm* were cut off from any good influence. So we stopped shunning him, even when he deserved it, out of concern for your welfare. But I'm not convinced we did right by you. No one wanted to separate you from your parents, but I truly believe we let you down. We should have found a way to protect you more, to show you the right path, and to give you the support that you so desperately needed."

"What?" Simon eyed Daet suspiciously. The words seemed to be slowly landing past his alcohol-induced fog.

"I'm here as a fellow Amish brother to support Menno," Daet said, giving Menno a nod. "And I will return with the bishop, the elders, and as many men from our community as I need to rummage up in order to make sure that this Amish man is not taken advantage of. We know who owns this property, Simon. If you have personal grievances against your brother, then we can sit down with you and help you to come to peace. But sitting in this house with your feet up while your brother works is not only dishonorable and disrespectful, but it goes directly against our *Ordnung*."

"You want *me* to muck out stalls?" Simon barked out a laugh.

"No, son, I want you use that cell phone that we all know you have and call for a taxi to drive you back to town. I want you to get a job, rent a room, and clean yourself up. You are no longer dealing with your brother in isolation. You are dealing with the Amish community as a whole, Simon Weaver. And we would like nothing more than to see you on the narrow path once more. But we will not abide by this life that you are living."

Simon, for once, was speechless, and Tabitha looked over at her father with a surge of pride.

"I will stay here with you until Simon has made his exit," Daet added, giving Menno a reassuring nod. "And I will report to the bishop and the elders just as soon as I am able. You can be sure that we'll come by to say hello, break a little bread, and make sure you're doing well on the regular, Menno."

"*Danke*, Abram," Menno said, and he looked a little stunned too. Then a smile touched his lips. "I do appreciate it."

Tabitha knew that her father did not believe in meddling in the romantic relationships with others, but it seemed that he was plenty ready to stand by an Amish brother in his time of need. This was the community support and stalwart love that she had returned home to find. And she'd found it between her father and a young, struggling Amish man.

Sometimes Gott provided in miraculous ways, but most times Gott provided through the community he'd already pulled together for his glory and his purpose. The Amish community was there for a reason—fenced in away from the influences of outsiders and determined to live plainly. This was the work of the church.

As Simon grudgingly pulled out his phone, and Menno and Daet headed into the house, Tabitha smiled to herself. She never could have gotten Simon levered out of this house, but her father managed it in five minutes.

Was this system perfect? No. But it had practical beauty all the same that had been working very efficiently for a very long time.

The foundational truth stood solid: There was strength in community.

34

Rose's kitchen had grown stuffy and overly warm, but Amanda was afraid to even move. This wasn't her kitchen, and somehow she felt like if she opened the windows or made cookies or washed those few dishes left in the sink or did anything in this space, she might break the tenuous thread that was holding everything together. This was Rose's kitchen, Rose's home, Rose's marriage . . . And it was all about to crumble.

So she'd sat there in a little pool of overly warm sunlight that made her feel damp and sweaty, and she'd waited, watching a fly bounce groggily against the windowpane. Amanda started to her feet at the sound of a buggy, and she leaned toward the window. It wasn't Rose's—it was her father's, and Daet and Tabitha sat side by side.

Amanda felt her hands start to shake. This was not good. She needed to tell Rose alone, not with anyone else who might see. This was shameful enough! Maybe Rose could fix it before anyone else had to know.

Amanda went to the side door, and she crossed her arms over her stomach, remembering with sinking clarity that the last time she'd seen her father, she'd defied him.

She'd thought she'd have some time before she was forced to discuss it with her father, but it looked like he'd come to find her, after all.

Her father met her gaze, but she couldn't figure out if he was angry or not. His expression was like stone. He and Tabitha both got out of the buggy.

"Daet, I'm sorry I left the way I did," Amanda began as she headed down the steps. "I should never have done that or spoken in anger like I did. I'm sorry. Menno dropped me off here, and I suppose I should have walked home, but—"

But things had just gotten terribly, terribly out of control, and Amanda had been left holding it all in her lap.

"It's okay, Amanda," Daet said. "I shouldn't have been quite so stoked up myself. We just came from the Weaver farm."

"Oh?" Her stomach clenched.

"We thought you were there," Tabitha added with an apologetic look.

"All the same," Daet went on, "I gave Menno a hand with something he needed done."

"Daet kicked Simon out," Tabitha supplied quietly.

"You did?" Amanda gave him a hesitant smile. "And Menno . . ."

"Was grateful," her father replied. "Although he's still got his hands full. But I think he's got a start in dealing with Simon, at least, and drawing those boundaries."

So her father had booted Simon off Menno's property, and no one seemed angry at Menno right now. That was all very good.

"Does that mean you approve of him?" Amanda asked. She needed her father to be very clear right now. She had enough uncertainties in front of her to try to guess at her father's feelings on the matter.

"Approve of him as what?" Daet fixed Amanda with a level stare.

"As a possible husband." Amanda had to push the words out. This was something Menno should be asking him about, not Amanda.

"That's a strong stance to take just yet," Daet said with a slow shake of his head. "I can support a young Amish man in his efforts to put together a righteous life, but for me to approve of that struggling young man for my daughter? I don't know about that." Daet looked around at the quiet property with a frown. "Now . . . where is your sister? Where is Aaron?"

Amanda licked her lips. "They aren't here."

"Then why are you here?" Tabitha asked.

Amanda knew it looked weird. Of course, she shouldn't just be hanging around in her sister's kitchen for no reason. As if on cue, another buggy turned down the drive, masked by some trees that stood in the way of seeing exactly who it was until they came past the big oak and into clear view. Amanda held her breath. *Let it be Aaron coming back . . . let it be Aaron . . .* Then all of this could be over, and Amanda would never have to say a word. The secret would die with her.

But it wasn't Aaron. It was Rose in their little courting buggy. She looked surprised to see her family standing there, and she cheerfully smiled and waved at them.

"Daet, Tabitha . . . I'm going to have to talk to Rose alone for a minute," Amanda said, her throat tight. She plunged past them toward Rose's buggy.

Rose reined in and hopped down, her running shoes crunching onto the gravel. She shook out her dress and tucked a loose tendril of glossy brown hair back under her *kapp*.

"What are you all doing here?" Rose asked.

"They're just here to pick me up. I came here because I was with Menno, and . . ." She sighed. "That's a long story, and it doesn't matter. I thought he could just drop me off here, and you and I could visit like old times. They're just here to bring me home again."

Rose headed over to her horse's side and started to unhitch, and Amanda sucked in a stabilizing breath.

"Let me help, Rose," Daet said, and their father came striding over to the horse and started unbuckling. The horse shuffled in pleasure as the tack started to loosen.

"Rose . . ." Amanda tugged on her sister's arm and pulled her away. "Come over here, would you?"

"What's going on, Amanda?" Rose asked. "You look like you're going to be sick."

That was about how Amanda felt, but emptying her stomach wasn't going to fix anything.

"When I arrived, Aaron was here," Amanda said, looking furtively toward Tabitha, who was watching them with her arms crossed. She didn't have much time to say this before they were interrupted again, she was sure. "And he was very upset."

"Oh?" Rose frowned. "Why? I told him where I was going."

"I don't know exactly what happened. He said you weren't happy." The words came out in a rush. "He said he didn't know how to fix things, and that he needed space."

"He has a whole farm." Rose spread her arms, then dropped them. "What do you mean *space?*"

That was the question, wasn't it? What did any man mean by *space?* Because the answer to his problems lay in his home with his wife. It lay in long talks and the sharing of feelings.

Even Amanda knew that. What would all this space do for Aaron? Nothing.

"He took a packed bag with him." Amanda sucked in a wavering breath. "He said he was going to his parents' place for a bit to . . . think. He said he'll come back and do chores so you don't have to worry about it."

Rose's face blanched, and she swayed on her feet. "What?"

"There's a note on the kitchen table," Amanda said feebly. "I didn't look at it, but he said it would explain."

"He . . . left me?" Rose whispered.

Amanda didn't answer because she wasn't entirely sure what was going on. Amish people didn't abandon their husbands and wives. They stayed, and they worked things out. When the Amish married, it was for life—for better or for worse. That was why they took such care when they married, wasn't it? So what was Aaron doing?

Rose's breath came in quick gasps. "What else did he say?"

"I don't know. . . . I don't remember—"

"Think!" Rose caught Amanda's arm. "This is my marriage, Amanda. What else did he say?"

"He thinks he can't make you happy!" As the words came out, she realized how loudly she'd said it.

Daet and Tabitha were both staring at them now, eyes wide. Tears welled in Rose's eyes, and her lips wobbled.

Amanda grabbed her sister's hand and propelled her toward the house. "Read the note, Rose."

Rose stumbled inside, and Amanda followed her. The screen door bounced behind them, and Rose snatched up the envelope on the table. She tore it open, and her eyes scanned the handwriting. She slowly sank down onto a kitchen chair just as Tabitha came into the house too.

"He says he doesn't know how we'll ever be happy,"

Rose said woodenly. "He says our marriage is broken, and he doesn't know what to do. He'll . . . be back for chores."

Tabitha stood frozen in the doorway. Amanda reached for her sister's hand. "Oh, Rose, I'm so sorry."

Rose tore her hand free, and her shoulders started to shake. Then she covered her face in her hands.

Daet came into the house next. He stopped short when he spotted Rose's tear-stained face.

"Rose?" Daet asked uncertainly.

"Aaron left me," Rose wailed. "What do I do?" Rose turned to face her father. "I know you don't want me to say a single word against the man I married, but what am I supposed to do when my husband writes me this?"

And she thrust the note into her father's hands.

35

Later that evening, Tabitha sat up in the kitchen with a mug of mint tea in front of her. The kitchen window was cranked open, and a welcome breeze filtered through. The tea sat untouched, a soothing habit more than a practical choice on a warm night. From the sitting room, she could hear the soft thunking sound of her father's rocking chair. The bottom of the worn rockers had flattened over the years, but he still rocked on it, thunking back and forth.

They hadn't eaten much for dinner—no one was terribly hungry—and Amanda had gone up to bed shortly after. All Tabitha could think of was what was happening over at Rose's place. Had Aaron come back? Was Rose okay there by herself?

Her own old pain kept rising up in unison with her worry about her sister. Rose was sitting in the house waiting, and how many nights had Tabitha done the same? Michael not coming home. Michael picking some pointless fight and then using it as an excuse to disappear for a weekend. How many nights had she been in a lonesome apartment, praying and wondering and trying to figure out why her marriage was such a chaotic mess?

The sound of the rocking chair stopped, and Daet came into the kitchen. He pulled out a chair opposite Tabitha and soberly sat down.

"Things have gotten out of hand," he said. "If your *mamm* were alive, she would have known what to do. She would have handled it all with so much grace and gentleness. I think I've done poorly."

"Daet, I know that Rose was trying to keep their problems private, but those two need help."

"I agree," he said. "I didn't want to intrude on a married couple's privacy, but it does seem that they need some loving support right now."

"I don't think I'm the right one to talk to her," Tabitha said. "If I go talk to her, I'm going there with all my fear and my trauma. I'm going to assume the worst—I already am. I'm going to think that Aaron is doing exactly what Michael did, and that isn't helpful right now."

Daet pressed his lips together, staying silent.

"This is what the beginning of a divorce looks like, you know," Tabitha said. "Two people who start pushing away from each other . . . one who moves out. This is what it looks like when people split up, Daet. That's why I'm so upset about this. I think you're the one to talk to them."

"Divorce?" he said. "That's what you see?"

"I do, Daet."

Daet rubbed his hands over his face.

"I'll tell you what," he said. "Tonight we pray, and tomorrow we stop by Rose and Aaron's home and see if Aaron is home yet. If he is, we thank Gott for his providence. If he's not . . . I will have a word with my daughter, and I will go to the bishop for some help. Those two love each other, but they might need some good counsel to see clearly again."

"*Danke*, Daet," Tabitha said.

Her father reached forward and patted her hand. "It's late."

"*Yah*. I'll head up soon, Daet. Goodnight."

Her father scraped back his chair and headed for the staircase, leaving Tabitha alone, bathed in the golden kerosene light of the overhead lamp. This was what made things different for an Amish couple. Every couple had challenges, but an Amish couple had a community ready to step in and guide them back together again.

And it was time for some community support.

36

When the bishop and the elders and their wives came together to help a struggling young couple, privacy was the key. Amanda knew that Daet had gone to talk to the bishop yesterday, and she knew what happened next. An elder would go talk with Aaron, and his wife would sit down with Rose. They'd listen with compassion, and they'd offer advice on how to get over the hurdle in the relationship. They'd help them sort things out, and they'd remind the couple of their vows.

For better or for worse. For life.

But it would be private.

So for now, everything grew quiet and still. Menno came by with some freshly smoked bacon as a gift, and he'd chatted with everyone for a few minutes while she hung up the last of the laundry on the clothesline. Then she and Menno had gone for a long walk together.

Amanda told the story of Tabitha saving Jared Blank's cattle with the hose down their throats.

"It was extraordinary, Menno!" she said. "My sister is really something. I didn't realize how skilled she was until I saw her working. If she hadn't known exactly what to do, those cattle would have died in that barn. But she knew, and she worked so fast. She kept giving me orders, and I just did as she said. She's impressive, you know."

"*Yah*," Menno said. "I can see that. You're rather impressive, too, for being able to assist her."

He took her hand, and she forgot about Tabitha and cattle. All she could think about was Menno's strong arm brushing against hers, and his warm hand wrapped around her fingers, and how the June afternoon felt just about perfect. If only they could stay just like this, held in the hushed quiet of a summer afternoon.

"I want to get a new courting buggy," Menno said. "I only have my big buggy, nothing smaller."

"A courting buggy?" she asked, studying his face. That was the common name for a two-seater buggy.

"It's the most appropriate way to take a woman out driving," he said. "To take you out driving, Amanda."

Her face grew hot, and a smile touched her lips.

"You'd be buying it to court me?" These open questions were getting easier now that she felt more certain of his responses.

"I do want to court you eventually. And when I do, I want to do things properly."

Maybe this was how things felt when two people were moving toward a life together. . . .

He asked to kiss her again, and her heart fluttered while he pulled her close just once before he left.

A couple of days later, Amanda went along with Tabitha on her veterinarian calls, and the morning seemed more hushed than other mornings. The birds twittered softly, and not even a breeze rustled the long grass that grew up along the fence posts the lined the road. It was like the whole earth was afraid to breathe.

They carried on past Aaron and Rose's place, and Amanda leaned forward to look for signs of movement. A whisper of smoke came up through the chimney, so Rose must be cooking. The windows were open, and there was an extra buggy in the drive. Someone was there helping, Amanda had no doubt.

The little house disappeared from sight behind a blind of trees amid the rhythmic clopping of hooves. Somehow, having somewhere to go and a job to do was helpful in calming her own anxiety today. If she'd been at home in the kitchen, schooling her thoughts into calmer places would have been almost impossible.

But despite her sister's current difficulties, Amanda's mind kept turning back to Menno and his tender kiss. Amanda knew that marriage could be a challenge. She knew it took stores of character that a woman often didn't even know she had. It took a great deal of love, patience, and understanding.

But not everyone went through these hard times that Rose was going through, did they? Weren't there some couples that just got married and had an easy time of it? Weren't there a few who paid their dues beforehand and then went into their vows peacefully? She wasn't sure she could survive what Rose was going through right now. If Menno married her and then broke her heart like that . . .

"Are you okay?" Tabitha asked.

Amanda pulled herself out of her reverie. "*Yah*. I'm fine."

"Are you worried about Rose?" Tabitha asked.

"I am," Amanda replied. "But I'm also thinking about myself. Everyone keeps warning me that marriage is hard and to be so very careful before entering into it. Does everyone go through this?"

Tabitha slowly shook her head. "I don't know. If they do, they hide it."

"But people still get married," Amanda said.

"Everyone hopes they'll skip the hard parts," Tabitha said.

"Don't some people? Isn't marriage pleasant and rewarding for at least some?"

"Rewarding doesn't mean easy," Tabitha replied.

Nothing worthwhile came easy—she'd been taught that all her life—but thinking about that fact in relation to a marriage? That was terrifying.

She had such pleasant times with Menno this week. They'd gone on another leisurely walk and taken a buggy ride—even though he only had his big buggy and not a smaller courting buggy. They talked now about so many things, and they were getting more comfortable together. And Menno's gentle eyes drew her in to every word he said. . . .

But once upon a time, Rose had been floating around while Aaron courted her too. And everyone had tried to warn Amanda that Menno was a risk. It might be wise to listen.

———

Later that afternoon, Amanda went with Tabitha into town again for her shift at the clinic. Dr. Brian was doing some spays and neuters, and Tabitha was seeing to the animals that were brought in for various complaints, which left Amanda with some time to herself.

Amanda had a few items she wanted to pick up from the shops downtown, and it was only about a twenty-minute walk to get there. Daet had promised her a new dress, after all, and she also wanted to pick up a birthday card for a friend. It was nearly three in the afternoon, and as she made it up to the bustling, cheerful center of town on Shepherd Avenue, she found her gaze moving toward the church. It had a tall white steeple, and a sign out front read *AA meetings Tuesdays and Fridays at 2:00 p.m., 6:30 p.m., and 9:00 p.m. You aren't alone.*

There was a buggy in the church parking lot, and several vehicles, but she paused at the sight of the buggy. She'd seen a buggy in the parking lot before, and there weren't many reasons why an Amish person would be in a Presbyterian church, unless they were just taking advantage of some parking while they shopped in the area. That wasn't unheard of. Amanda's gaze lingered on the buggy, and then she headed into the stationery shop to find the birthday card.

Was that buggy Menno's?

When Amanda came back out of the shop, a slim paper bag tucked under her arm, the first Alcoholics Anonymous meeting of the day was letting out. A side door had opened, and people were emerging from the building. She spotted Menno. It had been him! He had his straw hat in one hand still, having taken it off inside, and he paused on the sidewalk and looked up and down the street as if he was looking for someone. His gaze stopped at her, and he startled. Then he smiled, and Amanda felt a rush of relief at that smile.

She raised her hand in a wave, and Menno planted his hat back onto his head, then jogged across the street and headed in her direction. Amanda had associated that church with Menno ever since she'd seen him coming out of it that one day, but she hadn't actually expected to run into him here, and her heart pattered in her throat.

"Amanda." He reached out, and his fingers slipped over hers, then he released her just as quickly. Amanda glanced around. There were people around—always people around.

"Were you looking for someone?" Amanda asked.

"*Yah.* Simon said he might come today, and I'd hoped he'd at least try."

"He didn't, though?"

"No, he didn't." Menno shrugged.

Amanda looked down at her hands, suddenly feeling bashful.

"Do you want to walk?" Menno asked. "Do you have time? I have about twenty minutes, and then I have an appointment at the bank. I'm serious about getting that courting buggy. It would be useful for taking you driving, and also as a second buggy for when I have a wife to support."

Every time he mentioned that wife in his future, Amanda's stomach gave a flutter.

"I have a small certificate of deposit that is maturing," Menno went on, "and I want to use that money for the buggy. But . . . I'd like to walk a little."

She nodded. "*Yah.* My sister is busy at the clinic. You don't mind using that money on a buggy?"

"It's a different kind of investment into my future," he replied. "I'm sure."

They fell into step together, heading down the sidewalk. It was a busy day for tourists and *Englischers.* One family seemed to be all agog about an Amish buggy someone had left parked while running errands. They had their phones out and were taking photos next to it. When they spotted Amanda and Menno, they froze as if guilty until they walked on past, and then erupted in whispered relief. Amanda and Menno headed toward a less crowded area farther up the road.

An *Englischer* sauntered past them. He was dressed in a pair of jeans and a snug-fitting T-shirt—snugger than the Amish wore, that was for sure. For the Amish, just the fit of that shirt would be inappropriate.

"Hey, Menno. How're you doing?" the man said.

"Hey, Hank. Not bad. You?"

"Can't complain, buddy."

The man passed on by, and Amanda surreptitiously looked over her shoulder after him.

"Where do you know him from?" she asked.

"We worked a job together once when I was doing some construction. He's a carpenter."

"Oh." Amanda glanced over her shoulder once more. "Menno, why do you seem to get along with *Engslischers* better than Amish?"

"What do you mean?"

"That man—you're different with him. I saw it before when you were chatting with some *Englischer* in the street. You're at ease with them. You're relaxed."

"They don't expect much from me," he replied.

"Do you prefer that?" she asked. "I mean, given a ripe opportunity, would you go *Englische*?"

Menno paused, thoughtful, and for a moment her breath stuck in her throat. Finally he said, "No."

But that pause made her stomach tighten. "You don't sound sure."

"You asked a serious question, and I was thinking about it," Menno said. "I don't want to jump the fence. If I had, I'd have done it by now. I'm Amish. And, no, being Amish hasn't been easy for me, but it's who I am."

"What happens if Simon tries to stop drinking, and he comes back to your house?" Amanda asked.

"I don't know. . . . I guess I'd try and help him."

"And what if you're married, and Simon comes back wanting to stay with you?" Simon made her nervous, and she didn't believe his good intentions would be enough, but Menno might.

Menno slowed, and he looked over at Amanda uncertainly. "I can't know what will happen in the future. You know that. I don't know what I'd do. I mean, if I were married"—his gaze flicked up to meet hers at the word—"I suppose I'd have to consider my wife in the arrangement, but he's still my brother. I'd have to try to help him somehow."

"Would you . . . move him in?"

"I'd try not to."

"Would you believe him that he'd stopped drinking?"

"I know for a fact that men can stop drinking, Amanda, because I've done it. It's not easy. It comes with backsliding, but it's possible." Menno eyed her uncertainly. "What's this really about?"

"I don't know." She dropped her gaze down to her hands again. "Marriage is hard. Very hard. Sometimes people who have everything in common can still make each other miserable. You can have a man and woman from a good family, and they can have all sorts of support available to them and the same ideas about their future, and it can still get muddled."

"My family is the worry, then?" Menno asked. "Because I can't change them. That's a fact. Even if I wanted to."

"No, I—"

"So you have no issue with my family?" he pressed.

"Menno, don't make me say that!" Amanda said. Of course his family was a problem. He should know that better than anyone, but it sounded terrible coming out of her mouth. His brother scared her. And he had other brothers who'd grown up just like he had.

"I think you should say it," Menno said. "If we're talking about a future together, we'd better dump out the bucket, so to speak. Is Simon the problem, specifically?"

"I'm scared!" The words came out louder than Amanda expected, and she lowered her voice. "I'm scared, Menno. I can't tell you who I'm talking about, but there is a married couple I know rather well who are having problems right now. And they have everything in common. They're perfectly matched. I'd never have dreamed that behind closed doors they were battling the way they are. And if that couple could fall into such unhappiness, what guarantee do I have against it? I . . . I like you very much, Menno. I think you're kind and interesting and resourceful. But I'm scared too."

"Come over here." Menno caught her hand and led her quickly around a corner, out of sight of anyone for the moment. Menno looked searchingly into her face. Amanda's heart pattered in her throat, and she swallowed hard.

"I think every relationship comes with a risk," Menno said. "And I understand that I'm the risk here. I'm the one with the questionable family. I'm the one with something to prove."

Menno hadn't let go of her hand, and he squeezed her fingers gently.

"Don't you get scared?" she asked.

"A little bit. You're smart and insightful. And I like your bravery. But you're also strong, and I don't think you'd just let me call the shots. I can see that you'd have a few issues with my brothers. It's understandable that it would be . . . a point of tension."

So she wasn't quite his perfect ideal, either, and she found that his words stabbed deeper than they should. Tears stung her eyes. What did she expect, that he'd think she was perfection itself? That he'd think that life with her would be a walk through the garden? Maybe she wanted him to.

"But I find that I think about you all the time, anyway," Menno said softly. "I see you, and my heart stops beating for a second. I find myself going over all the little things you said. Tonight, when I'm mucking out farrowing stalls, I'll be going over this conversation—every word you say. I can't help it."

"My sister told me about how Simon was bullying you into getting his way before my *daet* stepped in. I worry that might happen again," she said, her voice shaking. "And I think you won't see that."

"Okay, so what would you do if Simon was bullying me?" he asked.

"I'd tell you."

"And what if I didn't agree with you?" he asked.

"I'd—" Tears misted her eyes. "I'd probably tell you louder. And that's terrible, isn't it? But it's also terrible if you put your drunken brother ahead of your wife."

"That's what scares you?" he asked. "That I'd put him first and you second?"

Amanda thought for a moment, then nodded. "*Yah.*"

"And if I promise not to do that?" he asked.

"I don't know if you can," she said. "If you disagreed with me and asked him to leave only because you'd promised, then you'd resent me."

"You do realize this argument hasn't even happened yet?" he said with a small smile.

"*Yah.*" But it felt real in her heart.

"Well . . . if I was really being bull-headed, you could bring

278

your father into it," Menno said. "I'd hate that a lot, but it would probably work."

"It's not about trying to make you do what I want," she said. "It's about issues that I think will become very big between us."

"And how I feel about you—" Menno lifted her fingers to his lips and pressed a soft kiss against her knuckles—"does that matter at all?"

"*Yah*, I suppose it does." She couldn't help but smile then.

"Because I've been thinking about what a life with you would be like ever since you arrived with those containers of baked goods. And . . . I've been thinking about you more than I have a right to."

"Me too," she admitted.

"I'd love you, Amanda," he said, his voice dropping low. "I'd love you, and I'd work hard to provide for you. Would I be perfect? I doubt it. But I'd try, and with you, I think I'd learn to be a better man than I'd ever be without you. I come with problematic brothers, and I grew up not learning half the things I should have learned from a mother. But if a loyal heart means anything, you'd have mine."

Amanda sucked in a wavering breath, and she stared at him, speechless.

"That's what I've got to offer," he said quietly.

She nodded, and for a couple of beats, there was just their mingling breath and the sound of chattering tourists moving closer.

"Menno, would I be worth the risk for you?" she asked.

A smile touched his lips, and he nodded. "Oh yeah."

It was an *Englischer* phrase, but her stomach quivered at those words, and then he looked over her shoulder toward the street.

"I'd better get to that appointment," Menno said. "I'll see you later."

His warm gaze met hers. "The next time I pick you up to go for a drive, it will be in a shiny new courting buggy."

But new buggies didn't change the challenges a couple could face, and Menno came with more challenges than most. Even the best men could fail to live up to their good intentions. It wouldn't be his fault. It wouldn't be hers. But would the obstacles be too many for them to really be happy together?

And if Menno was going to the expense of buying a new courting buggy, it might be best to be realistic now. He loved her, and all he had to offer her was his heart. And a heart was far too precious to toy with.

Was it kinder to both of them to end it now?

37

Menno stood outside in the warm evening, listening to the pigs grunting to one another and dumping bottle after bottle of alcohol into the compost heap. Most compostable material was fed to the pigs, except for grass clippings and weeds from the garden. This compost heap, away from the pigs, seemed like the safest place to dispose of the liquor Simon had forgotten to take with him. Where he'd rummaged up this alcohol from, Menno had no idea. When he'd arrived there had been none, and by dinnertime there'd been a stash.

It was worth a lot of money, and when Menno checked the coffee tin where he kept some extra cash in the kitchen cupboard, he found it empty. So that explained that. But this liquor was also a deadly temptation, and Menno wouldn't sleep another night with a drop of alcohol under his roof.

Gott, give me strength. Grant me the serenity to accept the things I cannot change, the courage to change the things I can, and the wisdom to know the difference.

It was a comforting prayer—a few words his own and the rest recited from the AA meetings that had saved his life.

What could he change in his life? He could let the community help him. He could determine to lean into their gatherings and find people he could be comfortable with. He could prove to Amanda's family that he could be trusted. He could try, at least. Abram was willing to help him with Simon, and that was a monumental step. Given time, Menno could show them he was a man who'd be good to Amanda.

What could he not change? His family. His brothers. His *mamm* . . .

Menno tossed the bottle into the box, glass clattering. Then he picked up the last bottle, unscrewed the lid, and began to pour. He couldn't even let himself sniff the bottle—that would be too much temptation.

Somehow this would be easier with a witness to watch him do it—someone to see if he cheated and took just one swig. But he did have a witness. Gott above was watching. And Menno wouldn't take any chances with backsliding into drunkenness again.

The last bottle emptied, he tossed it into the box. He felt better with this chore complete. He'd done it. He'd emptied out nine bottles without tasting a drop. That was a victory! *Danke, Gott.*

The sound of a car on his drive caught his attention, and he looked up to see a taxi creeping down the gravel lane. Was it Simon coming back, one last-ditch effort to share the farm? He half expected his brother to give it a try, just to see if Abram had been serious. Simon was no respecter of the Amish community.

But then the taxi slowed to a stop. The driver turned around and seemed to be conversing with the passenger. The door opened, and a middle-aged *Englischer* stepped out. She had graying hair cut in a bob around her face, and she wore a floral-patterned sundress.

Who would this be? Someone lost? Because she didn't belong here. He'd better find out before her cab left.

"Can I help you?" he called, taking a stride in her direction.

The woman looked up, her gaze locked onto his, and his heart skipped two whole beats.

"Menno?" she said.

"*Mamm* . . ."

The cab started to back up, and Menno took another step closer to his mother. Linda Weaver looked so different—the clothes, her hair, the lines on her face—she was like a completely different person, clean, well-kept, and healthy. She even wore a little makeup that softened her features and made her look even less Amish. But he could see his mother in there too.

"Menno, how are you?" Mamm asked, her voice shaking.

"I'm fine." Was this really what they were going to say after thirteen years of silence? "How are you?"

"I'm doing better."

"Good." He pulled off his hat and scraped a hand through his hair.

"Your brothers said that you're the one who straightened out," she said with a familiar lopsided smile. "I'm glad to hear that."

So polite. So pleasant. As if she hadn't walked out on him when he needed her most, and the grief of his adolescent self suddenly roared up inside of him. He'd missed his mother so much. He'd lain in bed at night—the nights he wasn't in a drunken stupor avoiding his feelings—and he'd cried bitter tears into his pillow. Because she'd not just left his father, she'd left them all. None of them had been worth staying for.

Green Pastures

"But it was no thanks to you, was it?" Menno snapped, and she recoiled as if he'd slapped her.

"Son, I'm so sorry," Mamm said. "I tried to practice what I would say to you. I wanted to explain myself. I was so beaten down. I was so broken. I ended up in a hospital for a long time, and when I finally got myself together, I didn't have the strength to face your *daet* again. I just couldn't."

"But you left us *with him*. You left us to deal with him day in and day out."

"I don't have a good excuse," she said. "I did come back once, and I saw you and your brothers all drunk just like him, and . . . I crept away again."

So she'd seen them at their worst. Maybe they'd scared her. He swallowed hard, and tears misted his vision. His mother was back, and after all these years of rehearsing the things he'd tell her when he had the chance, he found himself empty.

"Well, I stopped drinking," Menno said. "And I'm running this place now that Daet's dead. I'm making a success of it too."

"He's really dead," she whispered. "I still find that hard to grasp. I'm sorry."

"Are you?" he asked.

"Of course I am. I loved him once. But things got so bad."

"I can show you his grave," Menno said. "It might help to see it."

Sometimes Menno would go by the graveyard with its rows of simple Amish headstones and look down at his father's. He was dead now—beyond his addictions, beyond his mistakes.

"I'm proud of you," she said quietly.

"Simon's a wreck—you should know that," Menno said.

284

"He's drunk most of the time, and he's a burden to everyone. Emmanuel's got things together for himself, but he's not Amish anymore. Doesn't look like you are either. How's Daniel? I heard he's the one who got in touch with you."

"Daniel is married," she said. "He has a one-year-old daughter."

Menno blinked at her. He didn't know that. Daniel was a *daet* now?

"Did you want to come inside?" Menno asked.

His mother looked hesitantly toward the house, and it was like he could see her memories flashing before her eyes. No, she wouldn't want to come in—he could see that.

"Maybe we could go look at the pigs," he said.

She nodded then. "*Yah*, let's look at the pigs."

They walked side by side toward the nearest pen. The hogs were lounging in the summer light, luxuriating in the last of the warm sun. They stayed a couple of feet apart, and Menno stole another look at his mother.

"Mamm, I missed you," he said softly.

"I missed you too." Her chin quivered. "Oh, Menno. I was a terrible mother. I know it. I can't even forgive myself for it. I should have stood up to you boys and made you listen. I should have gone to the bishop and the elders. I shouldn't have run away—or maybe I should have taken you boys with me and done it sooner. I don't know. What I think I should have done depends on the day. But I've gotten stronger now, and I finally got the courage to come find you again. I just hope it isn't too late."

"You aren't shunned," he said, and it seemed like the most ridiculous thing to tell her, but it did mean something to him. The community hadn't judged her harshly. They'd understood.

"I'm not?" She frowned. "I should be."

"I think they were hoping you'd come back," Menno replied. "Abram Shrock told me that they felt bad for not helping you more."

"Oh . . ."

An image of Tabitha Schrock back in her Amish clothes with a pair of stout rubber boots on her feet came to mind. People got second chances . . . Gott gave second chances! Maybe his *mamm* could get one too.

"You're *Englischer* now?" he asked.

"*Yah*. I can't be Amish again, son. It's too much for me. I found a place where I can just be me, and I'm safe. I work a job at a department store, and I have a little apartment. I attend church, and I have some friends."

But she wasn't shunned, and that meant they could see each other. They had very strict rules in this community, but there was also fairness and compassion.

"Do you have a new man in your life?" he asked. "A boyfriend?"

She nodded. "His name is Ken. He's a mechanic. He's kind to me."

She could marry him now, if she wanted to. Now that she knew her husband was dead.

"But I had to come see you," Linda went on. "If I'm not shunned, maybe I can come again."

Menno nodded. "*Yah*. I could make you a meal. I could introduce you to my . . ." What should he call Amanda? "To my girlfriend."

"You have a special girl?" she asked with a smile.

"*Yah*."

"Are you in love?"

He nodded.

286

PATRICIA JOHNS

Tears welled in her eyes. "That's the most I could ask for my boys—that they have someone who loves them and takes care of them. I'm glad."

Menno looked back toward the house again. He longed to show her what he'd done with it, maybe make her a sandwich.

"Are you afraid to come in?" he asked gently.

Mamm nodded. "Maybe on my next visit I'll come inside. I'm just—" She licked her lips. "There are a lot of memories that still haunt me, Menno."

Yah, he had quite a few of those too. But he hadn't had the luxury of leaving them behind. Maybe she hadn't either, for that matter, since she couldn't even step inside the house.

"Could I ask for one thing?" she asked hesitantly.

Ah, here it was. The reason she'd come back. Was she an addict too? Maybe it was too critical of him, but it would explain her reappearance rather well. Unfortunately for her, his tin of cash was empty, thanks to Simon.

"Do you want money?" he asked tiredly. "Because Simon comes for money on a regular basis. I've stopped giving it to him, and I'm not giving you any either. Whatever it is you're wanting—"

"No." She shook her head. "I want to hug you."

For a moment he stood motionless. His chest filled with sadness and hope and love and heartbreak, so full that he thought he might burst from it all. Then he nodded.

Mamm stepped forward, reached up, and tugged Menno down to her level. She wrapped her arms around his neck and began to rock him slowly back and forth. It was then that the tears started.

Some were his, and some were hers, but outside in the lowering light of a rosy sunset, mother and son cried together.

When their tears were spent, they sat on the porch with kerosene light enveloping them, and they talked about everything they'd missed in the last thirteen years. Menno memorized her face again, every line, every wrinkle, even the way her lipstick wore away at the center of her lips, leaving only a pink line around the edges.

Mamm wouldn't stay. But she promised she'd come back again, and Menno realized that he would be all right with that.

Menno's heart was circling around another woman—Amanda Schrock—and he wanted to start a home with her, and they'd be each other's deepest comfort. Because Gott was the Gott of second chances, and he felt that with rock-solid certainty. But Menno longed to introduce his mother to Amanda. He had a feeling that Amanda would understand his mixed-up emotions. She might even give words to them. And then his mother could see the woman who'd stolen his heart.

Amanda was his future. . . . Oh, may Gott be willing.

38

Tabitha leaned over a pot and scrubbed hard. The plates were lined up next to some serving bowls, and the cutlery stood up in the plastic cup reserved for it. Supper was finished, and Daet was in the living room with a recent copy of the *Budget*. The gravy pot had boiled over and was burned on the bottom, so Tabitha was scrubbing with steel wool, the scrubber pushing into her fingers painfully.

It was strange. The more time she spent settling back into her community, the more she was convinced that her wisdom gleaned from her own pain was not what she needed to contribute to life in Shepherd's Hill. Even her career, while useful and interesting, wasn't enough either. Jobs could come and go. Making her whole identity a job was a dangerous thing to do.

There was a knock on the door, and Daet shuffled back from the sitting room to open it. Tabitha looked over her shoulder and saw Jonas in the doorway.

"Good evening, Abram," Jonas said. "I was hoping Tabitha might come take a look at . . . at our new horse."

So Fritz was sick again. The poor horse. Enough was

enough. If she had to use her own savings to buy the horse back, she was willing to at this point. Fritz needed to come home where she could care for him properly.

Daet stepped back and ushered the younger man inside.

"Is he getting worse?" Tabitha asked, wiping her hands on a dish towel and circling around the counter.

"*Yah*, he is, and the medication doesn't seem to be working this time," Jonas said.

She untied her kitchen apron and hung it on a peg. "I just need a couple of minutes to get my things together."

She looked over at her father, and Daet just stood there, his lips pressed together in a firm line. He wouldn't meet Tabitha's gaze.

"I'll stay and finish cleaning up," Amanda said.

Tabitha shot her sister a tired smile.

"I'll go with you to the Peachy farm," Daet said after a beat of silence. "I need to have a chat with Nathaniel anyway."

Tabitha glanced at Jonas, and Jonas raised one eyebrow in silent question. But Tabitha didn't know what her father had in mind, and Daet turned his back and set about putting on his boots.

"You two go on ahead, and I'll follow in our own buggy once I hitch up," Daet said.

"*Yah*?" Tabitha asked Jonas.

He nodded.

"See you there, Daet," Tabitha said.

Her father didn't look up, still not meeting her gaze. "*Yah*. See you there."

Maybe Daet was going to make it right—she could hope. She followed Jonas out to his buggy, and she tossed her bag up onto the passenger seat, then hoisted herself up.

"*Danke* for coming so quickly," Jonas said, flicking the reins so that they started forward.

"Of course," she replied. She looked over her shoulder as her father came out of the house. "Have you told your *daet* about who owned that horse before you?"

"I told you I wouldn't," he replied.

"So . . . you didn't?" She wanted to be absolutely sure what she would be facing when they reached the Peachy farm.

"I said I wouldn't, and I didn't," Jonas said. "You can trust my word, Tabitha."

They arrived at the Peachy farm in good time. Tabitha headed across the recently mown lawn toward the stable while Jonas unhitched his buggy. She spotted Jonas's *mamm*, Mary, pushing a mower through the backyard. The mower shushed along through the grass, leaving the fresh scent of grass clippings in the air. The older woman gave her a nod.

"Good evening, Mary," Tabitha called.

Mary waved, then started to push the mower again, and Tabitha carried on toward the horse barn beyond. She walked briskly, her anxiety leading tonight. When she got to the barn, she let herself inside.

What would Mary think when she found out about the horse? Her opinions mattered too. She'd tell her closest friends about it, and the news would spread.

But Tabitha was more immediately concerned about Fritz. The stable was dim but not too hot. There was a cooling cross draft coming in from the opened back doors that led out into a corral and some high windows that had been opened up for the same purpose. Fritz was lying down in his stall, and when she opened the stall door, he looked up at her and nickered wearily. The poor fellow.

"Hey, Fritz," she murmured. "I'm back. How're you doing?"

His side trembled under her touch, and his stomach was bloated. He was in pain—that much was very clear.

"What are they feeding you, huh?"

Tabitha opened her bag and pulled out the bottle of mineral oil. The horse had done better under her direct care, but that was beside the point now. He was no longer their horse. She filled the plastic syringe with a dose of mineral oil, and the horse shook his head as she eased the spout behind his teeth and squirted it toward his throat.

Then she stood up and looked into his feed bin. He had hay, but it wasn't the same high quality he was used to. This wasn't bad hay, but Fritz had a finicky stomach, and only the best would do. But she could only advise. What the owner did with his own animal was his own business, and that might be the most challenging part of this job.

She spent a few minutes petting Fritz and talking to him gently. It wasn't his fault that his digestion was so testy, and if he'd been with another family, they wouldn't have had the patience with him. Fritz was supposed to be a workhorse. His big liquid eyes shone with that depth of soul that horses had. Whatever his job was supposed to be, he was still a feeling, intelligent creature created by Gott.

"I'm going to find a way to bring you home," she said softly.

The barn door opened, and she looked over to see Jonas come inside.

"You've got to get him new feed," Tabitha said, rising to her feet.

"You said hay."

"*Yah*, and he needs higher quality, or this will keep happening. I'm sorry—I know it costs more, but this horse needs it. If you get him balanced on the best hay, you won't have these problems with his gut."

Jonas leaned against the rail, and Tabitha squatted down to put her supplies back into her bag.

"Your *daet* is out there buying the horse back."

"He is?" Tabitha rose to her feet. "Right now?"

"*Yah.* He brought a check with him."

"And your *daet* agreed?"

"Readily." Jonas smiled faintly. "I guess that means you won't have much reason to be coming by here. Not so often, at least."

"Are you saying you'll miss my pleasant company, Jonas?" Tabitha teased.

"I'll say this," Jonas said, thoughtfully. "You're not what I expected when you came back. I didn't think you'd find your place here again. I thought you'd be eyeing the fence. But you've . . . found a way."

"I'm not leaving Shepherd's Hill," she replied.

"I think I believe you."

Tabitha met Jonas's honest gaze, and a realization flooded through her.

"I've been struggling with where I fit in here, you know," Tabitha said. "I thought maybe my contribution in our community would be the wisdom gleaned from my own mistakes, but it turns out that my advice isn't as needed as I thought."

"No?" Jonas said.

"Shocking, I know." She shot him a wry smile. But all of her attempts at giving advice seemed to fall short for her sisters. It was humbling to realize the best thing she could do for her sisters was stand back and love them.

"You bring yourself," Jonas said with a shrug. "That's the

only thing any of us bring to this community. There is that verse that talks about storing up for ourselves treasures in heaven, where moth and rust can't destroy. The treasures—it's us. Relationships. People. You don't have to bring some big offering, Tabitha. It's great that you can be our veterinarian, but it wasn't the price of admission around here. You only had to bring yourself."

Tabitha bent down to stroke the horse's shoulder, attempting to hide the mist in her eyes, then she straightened. "Does that mean we're friends, Jonas?"

"I think we qualify." Jonas opened the gate for her to exit the stall and then closed it again after her.

"Are our fathers going to turn their swords into plowshares?" she asked, heading toward the stable door.

"It's definitely a start," he replied. "They're too old to keep battling anyway. And, Tabitha?"

She paused, her hand on the door handle.

"It's because of you, you know. If you'd never come home, they'd still be at it. Your *daet* would never have come to make peace. My *daet* would have done something in retaliation. It would have continued."

Maybe she had made a difference. She wasn't a girl anymore, and as a grown woman, she did have more influence. That was a comforting thought. Things had changed in good ways too.

Tabitha opened the door, and outside by the house, she could see the two old men standing a couple of paces apart. They seemed to be talking. Nathaniel was digging his heel into the dirt, and Daet had his thumbs in his suspenders. But they were conversing. Then Daet wiped a hand down the side of his pants and held it out to Nathaniel.

Nathaniel took a moment, but he reached out, and the men clasped hands and shook.

"It's probably just the deal for the horse," Tabitha murmured.

"Probably," Jonas agreed.

And maybe it was something more. Though friendship might be asking too much. Regardless, it was a beginning between these two men who'd been battling each other for decades. It was a step in the right direction.

39

That evening, in the warmth of the kitchen kerosene light, Amanda listened as her sister and father discussed their plans to hire a truck with a horse trailer to pick up Fritz at the Peachy farm. A moth fluttered up against the window screen, drawn toward the light, and outside Amanda could hear the trill of crickets.

Fritz was coming home, and Tabitha would give him the care he was used to. Amanda was glad to hear that. The poor horse had been suffering, although not because of neglect or mistreatment. He just needed Tabitha.

Amanda's gaze moved up to that embroidery hanging on the wall, and she let her mind sift through fragmented memories of their mother. The flash of a smile, the sound of her voice, the way she'd bang the door shut on her way out to gather eggs . . . It was funny what details a child's mind would hold on to.

Those careful stitches had become a part of their home, and somehow they held Vannetta Schrock in the center of things—the way she would have been had she lived.

The Lord is my shepherd; I shall not want.
He maketh me to lie down in green pastures: he lead-
eth me beside the still waters.
He restoreth my soul.

This psalm was one about peace and comfort, but Amanda wasn't yearning for peace right now. She needed more—something in her life to shake up and change. She'd wanted that to be a husband and a wedding, but maybe it wouldn't be, after all.

That thought brought a lump to her throat. She missed Menno even though she saw him just this afternoon. Just the thought of him touched a part of her heart so deep and tender that it ached. She loved him, she realized. She well and truly loved the man . . . as unhelpful as that was.

"What did you say to Nathaniel?" Tabitha asked, and Amanda tuned back in to her father and sister's conversation, trying to shake off her own sadness.

"I apologized. I said I thought the horse was well again, and I was wrong," Daet replied.

That was a big thing to admit to Nathaniel Peachy, even if Daet was pretending it wasn't much now. She knew what it took to humble himself before that man.

"It was the right thing to do," Tabitha said.

Her father shrugged. "I thought I had a miracle. I really did."

"Maybe the miracle was between you and Nathaniel instead," Tabitha said. "I'll take care of Fritz. He'll be fine with me. But you and Nathaniel talking again? That took Gott's intervention, for sure and for certain."

And Amanda knew that sometimes Gott's answers were complicated. Sometimes a person could pray for one thing, like a chance to marry a particular man, and Gott might have something else in mind altogether. Maybe Gott was simply bestowing wisdom through experience, like Tabitha had gotten. Was that all this had been with Menno—a chance to learn about people and relationships without going through a difficult marriage of her own? Was she supposed to be grateful to have avoided that heartache?

And while Amanda was glad that Nathaniel and her *daet* seemed to be mending fences between them, and while she was glad that Rose and Aaron seemed to be doing the same, her own heart was in turmoil. Because all she could think of was Menno—his kindness, his gentle eyes, his bravery . . . even that relaxed way he had around *Englischers* that was both admirable and unnerving at the same time. And from just the thought of ending their courtship, she missed him so much already that her throat closed off with the weight of it.

That night, Amanda lay in bed with a light quilt on top of her, her window cranked open, feeling the whisper of night breezes against her arm and face. She'd been naïve to think that she could simply choose a man and marry him. Why did everyone throw young people at marriage as if it was the most natural thing in the world? Without advanced warning about all the potential heartbreak awaiting, at that. They just told a young woman that if she loved her husband, was respectful, cooked meals he enjoyed, and kept a tidy house, that all would be well.

Nothing could be further from the truth!

Rose knew how to be a good wife. The best homemaking in the world didn't make for a happy home. What else did an Amish woman have to offer? They weren't like the *Englischers* who might have careers or other skills they brought to a marriage. An Amish woman brought her cooking, her cleaning, her handcrafts, her home economics. She brought her heart and her hopes and dreams. And if a man looked at all of that and couldn't love her? What was a woman supposed to do? Perhaps the best warning she could receive would be from Gott himself.

Oh, Gott, guide me, she prayed. *I don't know what to do. I do love Menno. That might be silly. It might be weakness on my part, but I do love him. And I'm terrified that loving him will not be enough. What are you trying to show me? Please be clearer.*

Amanda fell into a fitful sleep that night, without any answers from above, and she awoke the next morning feeling crumpled and tired.

She did her morning chores, and Tabitha helped make breakfast. This morning was corn bread with applesauce on top of it, boiled eggs, bacon, sausage, and oatmeal on the side. Everyone had a busy day ahead, and they needed the energy to do their work.

"Are you coming with me today?" Tabitha asked as she pulled the bubbling pot of oatmeal off the stove.

"*Yah*, I'll come," Amanda replied. It was better than sitting at home with her thoughts. And perhaps she'd better get used to working and finding her fulfillment outside of the home like her sister did. Not every woman got a husband and children.

"I'm going to start off here at home," Tabitha said. "Daet and I are going to change the cast on the bull's leg, then we can head out to my first call."

Amanda heard a buggy outside, and she looked out the window to see that Rose had arrived. Finally, she had come back to visit again. Did that mean all was well at home now?

Amanda opened the side door for her and waited while she hopped down and came up the steps.

Rose followed her inside, and the screen door clapped shut behind them.

"How is Aaron?" Amanda asked. "Is everything okay now?"

Rose nodded. "*Yah*, it's a lot better. We're working on it. Elder Yoder and his wife helped us a lot—just talking about how marriage works, and what we can expect from each other."

"So that's it?" Tabitha asked with a relieved smile. "Everything's fixed?"

"*Yah*. I mean, it was hours of talking, and a few other things that are too personal for me to talk about, but *yah*. We'll be okay."

"And his family?" Amanda pressed.

"He'll go talk to his parents and explain things." Rose sat down at the kitchen table. "This has been the worst time of my life. I've never been through a more difficult time, but I gained something through it in my relationship with Gott. When I was most alone, Gott was with me, and the comfort I got, and the reassurance that I needed to see this through— that came from him. I don't know how to explain it, exactly."

"Gott got closer?" Amanda asked softly.

Rose nodded. "So much closer."

"Menno said that it's like turning to Gott as a friend," Amanda said. It was more to herself than to her sisters, but Rose's eyes lit up.

"*Yah*, just like that."

"Gott gets closer in the valleys," Tabitha murmured.

Maybe they'd all experienced it lately—the intimacy with Gott that came through the hardest of times.

"Speaking of Menno," Rose said. "How is he?"

"Amanda has been seeing him," Tabitha supplied with a pleased little smile. "They've been spending quite a bit of time together."

"Are you two talking about marriage?" Rose asked.

"Sort of . . ." Amanda said. "But obviously I have a few hesitations. Menno comes with issues. He was raised in a very dysfunctional home. His *mamm* left. His *daet* abused them. His brothers drink. He didn't learn what a happy marriage looks like by watching his parents. He's a good man, and he wants a good Amish life, but he's . . ."

"A risk," Tabitha concluded.

"And, Rose, you and Aaron have everything in common. There was nothing worrisome about Aaron, and you and he still went through such a painful patch. What about Menno? What difficult valleys would be waiting for me? It's one thing to stumble into one, but it's another thing entirely to walk into it knowingly."

The women fell silent, and Amanda's heart clenched in her chest. She'd said too much, but all of it was true. And she needed answers.

"Do you love him?" Rose asked at last.

Amanda felt her face heat, but she nodded.

"And he loves you?" Tabitha asked.

Amanda nodded again.

"Aaron might appear to have everything together, but his parents didn't show affection at home," Rose said quietly. "He never even saw them sit on the same side of the table. So he thought that was how a godly couple behaved. And this morning, it was a big step for him to kiss me before he left to do chores. But he did it. And it's going to take time."

"And you're okay with that?" Amanda asked.

"That's what a marriage is . . . it's time," Rose replied. "I finally understand him better, and I'm grateful for that. Do I want him to just immediately become a warm and affectionate man? Of course. Will he, though? He'll try. I'll try. We'll do better. Maybe I'll learn to understand how he shows love and appreciate it. But I realized that I don't want to lose him, and our relationship is worth the work."

Tabitha smiled wistfully. "That's beautifully said, Rose."

"So . . . it isn't fixed?" Amanda asked. "I'm sorry to be so nosey, Rose, but this is important to me."

"It's not perfect," Rose said. "But we don't want to lose each other, so we're willing to keep putting in the effort. So I feel much better. I know that he loves me. I needed to know that."

Effort. Work. Marriage was not an easy path, was it? And yet marriage had matured Rose. This woman talking about marriage being about time wasn't the same younger sister from even a week ago. If Amanda ended their courtship, would someone else support Menno when he was tempted to turn to alcohol again? Amanda felt a jealous rush at that thought.

"How do you know if a man will cause you trouble?" Amanda asked.

Tabitha and Rose exchanged a solemn look.

"Sometimes you don't," Rose replied after a beat of silence. "Sometimes . . . he's just worth the challenges you will face."

"That's what you decide, I suppose," Tabitha said. "First of all, will he be faithful to you? And if he will, then do you love him enough that you're willing to work through the tough times to be with him? Only you can answer that."

Daet's heavy footsteps sounded on the stairs outside,

and that was their cue to stop talking about relationships. Amanda turned toward the stove to fetch the boiled eggs. The day was beginning.

Rose would go home to her husband and her own home. Tabitha and Amanda would head out to the day's veterinarian calls. Daet would work the farm.

But deep in Amanda's heart, a new question was brewing, mingled with the tenderness that just kept growing between her and the man she was afraid to trust.

Was Menno worth a lifetime of hard work and devotion? Somehow, she knew she was finally hearing Gott's voice after all this time of silence from above. And his voice was warm like green summer pastures, and deep and still like cool waters, and it echoed like love.

40

After breakfast, Tabitha and her father tramped out to the barn. The sun was high in the sky now, and the morning dew had dried. Beyond the barn, the cattle grazed out in the pasture, tails swishing. A calf ran around its mother, playfully kicking up its hooves. Tabitha paused to drink in the scene, and her heart fluttered in her chest at the sheer beauty of it all.

Even though her future would look different than she imagined, and even though she'd very likely never see marriage again, she did have a place here in Shepherd's Hill, and a place in Gott's plan. His ways looked different from theirs, and while life here was often about marriages and growing families, Tabitha was still someone's daughter.

Her rubber boots felt chilly against her bare legs, and she picked up her pace to match her father's stride.

"I hope the bull's leg is healing well," Daet said.

"I think it is, Daet. Once this cast is changed, we won't have to change it again until we take it off for good."

They headed into the barn. The bull was in a large stall, and he blinked at them and huffed a breath through his nostrils. They'd have to get him out of his stall and into the pasture, then into the squeeze chute again so that she could inspect his leg.

"You ready?" she asked.

"Ready as I'll ever be."

She opened the door to the barn, the scent of grass flowing into the stuffy interior and making the bull look longingly toward that open door. *Yah*, she could understand the pull toward freedom. She'd use it to get him moving in the direction she needed him to go. Then she pulled open his gate, and the bull lumbered in a limping gallop toward the outside door. Tabitha grabbed a flexible stick and jogged behind him.

"Tabitha, be careful," her father said behind her.

Tabitha didn't bother answering. Her attention was on the bull. This time he wasn't in pain—hobbled by the cast but not in pain. When an animal was in pain, it could lash out unpredictably, but it could also be corralled more easily. This bull would be able to think things through . . . and he might have a grudge.

"Come on, now," Tabitha said. She came up behind the bull, keeping within his line of sight. All she wanted to do was crowd him a bit, make him want to keep moving to stay out of her reach. And he did that but also shied away from the chute gate. They went around again, and Tabitha hung back a bit more this time.

"Do you want help?" her father asked.

"No, Daet, I'm good."

When the bull came close to the chute again, she took a step forward and spread her arms. The bull snorted and danced right into the chute. Her father leapt forward and swung the gate shut with a clang.

"Nicely done," he said.

"*Danke.*" She shot her father a grin. "Let's keep him moving."

They pushed the bull farther into the chute, and when his head came out the head gate, Tabitha pulled the handle that activated the squeeze chute.

"We'll need to dope him up just a bit." Tabitha reached for her bag. She had the syringe ready, and she pushed it into the muscle in his neck. She stood back. "Now we wait."

The bull was fighting the sedative, which only meant it would take a little longer. If he had the strength to be stubborn, then he was doing well. Tabitha crossed her arms over her chest to wait.

"So Rose and Aaron are going to be okay?" Tabitha asked.

Her father nodded. "*Yah.*"

"I thought they were going to split up, you know," she said.

"Because you did." Her father shook his head. "I'm not saying that in judgment. But you were seeing things through the lens of your own experiences. You were afraid for your sister. Your heart was in the right place."

"Are you telling me you weren't worried?" she asked.

The bull settled, his eyes half closed. The sedative was taking effect. Tabitha knelt in the grass and reached for that front leg. The bull allowed her to move the joint easily. She pulled out a little battery-operated saw to cut through the fiberglass, biting her lip as she focused on the awkward job.

"You said that's what a divorce looks like," Daet said.

"Because that is what divorce looks like in the beginning," she replied as she worked on the cast. "I know that feeling—the emptiness, the heartbreak, the loneliness . . ."

"Do you know what I saw?"

"What's that, Daet?"

"I saw the pain just before growth."

Tabitha eased back to a seated position and looked at her father. "Have you seen this before?"

"Of course. You've seen this with *Englischer* couples. I've seen this with the Amish."

And maybe Tabitha hadn't seen enough of Amish relationships and marriages. She'd left when she was old enough to think she knew everything and young enough to hardly know a thing.

"So what happens with Amish couples?" she asked.

"The husband and wife both grow up a little bit," her father replied. "Your mother and I went through it. I know others who have too. You go through a difficult patch. You see no way forward, you're both dug in. And then you realize that you're only hurting yourself. You figure out that you have to adjust somehow or break. So . . . you both bend. And both are better for it. They're stronger. They're wiser. They're more forgiving. When leaving is not an option, the only other choice is to grow. Marriage is like that. It forces two people to mature in ways they never would if they were apart. Sometimes that maturing process hurts, but it ends up bringing them closer."

Tabitha leaned back down to apply the little saw once more, her arm at an awkward angle as she cut through the last of the fiberglass.

"I didn't have that possibility with Michael," she said.

"I know," he replied.

"I would have worked through just about anything, but the other woman won." Even saying it now, there was a pang of pain that came with the acknowledgment. When things got hard, he'd chosen another woman. He hadn't chosen growth. It took two people, after all.

The cast finally snapped, and she muscled it apart and

eased it off the bull's leg. She moved the joint and felt for inflammation or any tender areas, then she pulled out more padding and another package of fiberglass wrap.

"How's the leg?" Daet asked.

"Doing really well," she assured. "We can return him to Leroy Lapp with this cast on when I'm finished."

Daet met her gaze. "*Danke*, Tabitha. This is a load of worry off my mind."

"It's what I do, Daet."

He was silent for a moment. "It's a good thing you're back. Your sisters need you."

"I'm not sure I was much help," she said.

"Don't sell yourself short," he replied. "Rose needed to hear that she could lose her marriage. Sometimes people need to know what they stand to lose. And Amanda is frustrated by being stuck at home with me still. I understand. She wants more, and you've shown her that a woman can make more for herself."

"She's thinking of marrying Menno, you know," Tabitha said.

Daet sighed. "He's a decent man, but his family is a concern."

They were both silent for a moment.

"She loves him," Tabitha said.

He nodded slowly. "She loves him."

"Not every woman can just sit at home and wait to be courted, Daet," Tabitha said. "It's not Amanda's fault that the men didn't see what she offers. Sometimes a woman has to be a little more creative in getting the life she longs for."

"I wanted an easier path for her," he murmured.

Easier than marrying a Weaver. Easier than loving a Weaver. Easier than what he'd watched Tabitha go through.

PATRICIA JOHNS

Tabitha understood that. But she wouldn't have been satisfied with staying in Shepherd's Hill and marrying a kind Amish farmer. She'd have always looked toward that fence. The most painful irony was that by going out and fully experiencing a life in the world, she'd finally recognized the value of what she'd left behind . . . one marriage too late. And Tabitha and Amanda were more alike than people thought.

"Amanda would get bored with an easy solution," Tabitha said. "At least Menno's Amish. She's got a fierce heart, and she loves hard. I think she'll be okay."

309

41

That afternoon after a busy day with her sister doing more vaccinations, Amanda squatted in the garden picking some peas and dropping them into a metal bowl. Tabitha and their father had the bull loaded up into a hired cattle trailer, and Daet stood talking with the driver, his arms crossed over his chest, his words not making it far enough for Amanda to overhear.

Amanda had been in a knot of nerves all day. What she wanted to do was talk things out with Menno, but there was only so much a woman could do to chase a man. And Amanda had done quite enough of that. Their last conversation, he'd been warm and spoke about seeing her again. He was buying a new buggy. That took time, and men took buggy selections very seriously. So she should wait.

Right? That was the right thing to do? Except the right thing seldom turned into results for Amanda. She'd done the right thing all her life and what had it gotten her? She'd asked her sister, and Tabitha only said that she couldn't give advice and Amanda needed to do what she felt she needed to do. Entirely unhelpful!

Amanda bent back down and continued to pluck plump, round pods. If she didn't pick them now, they'd only over-ripen. This might not be the home she shared with a husband, but it was her home, and like Rose, Amanda took pride in her ability to keep a tidy home and garden.

The driver got back up into the truck, and Daet slapped the side of the trailer in a farewell. The bull would be heading back to its owners, a job well done with the cows here and his leg healed well enough to travel.

And just as the truck started forward, it stopped again, and a buggy came past the truck. Then the truck revved to life once more and rumbled up the drive. Amanda's heart skipped a beat as she spotted Menno with the reins in his hands. It wasn't a new courting buggy—that would take a few more days, she imagined—but it was Menno. His tense gaze skimmed over the yard and landed on her. Then he smiled, all of that tension evaporating.

He'd come. She felt like her entire body was sighing in relief at the sight of him. But before she could even take a step in his direction, her father raised his hand in greeting.

"Menno," Daet called. "Good to see you. How are the hogs?"

Daet headed over in Menno's direction, and the younger man turned his attention to her father. Tabitha fell back and headed over to the garden. Amanda stepped over a row of cabbages and headed back out to the grass with her bowl of peas.

"Look who's arrived," Tabitha said with a knowing smile.

"*Yah*, I see that." Amanda watched the men standing there talking. Their voices were pitched low again, and she couldn't hear what was said. She wasn't supposed to bother with conversations between men. They weren't her business. But she was so tired of what she was supposed to do.

"I think he's come for you," Tabitha said.

"Then why am I not the one talking to him?" Amanda said, and she shook her head. "I get so sick of this, Tabitha. It's my life, my choice, my future. And yet I have to stand here and wait while the men who love me make decisions for my life."

"They aren't making decisions for you," Tabitha said. "I used to think that. I ran away from it. But do you know what's really happening over there?"

Amanda eyed the men—Menno nodding respectfully, and Daet talking earnestly.

"What's that?" Amanda asked.

"Daet is making peace with your choice," Tabitha said. "He knows he can't choose your future. We already talked about that, he and I. He's just trying to see what you see in Menno so that he can support you. That's all."

"Do you think?" Amanda asked.

"*Yah.*"

A lot had changed with Tabitha's return. A year ago, her father would have been giving orders. With Tabitha back, he'd stopped that. Tabitha's return to Shepherd's Hill had brought perspective.

The men parted, and Menno came over in her direction. He gave Tabitha a polite nod, then turned to Amanda.

"Would you let me take you for a buggy ride, Amanda?" His eyes said more, but they had people around them.

"*Yah,*" she said, and she couldn't help the smile that sprang to her lips. "When?"

"Are you free now?"

Amanda pushed the bowl of peapods into her sister's hands. "*Yah.* I'm free. Very free. Let's go."

She heard Tabitha laughing as she followed Menno toward

his buggy. Menno held out a hand to help her up, and she could feel her father's and sister's eyes on her as she put her hand in his. Menno was stronger than she thought, and he boosted her up, then headed around to the driver's seat. He settled in next to her and shot her a relieved smile. He flicked the reins, and they started around.

"I'm glad you came," Amanda said. "I thought you'd wait until you got your new buggy."

"Of course I came. I started looking at buggies, and I can't wait until I have the new one to show up in."

"Good." She cast him a smile.

"I said I would come see you. I'll always keep my word, Amanda."

As they went up the drive and out of sight of Daet and Tabitha, Amanda leaned back in the seat. Menno was silent as he steered them onto the road.

"I couldn't do this without your father's blessing," Menno said. "And he gave it."

"You're very proper, Menno," Amanda said with a low laugh. "Did you need his permission to take me out for a drive?"

"I need his blessing to court you." Menno looked over at her, and his gaze softened. "I don't want to waste time here. I'm not just taking you for a drive to get to know you. You know that. I want to court you properly, Amanda. I love you. I've never felt like this before, and I know that you're the one for me. I want to marry you." His voice broke then, and he looked away quickly.

The horse's hooves clopped at a steady rhythm, and another buggy passed them, but Amanda didn't even look to see who it was. Her heart hammered in her chest.

"My *mamm* came back," he added, and Amanda's mind

tumbled over the sudden change of topic. He wanted to marry her, and . . .

"She did? Is she at your farm?" she asked.

"No, she didn't stay, but she came to see me, and we talked."

"How do you feel about all of it?" she asked. Perhaps their talk of marriage could wait a minute or two.

"I'm okay." He gave her a warm smile. "It was good to see her. She'll come back again, and maybe given time, she'll even come back to being Amish."

"She's *Englische* now?"

He nodded, and maybe that wasn't a surprise. Linda Weaver had endured a lot.

"But after seeing her again, I realized that I don't want to waste time. I want to build a life with you, and I want to get married. I want to do this right—put some joy and happy memories into that old house."

"You want to marry me?" Amanda wanted to hear that part again, just so she could treasure it later.

"*Yah.* If you'd have me. Do you love me like I love you?"

"I do," she whispered.

He adjusted the reins into one hand and reached out to tug her closer against his side. She leaned into him, and it felt so very right.

"I'll keep our home private just for us," Menno said. "I'll get your *daet* and the rest of the community to help me with my brothers. I'll work hard, and I'll even be more social and go to the community events with you. I'll do whatever it is that will make you happy, if you'd just agree to be mine."

He took her fingers in his calloused grip, and her breath caught.

"What do you need to say yes?" he asked.

What did she need to be happy with this man? Suddenly, looking into those soft brown eyes, all of her previous fears faded away. Except for one.

"I need you to promise that we'll always talk things through," she said.

"That's it? Because that's easy."

Amanda cast about inside of herself, looking for some other key to the marriage she longed for, but there was nothing else.

"My sister and Aaron really struggled because they weren't hearing each other. They were battling each other. But they talked it out. I just don't want to get to that point before we talk things through. I want us to be open and say what we're feeling. That's what I want."

"Okay." Menno smiled. "You got it."

"Oh, and one more thing, we never sleep a single night away from each other. Not a single night. Unless one of us is in the hospital or something. But not by choice."

A mist came up in Menno's eyes, and he nodded, his chin trembling slightly. "Not a single night. You have my word."

"So . . ." She'd never done this before. She'd heard the stories girls told of how they'd gotten engaged, but they all seemed to know how this worked. Amanda and Menno were both a little awkward about it. "What does this mean?"

"I think it means we're getting married," Menno said, and he squeezed her hand. "*Yah?*"

"*Yah.*" She smiled, relief, happiness, and a wave of love flooding through her.

Menno leaned over and caught her lips in a kiss, but he couldn't linger and keep his eyes on the road. He straightened, and a shiver of happiness swept through her body.

"Do we tell my family when we get back?" she asked.

"Of course. It would hardly be official otherwise," Menno replied. "Besides, you need to plant more celery for wedding soup. I noticed your garden doesn't have nearly enough."

Amanda leaned her cheek against his shoulder, and suddenly a life with Menno didn't seem frightening at all. He was certainly worth all the work that marriage would entail. Because Amanda would be his, and Menno would be hers, and she could feel her heart closing around their future together in Shepherd's Hill.

With this man at her side, she'd found both the future she'd longed for and a deep, settling peace at the same time.

My cup runneth over.

EPILOGUE

That fall and winter, Menno worked his own farm, but he came down some evenings and helped Amanda's *daet* out with his chores too. Amanda knew he used it as an excuse to see her in the middle of the week, and she'd have fresh hand pies waiting for the men when they came back inside—made with love.

That time between Menno and her father seemed to do something for both men. Daet became more confident in his daughter's choice of husband-to-be, and Menno became more confident in his role as an Amish man in the community.

He started talking with the men more openly, and he told jokes that left them all in stitches. He was funnier than anyone realized, and with the support of Amanda's father, he seemed to be flourishing.

Normally, couples married in the fall, right after harvest. But Daet agreed that waiting to get married in the spring made sense so that they would have more time to prepare and more time for the families to adjust, namely Simon. So their banns were announced on a Service Sunday in April, and the Schrock farm was put in order for a wedding.

Menno had invited his *mamm* to the wedding, and she'd agreed to come. Amanda had met her twice over the winter, and both times she'd liked Linda Weaver a great deal. She even gave Amanda some Amish recipes she used to cook for her boys, and Amanda sensed the love and good intentions in the gesture.

So on the first Tuesday morning of May, Amanda stood in her bedroom—soon to be just a guest room here in her father's house—and adjusted the pins in her blue wedding cape dress in front of a mirror.

This morning, she missed her own mother a great deal. Her aunts had been standing in for Mamm's absence, but it wasn't the same.

Amanda leaned closer to the mirror to get a better view of the pin, when there was a tap on the door.

"Come in," Amanda said past another pin she had pressed between her lips.

The door opened with a familiar creak, and she looked up to see Tabitha in her *newehocker* pink dress.

"Do you need help?" Tabitha asked.

"*Yah*, this pin—" She let her sister adjust it for her, and then Tabitha stood back.

"You look lovely, Amanda," she said.

"*Danke*." She smoothed her hands over her new starched apron.

"Menno is a good man," Tabitha said. "You're going to be very happy."

"I know." She had no doubt of that. Over the last few months of their courtship, Menno had proven again and again how much he loved her. "*Danke* for coming home,

Tabitha. I don't think I would have had the courage to do what I did if it weren't for you coming back."

"When you and Menno start a family, just remember that you've got a sister who needs to dote on your *kinner* a whole lot, okay?" Tabitha said, tears in her eyes.

"Of course!"

Outside the window, Amanda could see more guests arriving. There was a big tent set up for the ceremony, and the young men and boys were arranging benches as if it were Service Sunday. Everyone knew what to do, and all a bride had to take care of was her own fluttering heart.

Her *newehockers* were all dressed in matching pink. Her sisters were standing in the role of bridesmaids for her wedding, along with a few of her friends. Out the window she spotted Katherine rushing past her field of view in a blur of blue cotton, chasing after a toddler. Life went on. There was another tap on the door.

"Amanda?" It was Rose this time. She was in her *newehocker* pink, too, and it brought out the blush in her cheeks. "Are you in there?"

Rose opened the door and poked her head inside. "Come on now, it's almost time to start. Time to come down."

Amanda sucked in a wavering breath. "Okay . . . Okay . . ."

"You look beautiful," Tabitha said.

"Come on," Rose said. "Let's go. People are getting seated. Menno's in the kitchen waiting for you."

Outside the window, Amanda heard the sound of voices rising a cappella in a hymn, but it was mention of Menno that calmed her nerves. He was waiting for her . . . and she wanted to be nowhere else but right by his side.

"I'm ready," Amanda said, and she meant that in every way possible. She was ready for all of it—the love, the adventure, the home together, the children, the mountain peaks, and the valleys.

Amanda headed for the staircase and for the man she adored. Today began the rest of their lives together, and the deepest prayer of her heart was answered.

Discussion Guide

1. When Tabitha returns to the Amish faith, she has to stand in front of the church community and confess her mistakes. How hard do you think it would be to tell everyone your biggest mistakes? Would you be able to do it?

2. When Tabitha left the community and the faith, her decision deeply affected Amanda's ability to get married and start her adult life. Was this really Tabitha's fault? How much responsibility for this should Tabitha take? And how much was because of Amanda's own choices?

3. Amanda decides to pursue Menno when she learns that he's looking for a wife. This is considered shocking in their community. Would you have taken such a daring step? How would you have handled it in her position?

4. Menno has a difficult past and comes from a problematic family. How cautious do you think Amanda should be considering those things? What questions do you think she should ask before letting her heart get involved with Menno?

5. Abram and Nathaniel have been feuding for years. It isn't Christianly, but because they haven't caused

trouble for anyone else, no one has sat them down and forced them to make peace. Do you think the community should have stepped in earlier and insisted the men made up? Or is it understandable to let grown men sort themselves out?

6. Tabitha returns to Shepherd's Hill as a full veterinarian. If she hadn't left the faith, she never would have been able to fulfill this lifelong desire. And she's good at her job and good for the community. Do you think it was God's will that she leave the community for a time? How do you reconcile this?

7. Tabitha's job as a veterinarian is considered a man's job to the Amish community. Have you ever worked a job in a male-dominated industry? What was your experience?

8. Tabitha wants to help Amanda find a husband, in part because she feels responsible for Amanda's single status. Have you ever tried to set a couple up before? What are the pitfalls?

9. Rose has been married for two years, and she's struggling to find happiness in her marriage. Have you ever experienced a tumultuous time in one of your relationships? What advice would you give to Rose?

10. Abram doesn't want to interfere in a young married couple's relationship. Do you think that Abram was right in his position that married couples require privacy?

11. Tabitha must live a single life in her community. Do you think this is fair? Do you think second chances should apply to people in her position too?

*Read on for a sneak peek
at the next book in*

THE AMISH OF
SHEPHERD'S HILL
SERIES

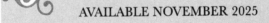

AVAILABLE NOVEMBER 2025

1

~~&~~

Friesen Lake was still and deep, nestled with the quietness of a prayer in the middle of the treed hill country on the far edge of Shepherd's Hill Amish church district. Chilly water lapped the rocky shore, and the pebbled lake bottom sank down in quick decline into the water, disappearing into crystal depths. At ninety feet at its deepest, where an underground spring fed the lake, even the summer heat never completely warmed the water, but that vast, sparkling expanse was tempting all the same, and Beth Peachy longed to swim.

In her many visits to see her grandmother in Shepherd's Hill, Beth had never been permitted to swim in this lake. Not when the weather was sweltering hot in the middle of August. Not when the *Englischers* in the cabins farther down the lakeshore were paddling around by the wharf, their laughter surfing the breeze. Mammi had forbidden swimming in this lake. Beth's *daet* had supported the rule, and no one in her family explained.

But that was what this family did—they kept secrets. Daet had never spoken about his childhood here, and there was no explanation for that either. Beth had been plying her mother with questions since Daet's death, though Mamm knew very little. But *why*? That question had plagued Beth since her father's passing last year. Why all the silence and secrecy surrounding their family?

Farther along the lakeshore, there was another Amish home nestled in next to the old ice house. Decades ago, the ice house used to provide ice for Amish ice boxes. They would harvest the ice in the winter and keep it in the insulated ice house all summer. But those days were past, and their community now used propane-powered refrigerators and freezers for their families' needs. The Lapp family owned those cabins beside the lake, where *Englischers* liked to stay, and they had recently renovated the old ice house into an attractive little cottage too. Beth could make out both the two-story house and the newly whitewashed cottage from here.

Beth shaded her eyes. Did Danny Lapp still live there with his parents? They had been friends, but Beth hadn't been to Shepherd's Hill in about three years—Mammi had come to them in Strasburg instead—and a lot could change in that amount of time.

Goldie barked hoarsely from the yard behind her. She was a twelve-year-old golden lab. Her face was white, and her torso was thick. She plodded around the property with the gate of a regal old woman. Mammi said that at their age, neither of them could be expected to have waistlines anymore.

"Beth?"

Beth turned back to wave at her grandmother, who bustled out the back door of the house. Mammi was as portly as Goldie was, with a round face and eyes that squinted so that they almost disappeared when she smiled. But she wasn't smiling now.

"Beth!" Mammi puttered over the grassy lawn, beckoning toward Beth. "Come away from there, Elizabeth. Come away. Come, come."

Mammi flapped her hands at Beth as if she were one of her chickens. Beth grinned but cooperated all the same. She'd arrived this morning to help her grandmother with housework and chores for the summer. Now in her late seventies, Mammi was starting to struggle with more than just the physical work. She'd been getting more forgetful lately, and she'd been having bouts of confusion. Beth's mother had told her that their family was looking for a grandchild to help Mammi, and Beth had volunteered for the task. It would provide Beth with some space and time to make her own decisions too.

"Mammi, I'm twenty-one," Beth said, crossing the rocky shore and heading back up to the grass. "I'm not a little girl anymore."

Surely those rules about swimming wouldn't apply now.

"The lake doesn't care how old you are," Mammi said. "Come sit on a chair on the lawn. You can see the water from there. It's a very nice view."

As Beth's feet touched the grass, a smile returned to her grandmother's weathered face, and the old woman turned around and bustled past a pair of white Adirondack chairs that sat in the shade of two cherry trees. Mammi had a large garden, too, and at only the beginning of June, her rows of vegetables were already flourishing.

"I'm a strong swimmer, you know," Beth said. "You don't need to worry about me, Mammi."

She'd brought her homemade bathing dress with her. It had a high neckline, short sleeves, and shorts underneath the knee-length skirt, so she was modestly covered. Her bishop back home in Strasburg had permitted them, as long as boys and girls weren't swimming together. Besides, no one from the Lapps' section of the beach would see what she was wearing once she was in the water.

"It's not safe," Mammi said.

"That's all you've ever said about it," Beth said. "But my *daet* taught me to swim."

Mammi silently met her gaze for a moment, pursing her lips.

"There are people who have drowned in that lake who were never found," Mammi said finally. "That lake holds more secrets than you can imagine. While you are here, Beth, you need to listen to me, or I will send you straight home. If you really are so grown up, then you'll understand that life is fragile, and it's prideful to take unnecessary risks. You are not less mortal than anyone else."

Beth looked at her grandmother in surprise. That was the most her grandmother had said about the lake in Beth's hearing. Ever.

"You'd send me home, Mammi?"

"If I have to." Mammi crossed her arms over her chest.

Beth cast the glistening lake one last look of longing, then put an accommodating smile on her face. She was here to help Mammi, not upset her.

"All right, Mammi. I won't swim."

"*Danke.*"

She followed her grandmother back in through the side door of the big three-story house. Goldie plodded after them, her back legs looking stiff. The dog stopped a couple of yards from the door, and when Beth bent down to give her a pet, Goldie yipped and shied away.

"Careful with her back end," Mammi said. "The poor girl is awfully sore these days."

"I'm sorry, Goldie," Beth whispered. She held a hand out to the dog, but Goldie wouldn't come close again. Beth straightened. She didn't blame her. She'd have to regain Goldie's affection. On her last visit, they'd had a lot of fun together. The dog padded stiffly over to Mammi's side.

This three-story house was big enough to house a large family, but it had only been home to Mammi and Beth's *daet*, Mose. Which bedroom had belonged to Beth's father? She didn't even know that. Had he slept on the second floor or the third? What had they done in this big rambling house, just the two of them? No one had ever said.

The side door led into a spacious kitchen. The windows were propped open to let in the cool air coming in from across the water. The wooden floors were polished to a glow with linseed oil, and the cupboards were freshly painted a bright white. The counters were a little cluttered, but Beth could help with that. Goldie plodded in after Mammi. The old dog stopped at the water bowl and took a slow drink.

A plate of glazed donuts waited on the counter, but Mammi went to a cupboard and pulled it open. Beth looked over her grandmother's shoulder. There were mugs, plates, and a single black walking shoe sitting on top of the plates.

"Mammi, why is that shoe in the cupboard?" Beth asked.

Her grandmother blinked at the shoe in confusion. "I don't know."

"Here, I'll take care of it." Beth pulled the shoe out and tucked it under her arm, then pulled the dishes out too. "I'll wash these for you."

"You should eat something," Mammi said, her cheeks growing pink in embarrassment, and she gestured toward the plate of donuts.

"Of course, Mammi. I'd love one," Beth said. She put

the dishes in the sink, and then brought the shoe over to the rack by the door. She didn't see its mate, but she put it into a free space all the same. Beth then went back to the sink and washed her hands.

"These are very good donuts," Mammi said. "Your *aent* Mary made them. She wanted you to have something special when you arrived."

Aent Mary was actually Mammi's niece and Beth's father's first cousin, but she'd been close in the family, and they'd lovingly dubbed her *aent*. The donuts did look delicious. Beth picked up a plump pastry and took a bite. She chewed slowly and nodded her appreciation.

"Good?" Mammi asked with a hopeful smile.

Beth nodded again. "Delicious."

"Aent Mary will come by to say hello," Mammi said. "She was so happy you were coming."

"That will be nice," Beth replied. Aent Mary was more open and talkative than most of Beth's extended family on her father's side. She was always fun to visit with, and she was full of news from all corners of the family, and that was why Beth liked her so much.

"I'm so glad you came too," Mammi said. "I've missed you, Elizabeth."

"I've missed you, too, Mammi. It was so nice when you came to see us, but I missed this house and Goldie and your good cooking."

Mammi smiled in response.

"I was hoping you'd tell me stories about my *daet* while I'm here," Beth added. "Ever since Daet passed away, I realized I don't know much about when he was little. I should have pestered him more to tell me stories."

"You miss your *daet*," Mammi said softly.

"I do. And I wish I knew more about him."

"What do you want to know?"

"What was my *daet* like as a *kind*?" Beth asked. That was an easy enough question to answer.

"He was a sweet boy," Mammi said, tears misting her eyes. "He was kind to everyone. To animals, to friends, to me . . . He was a very gentle child."

"What about when he was a baby?" Beth asked.

Mammi didn't answer. Was that her confusion, or the old refusal to speak of the past? Beth wasn't sure.

"What was his first word?" she pressed.

The old woman pushed herself to her feet and went over to the fridge. "I'll get you some milk to go with your donuts."

Evasion. It was like everyone except Aent Mary was so used to keeping secrets that they forgot how to talk about ordinary everyday things.

"Daet was like this, too, you know," Beth said. "I don't understand it. Why does no one talk about the past?"

"There's nothing to tell about your father as a baby," Mammi said, returning with a pitcher of milk. "Every mother thinks her baby is wonderful. The stories don't get interesting until the *kinner* are older, though."

That felt like more evasion to Beth, but she'd given this some serious thought over the years, and she had a theory. Mammi seemed to have raised her son alone. There wasn't a *dawdie* in the picture—at least none that had ever been mentioned. Had there ever been a husband? Had he died? Had he abandoned her? Beth didn't know because no one spoke about that, and when Beth asked questions, she was hushed. Apparently, Mammi didn't have a husband that anyone had met, and Daet had never mentioned his father. Not once. But Mammi did have a son. If Mammi had had her son out of wedlock, that would have been a deep disappointment to her conservative Amish family. Had Mammi been a single mother? Was that the big secret?

"I want to hear about you," Mammi said. "Tell me how you've been doing, Elizabeth."

"I've been working at the flour mill," Beth said. "And I've been learning some new quilting blocks. I'm making a Star of Bethlehem quilt to sell at the spring mud sale."

"Very nice," Mammi said with a smile. "Are you making it alone?"

"My *mamm* is helping me get everything pinned. And my sisters are doing some edging for me. But the hard work—that's mine."

"It's important to know how to quilt," Mammi said. "One day, you'll be making quilts for your own home with your husband and *kinner*."

"One day."

"Is there a young man who's caught your eye?" Mammi asked with a coy little smile. "Your secret would be safe with me."

"There was a boy I liked a lot," Beth said, "but it didn't work out."

"I'm sorry."

"It's okay."

They both fell into silence, and Beth took another bite of the donut, tearing the soft bread with her teeth.

"Did you ever get disappointed like that?" Beth asked.

"Me?" Mammi blinked a couple of times. "Oh . . . that was a long time ago. I hardly remember."

A lie, Beth suspected. Old women remembered everything, at least until senility swept those memories away.

Mammi smiled sadly and pushed the plate of donuts

closer still. "Have another one. It's been a long time since I've had a young person to feed."

Beth shook her head. "I've had enough. *Danke.*"

Everyone back home wanted her to get baptized, to make her decision for the church once and for all. During her lengthy *rumspringa*, Beth had several *Englischer* friends from town, and they were much more open about their family stories. They knew the good, the bad, and the embarrassing about their family histories. It was refreshing how open and honest *Englischers* seemed about those things. It didn't matter to Beth if Mammi had been a single mother. She just wanted her family to trust her with the truth.

All Beth knew was that she had a choice to make about her own future, and she couldn't make a decision one way or the other. She felt stuck on the fence, sometimes leaning toward her Amish heritage, and other times leaning toward *Englischer* freedom. She loved her Amish life, but she could feel the secrets just out of reach, and it was unrealistic of her family to expect her to vow the rest of her life to the faith when they were hiding things from her. If she was grown up enough to make a choice for their faith, then she was also ready to hear the stories that the adults kept hushed around the *kinner*.

"Mammi, can I ask you something?" Beth said.

Her grandmother raised her gray eyebrows. Again there was that hesitant air. "*Yah.*"

"What bedroom belonged to my *daet*?"

Every time they'd visited, the *kinner* would play outside or hang out together in the kitchen, and the adults would chat. If they did ask a question, Daet used to joke around. He'd say something like, "Me? I slept in the barn," or "Your *mammi* gave me a mat to curl up on next to the dog." And

Mammi would playfully swat his arm and shake her head, and the conversation would move on. Beth still didn't know what bedroom had belonged to her father when he was growing up. Such a small detail to just *not know*.

Mammi pointed directly above them. "That one."

"The bedroom above the kitchen?"

"*Yah*, that was his."

Finally, a fragment of information. It was a start. Beth was here for the summer to help Mammi, and that gave her three months to wheedle out more details. The time for secrets was past. Mammi was becoming more confused and muddled, and there might come a time rather soon when she wouldn't be able to tell those stories anymore. They'd be lost, and as heartbreaking as Mammi's decline was, Beth didn't want to waste a moment of this summer with her grandmother.

Daet had had both a childhood and a father. Maybe the story was going to be a hard one for Mammi to tell, but Beth was determined to find out about both of them.

Patricia Johns is a *Publishers Weekly* bestselling author of more than fifty books. She writes Amish fiction with tight Amish communities, outspoken Amish heroines, and the handsome, rugged men who fall in love with them. She lives in Alberta, Canada, with her husband and son. Learn more at PatriciaJohns.com.

Sign Up for Patricia's Newsletter

Keep up to date with Patricia's latest news
on book releases and events by signing up
for her email list at the website below.

PatriciaJohns.com

FOLLOW PATRICIA ON SOCIAL MEDIA

Patricia Johns Author   @AuthorPatJohns   @AuthorPatJohns